M000196209

the Merchant of venice beach

Books by Celia Bonaduce

The Merchant of Venice Beach

A Comedy of Erinn

the Merchant of
venice beach

CELIA
BONADUCE

KENSINGTON BOOKS
www.kensingtonbooks.com

KENSINGTON BOOKS are published by

Kensington Publishing Corp.
119 West 40th Street
New York, NY 10018

Copyright © 2013 by Celia Bonaduce LLC

All rights reserved. No part of this book may be reproduced in any form or by any means without the prior written consent of the Publisher, excepting brief quotes used in reviews.

All Kensington titles, imprints, and distributed lines are available at special quantity discounts for bulk purchases for sales promotion, premiums, fund-raising, educational, or institutional use.

Special book excerpts or customized printings can also be created to fit specific needs. For details, write or phone the office of the Kensington Special Sales Manager: Kensington Publishing Corp., 119 West 40th Street, New York, NY 10018. Attn. Special Sales Department. Phone: 1-800-221-2647.

Kensington and the K logo Reg. U.S. Pat. & TM Off.

First Electronic Edition: August 2013
eISBN-13: 978-1-60183-122-4
eISBN-10: 1-60183-122-6

First Print Edition: August 2013
ISBN-13: 978-1-60183-123-1
ISBN-10: 1-60183-123-4

Printed in the United States of America

For
Elizabeth Steck-Bonaduce,
a great mother, a great writer, a safe harbor.

ACKNOWLEDGMENTS

This is my first book—and there is an entire world to thank. Actually, several worlds. Let's start with my dance world: First and foremost, to Ron Okubo, the most talented and patient dance instructor on the planet. Truly, "you taught me everything I know" is not an exaggeration. Many, many thanks to my other brothers and sisters in dance: Vladimir Estrin, Sonny Perry, Sandor and Parissa, James Riley, Sergio Coronado, Dori Berman, Ron Slanina, Gilmore Rizzo, Richard Bruno, Bryan Titan, Stephanie Jenz and to the wonderful people who inhabit my dancing venues at The Dance Doctor, 3rd Street Dance, and L. A. Dance Experience.

To my friends who read and read and then read these pages some more—another world of thanks: Suzie Segal, Mary Asanovich, Lisa Sichi, Anne Etheridge, Stella Rose, Lisa Medway, Laura Chambers, Sheryl Scarborough, Lisa Ely, Jill Roozenboom, Beverly Beven-Florez, all the ladies in Jodi's Pioneers and of course, my mentor and friend, Jodi Thomas. Thanks to Beth Kinsolving for not charging me for proofreading—what a pal.

To Eileen, Amy and Sandra Bonaduce, Kelly Mooney, Alessandra Ascoli, and David Traub—thanks for your unswerving faith. To Clare O'Donohue, thanks for setting this amazing adventure in motion.

To my father, Joseph Bonaduce, who sadly did not live to see this acknowledgement. The man knew a lot about writing. Thanks, Dad. I hope I did right by you. A big thank you to my brothers, John, Anthony, and Danny: just being in your company keeps me honing my craft. To my mother, who inspires every avenue of my life and sees "the good story" that can be woven out of any experience or misstep. To my nieces and nephews, thanks for keeping me open to everything.

To my sister-in-law, Clare O'Hoyne: this book would never have entered my mind without the fantastic stories of your tango lessons.

To my agent, Sharon Bowers, and the wonderful people at Miller, Bowers and Griffin: my eternal gratitude for making me feel like I knew what I was doing at a time when I was convinced only my mom and girlfriends thought I could write. And to Martin Biro and Kensington Books: I never, never thought I would get this far. You guys are *awesome*!

Billy is my husband, around whom all my worlds revolve. I may not always jump to his tune, but his is the music to which I dance.

Now for the tea of our host, now for the rollicking bun, now for the muffin and toast, now for the gay Sally Lunn!

—W. S. Gilbert

PROLOGUE

Suzanna tended to cut herself a lot of slack, but to say she was thinking about stalking a dance instructor put her in a bad light—even to herself.

Her chance encounter with an amazing man who (it turned out) taught dancing definitely needed some spin. She decided to think of it as the universe's way of saying she needed to get into shape.

Suzanna was standing in line behind him at Wild Oats in Venice, California. The first thing she noticed about him was that he didn't have his own grocery bag with him. *Was he actually going to use a store bag?* Suzanna wondered.

He was a rebel—no doubt! She could tell he was gorgeous, even though she could only see him from the back. He had long black curly hair slicked back in a shiny ponytail. Suzanna didn't go for ponytails as a matter of course, but she could have written sonnets to this ponytail.

Except she couldn't write sonnets. But if she could have, she would have.

She tried to stand as close to him as possible, to judge his height. She guessed he was in the almost-six-feet category, and he had broad shoulders. Fernando, her best friend and co-worker, would have been smitten as well. He loved what he called "those lean, long-limbed gods." *Lean* was a good word, but to Suzanna's ear, it verged on *skinny,* which just wasn't sexy no matter what you called it. But this guy was not skinny. He was flawless. In the old days, she and Fernando would have spent hours giddily agreeing on the perfection of this man. They used to have the same taste in men. But their opinions about almost everything seemed to be going in different directions these days.

The man was wearing a white dress shirt—one that had been professionally laundered. You could have spread butter with the razor-sharp crease in the sleeve. He was also wearing black dress trousers . . . not pants, trousers. Suzanna was impressed. She always thought you could tell a lot about a man by his laundry. Eric, Suzanna's other best friend and other co-worker, probably would have said the guy was trying too hard and looked like Zorro. Suzanna could feel herself becoming irked with Eric for his snide comments, but she pushed the emotions back down. After all, he hadn't actually said that her fantasy man was trying too hard . . . she just figured he would.

What can you expect from a straight man?

There was a large, round security mirror in one corner of the store and Suzanna kept trying to angle herself so she could get a look at his face, but all she managed to do was knock over a display of organic oatmeal cookies. By the time she had finished paying for her groceries, he was gone. She sprinted, as casually as possible, into the parking lot, but he was nowhere to be found. Dejected, she hopped on her bicycle and headed out of the parking lot.

And that's where fate took a turn.

He hit Suzanna with his car.

Suzanna was sprawled on the ground, trying to catch her produce as it rolled by. She knew the man must be horrified by what had just transpired, even though he didn't get out of the car. He just opened his door and leaned out. Suzanna noted the BMW insignia on the hood. It was an older model, but very well-maintained, she noticed. She smiled at him to let him know that she was fine, but he didn't smile back.

He's just hit me with his car. Maybe he thinks it would be rude to look like he's taking the situation lightly.

Once Suzanna was on her feet, she realized he was as handsome as she'd imagined: deep-set, smoldering eyes and a slightly bored look. She was impressed that he could manage to look bored even though he had just hit somebody with his car.

Nerves of steel.

She walked over to the car window, showing off her hearty good health. By this time he had gotten fully back into the car, but he handed her his card and said in a mysterious accent:

"Call me if there is a problem."

And he drove off. She stared at the card. It had no name on it, just DIAGNOSIS: Dance! and the studio's address and telephone number.

Suzanna stared after the car.

She was shaken *and* stirred.

PART ONE

VENICE BEACH

CHAPTER 1

Suzanna knew she was out of her element as soon as she walked up to the dance studio. She couldn't help but compare the place to her own little run-down business on the other side of town. Her combination tea shop and bookstore was her pride and joy. Or the bane of her existence, depending on her mood. The place could have subbed as a location for *Fried Green Tomatoes: The Sequel.* A location scout had actually asked Suzanna about it. While the tea shop sat smack on the rundown boardwalk in Venice Beach, DIAGNOSIS:Dance! was on more ritzy Main Street—uptown in every sense of the word. Maybe not as uptown as Santa Monica, but Main Street was the best Venice had to offer.

As she walked into the dance studio, the wooden floors gleamed at her and the disco balls suspended from the ceiling threw off sparks of promise. The mirrors—the endless walls and walls of mirrors— showed nary a ghost of a fingerprint. Suzanna sneaked a peek at her reflection because, in all honesty, there was no escaping her reflection. She became instantly aware of the little muffin top peeking out between her T-shirt and jeans.

I look like someone who could use some dance lessons.

She hovered in the back of the studio and checked out the dancers as casually as she could. Some of them were clearly professionals, but Suzanna was relieved to see there were others who seemed like regular people . . .just ordinary folks who'd decided they needed to dance. Except even the regular people were beautiful. Everybody was in shape. Everybody had perfect hair. Even the janitor and the staff were fabulous. She could feel her nerve ebbing away.

Suzanna eyed the front door.

Too late for a graceful exit?

She started to leave, but caught sight of the gorgeous dance instructor from the Wild Oats entering through her escape route. He took her breath away, and she doubled her resolve to become a dancer as he glided past. She inhaled his exotic cologne, an intoxicating blend of lavender, peppermint, roasted coffee, tonka bean, and chocolate. Being raised in Napa Valley and running a tea shop gave Suzanna an edge when it came to identifying scents. She tried to focus, looked around, and located the front desk. She was determined to speak to a Beautiful Person in person.

This is going to be worse than signing up at a gym. That's not true. I don't think they are going to weigh me at the dance studio.

Dancers were swirling around in gaspingly ethereal pairs as she beat a path to the front desk. She felt like a colossus bushwhacking her way through gracefully swaying weeping willows.

The Beautiful Person looked up from her computer, looked at Suzanna, and screamed.

No, she didn't. But Suzanna was braced for it, and when it didn't happen, she was grateful for the woman's tiny benevolence. The Beautiful Person was so fragile, she appeared to be made out of lace. She looked like a faerie.

Suzanna started to swell.

"May I help you?" the faerie inquired in a whisper.

"I'm thinking of taking some dance lessons," Suzanna whispered back, trying to keep her feet on the ground. She was swelling so much, she was sure her feet wouldn't stay there for long.

"Private or group?" the faerie continued. Her voice was so wraith-like that Suzanna could barely hear her, even though Suzanna reckoned her ears might be clogged from the swelling. She didn't know which.

The faerie tactfully ignored the fact that Suzanna appeared to be ingesting several canisters of helium. The studio was a business, and Suzanna guessed the girl had seen all kinds. Suzanna knew about that. She owned a business herself.

Suzanna tried to keep her eyes from squeezing shut—the pressure was awful. She felt as if she were about to tip sideways and float to the ceiling, a bouncing, bloated gargoyle looking down on the Beautiful People below.

She hated when this happened. Eric and Fernando always insisted that she wasn't really bloating and floating, but Suzanna thought they were probably just being polite.

The first time she had what she referred to as a "panic swell," she was in junior high school and madly in love with a boy named J. Jay. They had a drama class together and were cast opposite each other as the leads in *Romeo and Juliet*. In rehearsal one day, Suzanna was standing on a ladder that was serving as the balcony and looking down at J. Jay, with his blond hair and blue eyes. She poured her heart into the dialogue, trying to convey that this was not just Shakespeare talking, but her—Suzanna. She infused adolescent passion into every syllable:

> My bounty is as boundless as the sea,
> My love as deep; the more I give to thee,
> The more I have, for both are infinite . . .
> I hear some noise within. Dear love, adieu!

Wildly in character, she turned on the ladder to determine what noise she was hearing from within, and *bammo,* she bumped down the ladder and fell to the floor in a heap. A gasp rose, in unison, from the other kids. As soon as it was clear that she was not dead, this being junior high the gasp turned into suppressed giggles and predictable guffaws. This was not the end of her humiliation, however. A collective gasp once again filled the auditorium as she picked herself up off the floor. She looked around at all the kids laughing and pointing, and that's when she started her first panic swell.

It started, as always, in her ears. She could no longer hear the kids laughing, making it doubly hard to determine what was so hilarious. Then, her body started to expand as the kids continued to point and the full weight of what was going on became clear. . .

The straps of her training bra had somehow come loose on her descent into hell, and her bra was circling her waist. At this point, she had liftoff. Her toes could no longer stay on the ground. She floated to the ceiling and bounced along the tiles until she managed to pull her shirt over the offending undergarment. To add insult to injury, J. Jay was leading the pack in their hilarity. Suzanna prayed that she would be able to stay on the ceiling forever, but suddenly, *pop!*—she was back on the ground, pretending to find the whole thing hysterically funny.

Suzanna pretended to laugh. Then she pretended to laugh harder. In the kill-or-be-killed world of junior high, Suzanna came up with one of her lifelong survival skills. In times of severe humiliation and mortification, she would laugh so hard it looked like she was crying. That way, when she *was* crying, no one could tell that her heart had been broken into a million pieces. It was really very effective, not to mention a great cover. It was something that she used many, many times in her life.

She recommended this approach to Fernando, who took it with a grain of salt—he had no problem weeping copiously when he was unhappy—and to Eric, who disregarded it. Suzanna thought grimly that she'd had to use this strategy when it came to Eric more than once in her life and that perhaps things would have turned out differently if he hadn't ignored it.

Through swollen eyes, she looked around the studio and saw that the dancers all seemed to be having private sessions. She thought of the hot dance instructor and how much fun it would be to have his entire focus. Even though she would, of course, have to pay for his complete focus.

Would it feel like going to a dancing prostitute?

But dancing was a wholesome, healthful activity . . . she wouldn't really be a "john," would she? Another possible plus: a private lesson would lower the risk of public humiliation.

"Private or group?" the faerie inquired again, sounding a little less serene.

Suzanna tried to steady her voice so that she sounded normal; the panic swell brought an elevated timbre to her voice.

"Private . . . I guess."

"Great! They are $120 a lesson."

The faerie beamed up at Suzanna, and *pop!*—she was back on the ground.

"Did I say private? I meant group."

What's a little more public humiliation anyway? I mean, after the bra incident, I'm a veteran.

"Groups are great, too," squeaked the faerie. "We have several different classes. Salsa, ballroom, tap . . ."

"Wow . . . so much to choose from."

"Level?" the faerie asked, switching gears.

Suzanna was momentarily stumped, but noticed a small anteroom at the studio, where a class was being taught by her handsome dance instructor. He didn't notice her staring as he whirled on assured feet and with his alluring hips.

'Who is . . . what is that class?" Suzanna asked.

"That's beginning salsa."

Watching the dance instructor in action, Suzanna felt remarkably . . . inspired.

"I'm a beginner," she said. "And I am going to start with salsa."

Suzanna rummaged through her purse and pulled out a credit card. She held it out to the faerie and then snatched it back. Her roommate, co-worker and co-best friend, Eric, in the midst of earning his business degree, had made their method of paying for things so elaborate that she could never keep her credit cards straight. She pulled out another card and handed it over. Suzanna took her receipt and looked at it with pride. She was signed up for classes on Monday nights at seven-thirty.

The faerie breathed, "You don't have to limit yourself to Monday evenings. You can come whenever you want. There are continuous salsa classes here and you can take any of them."

Suzanna felt all warm inside, as if the dance studio wanted to become her second home.

Classes were $15 a session (what a bargain!). The faerie told Suzanna to wear comfortable clothing and, if she were really serious about this, to get dance shoes. This sounded like sage advice: the faerie knitted her tiny brow when she said it. Suzanna stared mutely at her. Dance shoes. She should get dance shoes. But Suzanna had absolutely no idea what that meant.

Shoes in which I will dance, perhaps?

As Suzanna continued to ponder the mystery of dance shoes, the faerie slid a brochure toward her. Suzanna opened it. It was from a store called Dante's Dancewear, where she could buy dance shoes.

She choked when she saw the prices. There was nothing in the catalog for less than $130! Maybe she'd see about buying them later, when she was more in the swing of things.

Suzanna thanked the faerie and let her know in no uncertain terms that she would see her Monday, lest she think Suzanna a quitter. She slipped the brochure into her purse and headed toward the door, where she collided with her dance instructor.

"Oh, hi," she said. "We always seem to be running into each other."

The dance instructor blinked languidly at her.

"I'm going to start taking salsa lessons with you," she added.

He looked at her feet.

"Bring the right shoes."

Quivering from her encounter, Suzanna left the studio and the beautiful dancers behind, happy and terrified that she and her new dance shoes—which were now definitely part of the agenda—would be joining their ranks in a few short days.

Suzanna had never been much of a shoe girl. Even during the *Sex and the City* years, she couldn't imagine hobbling along the mean streets in four-inch heels. Plus, an upbringing in Napa in the eighties and early nineties didn't really lend itself to shoe lust. Napa was a big jeans-and-T-shirt kind of valley. The only place more casual than Napa, as far as Suzanna knew, was Hawaii. She had a friend from there who said he wore flip-flops and shorts every day all the way through high school. The school made the students wear long pants and closed shoes for graduation. Suzanna wondered if they had ever even heard of dance shoes in Hawaii.

It was evening and Suzanna had the bench outside the little library on Main Street to herself. She pulled out her dance shoes catalog and smoothed it open on her lap. She had stopped at Coffee Bean and Tea Leaf, ordered a Moroccan Mint Tea Latte, and poured it carefully into her bright-red travel mug. She wasn't exactly hiding the fact that she drank tea from a corporate chain, but she knew that many of her own customers would be more than a little surprised—and judgmental—if they knew she patronized such a place when she owned a tea shop herself.

One of Suzanna's little rebellions (and secrets) was that she loved the Bean. Suzanna knew there was no way to whip up those chemical-infused concoctions in her traditional space, but it was always fun to slip off to the Bean and sample whatever new, weird thing was being offered. She hadn't been in love with the Strawberry Crème tea, but, honestly, this chocolate-mint concoction was delicious . . . and the pomegranate-blueberry latte was a keeper.

Suzanna thought about her other secret. She had never kept anything from the guys before, and deciding to keep these salsa lessons on the down-low made her feel both guilt-ridden and exhilarated. Sort of like Diane Lane in *Unfaithful*, when she'd slept with Olivier Martinez and was horrified and proud of herself at the same time. Suzanna flushed. She knew just how Diane Lane's character felt. Powerful, for the first time in ages. Alive. Taking a chance, no matter what anybody thought. Ready for a change.

But too chicken to say it.

Taking a long, soothing sip, she thumbed through the dance shoes catalog, already feeling as if she'd been accepted into a secret club.

I am one with the dance world . . . or I will be when I settle on some shoes.

There was much to absorb. There were ballroom shoes, jazz shoes, tap shoes, and various rounded-toe versions of athletic shoes. Suzanna immediately discarded the jazz and tap shoes as they were footwear for avenues she was sure she was not (at this time) prepared to dance down. She was drawn to the athletic shoes, but something told her that these were not going to fly in the steamy world of Latin dancing. She didn't think athletic shoes were what the instructor had in mind when he sneered at her feet. Next, Suzanna rejected the ballroom shoes. They were too fancy, too high, too Beyoncé.

And then she saw them. A whole category called "character shoes." These were the perfect shoes for a woman in her thirties. A woman—grounded and with modest goals.

Well, if you called wanting to nail your new dance instructor a modest goal.

CHAPTER 2

Suzanna was a compulsive watch-checker. Over the years, the checking had become a habit, much like twirling one's hair without thinking. The time didn't always sink in as she twitched her wrist for a quick peek. As she sat contemplating shoes and sipping her tea, she pivoted her wrist and looked at her watch. She was wearing one of her favorites—a Fossil brown-leather cuff that lit up. She loved watches that lit up at night because, even groggy with sleep, she loved to see the time. For Christmas, Eric and Fernando had bought her a clock that projected the time on the ceiling. She thought this was an incredibly thoughtful gift, but when the boys were practically crying with laughter after they gave it to her, she realized they thought it was a big joke.

She took another sip of her latte, then flipped her wrist again. In this instance, the time did register, and she almost choked.

It was three o'clock, the busiest time of day in the tea-shop half of her business. Well, the busiest time of day for the tearoom, anyway; afternoon tea would be in full swing.

Suzanna pedaled to the shop as fast as she could, weaving through the stop-and-go traffic that clogged Main Street, then down Rose Avenue to the boardwalk. She wheeled quickly around the front of the store, glancing up proudly at her six-foot-high hand-carved wooden sign that announced THE ROLLICKING BUN: HOME OF THE EPIC SCONE. She dismounted, walked to the back and, dropping her bike, snuck in through the backdoor and took a peek into the little section that served as the bookstore. They had taken to calling the alcove "the book nook" as a sort of whimsical joke, but the moniker had stuck. Eric was manning the nook and, thankfully, having a quiet afternoon. He had his long legs stretched out on the weather-beaten counter. Suzanna could see the pencil tucked behind his ear—a clear sign that he was studying. He looked up and waved. Suzanna jerked her thumb in the direction of the teashop . . . she could hear the din of afternoon tea going full force.

Gotta go!

Suzanna slipped into the teashop in time to hear Fernando arguing with Mrs. King, a regular customer who always called Fernando out of the kitchen to discuss the day's offerings. Unfortunately, Fernando's sniping at the customers was business as usual. Suzanna had tried to get used to it, but every time a ruckus broke out, she instinctively held her breath.

"De-ah," Mrs. King said as she slathered clotted cream and raspberry-rhubarb marmalade on her scone, "could I have some strawberry jam?"

"No," Fernando said. "I didn't make jam today. Besides, you have that divine clotted cream and marmalade . . . you don't need strawberry jam."

Mrs. King giggled and slapped at him playfully.

How was this possible? Had I been the customer, I would have slugged him.

Fernando kissed Mrs. King on the top of her gray head and headed back to the kitchen. He spotted Suzanna, who was stacking menus as if she'd been there the whole time. He stalked over to her, his tight soccer player's body tensing with every stride.

"Where have you been?" he asked.

"I was out," Suzanna said, quickly remembering that she had gone to Wild Oats for him.

She tried to sound indignant.

"Grocery shopping for you!"

"That was hours ago," Fernando said. "I wasn't able to make jam!"

Suzanna could feel the color in her cheeks. Fernando had been covering for her.

"Oh, Fernando, I'm so sorry."

"Well?"

"Well, what?"

Fernando puffed out his cheeks in frustration.

"Where are the strawberries?"

"Oh! I left them in the bike basket! I'll be right back."

"No rush," Fernando said, his hands on his hips. "It's too late now."

Suzanna escaped the tearoom. She couldn't believe she'd let the day get away from her like that! As she headed back toward her bike, she saw a slim young blonde woman in tight jeans going into the book nook. Suzanna detoured into the alcove behind her.

As she suspected, Eric's radar was on high alert. His nose came out of his book in record time. The blonde smiled at him. Or Suzanna imagined that she smiled; she couldn't actually see the woman's face. Just the long blonde hair and perfect butt. Suzanna ducked behind a tall shelf to watch their interaction.

"Hey, Eric," the blonde said. "I came in to say hi."

"Great!" Eric said. "I'm glad you did."

The blonde looked around the store.

"This is a cute place," she said.

"Yeah."

"Well, I guess I'll see you at the gym sometime."

Aha! So that's the connection.

"Yeah. Did they reopen the spinning room yet?"

"I think so. I'm going later today. I'll let you know."

"Thanks," Eric said, coming around the front of the counter. "So, listen . . . can I interest you in a book?"

"No, thanks," she said as she headed out the door. "I've got a book."

I've got a book?

Suzanna snuck out of the nook before Eric saw her. She leaned against the wall. She closed her eyes and pondered . . . how could Eric possibly be interested in a woman like that?

Not that he had said he was interested, but he did try to sell her a book. That must mean something. When Suzanna opened her eyes, she was standing toe to toe with Fernando.

"Where are my strawberries?"

"On my way! I'm on my way!"

Gentrification had shambled its way into Venice, doing battle with the old hippies and the new legal-marijuana shops. The end result was that the boardwalk was now in vogue with just about everybody. Suzanna and her co-workers had held their breath, literally, when marijuana was legalized for medical use and medical-herb shops started cropping up on the boardwalk. Luckily, the Rollicking Bun (or "the Bun," as locals called it) was situated in an old wooden cottage on one of the less populated portions of the boardwalk. The medical-marijuana users had their section and the tea drinkers had theirs. And, as Fernando pointed out, marijuana tended to give people the munchies; sales of pastries and scones had certainly perked up since the new neighbors moved in.

People often complimented Suzanna on her foresight. Buying the place for a song and turning it into a profitable business made her seem something of a financial soothsayer. But she would be the first to admit that it was just dumb luck. She couldn't have guessed in a million years that a bohemian landscape and a run-down teashop that had enough square footage to throw in a stuffy bookstore would somehow turn a profit. When she and her friends Fernando and Eric first set up shop, Eric thought they should call the place Plenty O'Mistakes. At the time, she thought this was funny, but now that she thought about it, it was a very insensitive remark. After all, it was Suzanna's money—well, all right, Suzanna's older sister's money— that had gone into the place. Just another example of Eric's cavalier attitude, Suzanna thought defensively. After all, at the end of the fiscal day, she had always managed to keep the doors open—and paid Fernando and Eric a salary, too!

Suzanna's place was surrounded by other unusual little stores. Compared to her neighbors, the Bun's inventory of teas and books was actually pretty diverse. There was a shop that sold only candles, another that was dedicated solely to prisms, and there was a kite store, to name just a few of the oddities in the immediate environment. There were also a few new restaurants popping up on the boardwalk, running the gamut from chrome monstrosities to quaint little cafés with European-looking courtyards. One of the restaurants had a pet possum, which ran around between the feet of surprised patrons. At night, Corky was often mistaken for a rat, and the relieved guests were so happy to find out they were not being menaced by a *rattus domesticus* that they forgot to call the health department.

In all honesty, if it were anywhere else, the shop would probably be considered an eyesore, but the Bun was chicly ramshackle. Or at least it was in Suzanna's eyes.

The building itself was an oddity in Southern California architecture. It looked more like an old-fashioned house from the New England coast. White, weather-beaten shingles covered the entire two-story house. Suzanna's pride and joy was the round tower tucked into one corner. That turret was the focal point of the Bun and drew people like a homing device. A wide porch stretched from one end of the structure to the other and looped enthusiastically around one side. A massive door stood at the top of five steps—the staircase could easily manage several people coming and going, all with books or pastries in their bags. The door served both the tea shop and the bookstore. It wasn't until you were inside that you determined your destination. To the right was the tearoom, to the left, the little book nook.

The teashop was cute without being cloying. The walls of the tearoom were a very pale mountain laurel, not pink and not lavender and, while Suzanna had lots of china, none of it matched. She pretended it was a design choice, but in reality, she hadn't had a ton of money to drop on cups and little plates. Most of her stuff came from Big Lots and Goodwill.

Suzanna was determined to put her mark on the place when she bought it, but she had no money, so decorating the Bun was a challenge. Besides having no money, the building itself presented something of a decorating challenge. The shop was oddly shaped. It had a couple of . . . well, to call them rooms would be a highly inflated statement. They were more like a couple of alcoves, which would be great if Suzanna and the guys were running a romantic little hideaway, but very few people have their smoldering tête-à-têtes in tearooms.

After much deliberation, Suzanna blew her entire decorating budget on long, slender rectangular sketches of antique-looking flowers that she found in a thrift shop. One of her tea drinkers who was very handy with calligraphy added some great swirly descriptions of the flowers. When she framed them and finally got them positioned among all the windows, Suzanna felt the whole room come together. Fernando always called them the Stations of the Carnations, which only amused Catholics, but that never seemed to stop him.

The other side of the store had a different vibe altogether. The basic atmosphere was rustic, with redwood bookcases lining the walls. Books overflowed from the shelves and more books were stacked in every corner and heaped in hemp baskets that dotted the narrow aisles. Customers probably thought there was a method to the madness, but in reality, there was only madness.

Although Suzanna owned the place, she had always been the first to admit it took the three of them to make a go of things. Fernando worked as the chef and supervisor in the tearoom (providing both the "bun" and the "scone" half of "the Epic Scone") and Eric managed the books (providing the "epic"). Currently, Eric was studying to get a BA in business management through UCLA night courses, which might make him better with numbers, but as far as Suzanna could tell, none of his classes inspired him to thin out the rows upon rows of books.

"I'm not surprised Eric is going to business school," Suzanna's mother had said during one of their lengthy phone calls. "He's always been the mature one."

Eric had always been the most practical of them all—which wasn't saying much—but Suzanna sometimes thought that he got stuck with the role of "the mature one" through his looks as much as his demeanor. At five-feet-ten, with perfect posture and soulful eyes, he just gave off the vibe that he could take care of things.

Suzanna sort of flitted from establishment to establishment. She referred to herself as the "ing" specialist: waitressing, hostessing, ordering or stacking books. If the word had "ing" in it, she probably was in charge of it.

Lately, Suzanna found her temper getting short with Fernando and Eric for no apparent reason. Everything the men did seemed to drive her to distraction. She chided herself when she thought about how much effort the guys had put into making the enterprise a success. Fernando was forever trying new recipes and poor Eric was like a man on a mission, attacking the mildew that was always threatening the books.

Fernando was the darling of the neighborhood and Eric breathed customer service. If she were working in the nook and a customer were looking for a particular book the store didn't have, Suzanna would shake her head sadly and say they didn't carry that particular tome. Eric, on the other hand, would offer to track down the title, no matter how obscure. He would jump on the computer and spend hours searching for a book that would probably turn only a dollar or two of profit. Whenever Suzanna mentioned this, Eric said that that was beside the point.

They stood shoulder to shoulder making the Bun a success.

"We stick together . . . I'll say that much for us!" Suzanna would often say to herself. But by the end of any given day, she was totally exasperated with them. She remembered overhearing a woman telling Fernando that she was falling out of love with her husband and that she felt powerless to stop the slow ebb of affection. He wasn't doing anything wrong or even doing anything different. There had just been some subtle shift in her feelings, and there didn't seem to be anyway to set things back the way they had been.

"I want to stab him with a fork when I hear him chewing," the woman almost wailed. "Everything about him drives me nuts, and it isn't his fault."

Suzanna had strained to hear Fernando's response, but couldn't make out what he said. She wanted to heed his advice, whatever it was.

Because that's the way she was feeling about her two best friends. They were driving her nuts, and yet she couldn't put her finger on why.

The three of them had known each other since high school, in Napa Valley. That was in the mid-nineties, when Napa was just becoming the zoo it is today.

"You know that traffic and noise pollution have gotten out of hand when you move to Los Angeles to get away from it all," Eric would tell customers as he regaled them with story of "the three musketeers."

The fact that Suzanna was inseparable from her two male counterparts caused some buzz, she knew. The fact that Fernando was gay didn't seem to stop the guesswork. In fact, it probably added to it. Were Eric and Fernando a pair? Suzanna and Eric? It didn't really bother any of them. Speculation, as Fernando would say, was probably good for business.

Suzanna and Eric always joked that they had a *When Harry Met Sally* relationship—only without the sex.

"We have all the good things about marriage," Eric would say, throwing an arm around her, "without the great things about marriage."

Haha.

After they had graduated from high school, Fernando, Eric, and Suzanna each had a vague idea that they might find their collective self in L. A. , so they just loaded up a U-Haul and moved to Southern California. None of them really envisioned the whole story, thought Suzanna. They just couldn't imagine life without one another.

Now, whenever Suzanna did imagine life without them, she felt guilty.

She turned the DIAGNOSIS:Dance! business card over and over again, staring at it as if it were about to impart some great wisdom. Or give her permission to claim these dance classes as her own.

A little time apart will be good for all of us. . . . Besides, don't I deserve my own space?

Suzanna looked up "character shoes" on eBay. Suzanna adored eBay and never bought anything without checking it out on the on-line auction site first. Fernando introduced her to it as a way of getting some great deals on stuff for the Bun's kitchen. Eric, ever the poetic soul, at first eyed the website suspiciously, but after Fernando pointed out that you could buy leather-bound books for a veritable song, he was in. The three of them had gone through an eBay-buying-frenzy. Suzanna feared they might need a twelve-step program to disengage, but luckily, things settled down. While the three of them now had a more sensible relationship with it, Suzanna was not about to go shoe shopping without seeing what eBay had to offer.

Both the tearoom and the bookstore were locked up for the night, but Suzanna let herself into the tiny office at the back of the bookstore half of the establishment. Eric often worked late hours even after he'd hung out his "Closed" sign, and after determining he was nowhere in sight, she jumped on the Internet and started scouting through eBay's "clothing, shoes, and accessories" category.

Typing in the words "dance shoes," Suzanna gasped when over twenty thousand choices appeared. Through much trial and error, she finally made her choice: a great pair of black-and-white dance shoes. She was about to bid on them when, in small print, she read, "These shoes will signal to the world that you are ready to SWING or HOP."

Well, that's not for me. I'm not big on signaling the world about anything I do, let alone swinging or hopping.

She narrowed her search to include the word "character" and was so absorbed in the process that she didn't hear the boys walk in.

"Hey, want to just grab a pizza this—" Eric started to ask, but Fernando interrupted him.

"What are you looking at, Moan-a?" Fernando asked.

Suzanna bristled inwardly at the nickname. Fernando had been calling her "Moan-a" since high school because he thought Suzanna had a tendency to be a downer. Suzanna's parents had worked relentlessly to ensure that Suzanna's full name was never bastardized to "Suzy" or "Sue" or "Suzie-Q," but you can't stop nicknames, no matter how hard you try. Suzanna wished the boys would have settled on something as innocuous as a "Suzy" derivative. The only nickname that was worse than "Moan-a" was Eric's little pet name for her. He called her "Beet" because Suzanna tended to flush easily. When they were teenagers and a bunch of the kids were hanging out, Eric would turn to Suzanna and say, "Hey, everybody, watch this: Beet, turn red."

And then, as hard as she tried not to turn red, she would turn red.

Suzanna didn't think the boys ever thought about the origins of these monikers, because they continued to use them affectionately.

"Nothing important," Suzanna said.

"Come on . . . You've got on your eBay face," Fernando said.

There was no denying "eBay face," so Suzanna quickly clicked on the Health and Beauty section to throw the guys off the track. Suzanna looking on eBay for anything (but especially for beauty products that would make her look younger, thinner, sexier, shinier, or somehow more glorious) was business as usual around the Bun.

"Hey, guys," she said, peering casually at the screen. "Did you say something about pizza?"

"Let's see what you're up to," Fernando said, and put his chin on top of Suzanna's head, a gesture that Suzanna used to find endearing but that now aggravated her.

Why can't I have any privacy?

Since Suzanna had no idea what she had pulled up, she looked at the screen, too. She blinked in fascination as she found herself looking at a lip plumper that worked in seven seconds.

"I'm looking at a lip plumper that works in seven seconds," she said casually.

"Hell, Suzanna," Eric said. "I wish you would just accept the fact that you're fine. You're fine. You don't need plumper lips. Or stronger nails. Or shinier hair."

"Don't listen to him," said Fernando. "Let's have a look . . ."

Fernando let out a snort.

"Oh. My. God. Suzanna! This is too fantastic! How did you hear about this?"

"I just . . . stumbled on it."

Suzanna had randomly landed on a creation that would give a person lips that looked as if she had been stung by a thousand bees. Not only that, but its "secret ingredient" was also used in products that promised penile enlargement. Apparently the inventor of the lip plumper decided that the skin on her lips was very similar to the skin on a penis, so she wondered if her lips would grow if she created a serum using the same ingredients, and voilà! Pouty Enhancer was born.

"Her lips are similar to the skin of a penis?" Eric said. "That's a pretty gross comparison."

"Speak for yourself," Fernando said.

Although the inventor's story went on and on, with words like *pulsating* and *swelling*, she swore her lips actually grew. Suzanna sat smoldering in embarrassment at the computer. Eric continued to look perplexed while Fernando had tears in his eyes, he was so amused by the copy.

"I'm not sure I want my penis to feel as if it's been stung by a thousand bees," Fernando said.

"This isn't about your penis, Fernando," Suzanna said.

"Darling, it so very rarely is, these days," he said.

"OK, I'm done here," Eric said. He tended to be the most reticent of the three to start comparing sex and love-life details. "I'll order the pizza."

"Oh, no, you don't," Fernando said as he took off after Eric. "Last time you ordered whole-wheat crust. That's a sacrilege!"

Suzanna took a deep breath and went back to looking at dance shoes as soon as the boys were gone—but not until she had purchased two Pouty Enhancers.

CHAPTER 3

Suzanna was in a panic. After several futile attempts at finding shoes online, it became clear she was never going to have enough alone time to really investigate the subject properly. All the research she did manage just brought about more questions, not fewer, and Suzanna had to admit that she really needed some expert help in finding the right shoes. Now her first salsa lesson was looming, and she had somehow not managed to find the time to go to Dante's Dancewear. She didn't know exactly what she wanted, but she knew she couldn't show up at the studio in the "wrong" shoes . . . whatever that meant!

Slipping away from the Bun as soon as the afternoon tea crowd had settled down, Suzanna pointed her Smart Car toward Westwood Boulevard, where Dante's Dancewear beckoned. Suzanna walked quietly into the store, ready to appear confident and assured. After all, she didn't know everything, but she knew she wanted character shoes.

"You don't want character shoes," said the stone-faced skeleton behind the counter.

It was at times like these that Suzanna remembered why she never left her comfort zone. When she was managing the Bun or hanging out with Fernando and Eric, curveballs like this were never hurled at her. Now, little self-doubts pricked at her like tiny toothpicks, but she pulled herself together, arched an eyebrow, and breathed, ". . . Oh?"

"A character shoe has a leather sole. You want a suede sole for classes."

"Oh." She paused emphatically. And then, because she couldn't stand not knowing, she added, "Why?"

"The suede glides on the wood floor," the skeleton replied, "and a suede-soled shoe is lighter and easier to dance in for long periods of time."

It took Suzanna a moment to let go of her character-shoes dream, but since her character-shoes dream was only about a week old, she found she could easily replace it with the new, more-dance-centric suede-sole dance-shoes dream. Because, make no mistake, she planned on dancing for long periods of time!

She asked the skeleton to show her some suede-soled dance shoes that would lend themselves to sensuous salsa.

"What color?" she asked.

Red? Too showy. White? Too virginal.

"Black!" Suzanna said.

"You don't want black."

Suzanna left Dante's Dancewear a little more unsteady and a lot less sure of herself than when she had arrived, but she had to congratulate herself. She had bought her dance shoes.

They were beige.

Apparently, in the dance world one referred to shoes in the singular. You bought a "shoe" and somehow your other foot magically got shod. According to the skeleton, one did not want a shoe that stood out. One wanted a shoe that blended in. Suzanna argued that the whole point of dance lessons was that she was damn *sick* of fitting in. The skeleton replied that she wanted her form and her self to stand out, not her feet.

"Beige hides footwork mistakes," she said.

So Suzanna bought beige.

Suzanna clicked off the alarm in her Smart Car and hid her clandestine purchase in what passed for a trunk in the vehicle that passed for a car. Suzanna wondered briefly if the hot dance instructor would be impressed with her wise choice of a beige shoe. She looked down at her iPhone calendar—she'd find out in less than four hours.

The rest of the afternoon passed by in a blur. The sink stopped up in the tea shop, and this filled Fernando with anxiety. Suzanna and

Eric knew from experience that the best thing to do in situations like this was to distract Fernando and get him away from the problem before he decided to take matters into his own hands. He was inclined to do things like poke wooden spoons down the drain, trying, as he put it, to "shove the problem out." After exchanging a knowing look with Eric, Suzanna sent Fernando to the computer to look up an exotic white tea she thought might be interesting for the shop. She then manned the book nook while Eric fixed the plumbing.

The sink took longer to fix than Suzanna had thought it would, and by the time Eric was washing up (and the water was happily splashing down the drain), Suzanna was desperately eyeing the wall clock in the bookstore. After all her careful planning, was she actually going to be late for her first lesson?

Fernando popped back into the tea shop kitchen to admire Eric's handiwork, and Suzanna stuck her head in to say that she had closed up the bookstore and was heading out for the evening. She withdrew as quickly as she could. She didn't want to have to lie to them.

"Where are you going?" Eric asked, before she could escape.

"Just out to . . .. buy some new bras."

That shut Eric up, but Fernando's ears perked up.

"Oh? I'll go with you. That last bra you bought gave you uniboob. I'll come as your consultant."

"Thanks, Fernando," Suzanna said. "But I'm meeting some of the girls."

Suzanna saw them exchange a confused look. There were no "girls" . . . and the boys knew it.

Suzanna grabbed her keys and ran down the gravel path to her car. She felt terrible about lying, but they had driven her to it!

By the time she drove across town, Suzanna's nerves over lying to the boys were replaced by nerves about walking into the dance studio for an actual lesson with her dream man. Clutching her beige shoes to her chest, Suzanna took a deep breath and pushed open the door. She had made up her mind.

There was no turning back.

She sat on a bench along the back wall and put on her dance shoes, sneaking a peek at the other feet in the room. She noted that a high number of the women were wearing black shoes. Suzanna felt a touch of magnanimous pity for them—they clearly didn't get the memo. She also noticed that many of the students were just wearing street shoes. Well, perhaps they were not as serious about this as she was.

Suzanna tended to latch onto anything that would bolster her ego when she felt her self-confidence lagging, and while she was well aware that feeling superior to other people because she had the right shoe was pretty pathetic, she did recall reading that bouncers at fancy clubs often decided if they were going to let a particular person inside the velvet-covered chain based on whether he or she had the right shoes. If nothing else, she had the right shoes to get into the club.

A man and woman who were taking a private lesson in an adjacent glass-enclosed room practiced a tango. A year ago, Suzanna wouldn't have known what name to attribute to the dance, but *Dancing with the Stars* had changed all that. The couple was young and obviously learning a choreographed dance for their wedding. A few years ago, Suzanna wouldn't have known that, either, but there had been about a million wedding showers at the Bun, so she was now in the "first dance" loop, big-time.

The groom-to-be was clumsy, stiff-limbed, and looked miserable, but appeared to be a good sport. His bride-to-be was lovely, but seemed to be seething with impatience at her man's lack of grace. The instructor, an agile-looking fellow with an earnest smile, tried to show the couple what they were doing wrong. He took the woman in his arms and danced effortlessly around the studio. The bride-to-be was glowing as her fantasy dance was fully realized . . . except for the fact that it was being executed with the wrong man.

Suzanna made a mental note not to get caught up in any such foolishness. Once she got the attention of her instructor, she was going to keep it real.

Almost by magic, everyone in Suzanna's section of the studio settled down and turned their attention to their instructor—her instructor—who had silently entered the room. He hadn't even spoken, and yet the command he had over the room was evident. Chills ran up and down Suzanna's spine as he began the class.

"Hello, everyone," he said in his slightly accented English. "I'm Rio."

Suzanna was about to say, "Hi, Rio," the way they do at summer camp, but realized that there was an ultra-cool vibe going on in the room and that chirpy greetings probably didn't work here.

He continued, ". . . To anyone who is new . . ."

He stared right at Suzanna with his liquid-mercury eyes.

"You're new," he said.

Suzanna was disappointed that he didn't mention their interlude in the Wild Oats parking lot, but maybe he thought it would be rude to bring it up. Maybe he thought it would embarrass her.

Or maybe he just doesn't remember.

Suzanna was about to say "Yes, I am new," when she realized he had not asked if she was new. Since he had stated that she was new, his comment did not require a response, although making no response seemed unfriendly and closed off. Fernando had often accused Suzanna of overthinking, which, she had to admit, was what seemed to be going on at the moment. Suzanna shook her head and tried, as Eric would have said, to be "in the moment." She felt tongue-tied, but was relieved to see everyone smiling at her. In the midst of her tumultuous inner chatter, Rio threaded his way toward her and put out his hand. She extended her hand to shake his, but quickly retracted it when she noticed that his hand was offered palm up.

The entire class was watching and Suzanna had no idea what to do. Instinct (what instinct? . . . is there a salsa instinct?) told her to just lay her hand, like a delicate tropical flower, in his hand.

Apparently, her guess was right because, her hand in his, Rio led her to the middle of the floor. Suzanna was so happy she almost started floating toward the ceiling again—she floated in times of euphoria as well as anxiety—but stayed grounded. Using just his hand to guide her, Rio spun her gracefully around to face him. He pulled her firmly against his hip. She let out a tiny gasp and could feel the color in her cheeks rising as she shyly looked into his eyes.

Those eyes!

"Let's review," Rio said to the class.

The class reviewed what they had learned in the previous weeks. No one seemed the least bit interested that Suzanna was standing in the middle of the room, attached to their dance instructor. Suzanna recalled the time when, as a kid, she had had her appendix out. A doctor came in with a bunch of young interns and they discussed her incision as if she wasn't there.

This is like that, only I get to keep my clothes on.

Suzanna doubled her resolve to stay focused. Rio gently adjusted her posture. Suzanna told herself that she should not get her hopes up, that he was a professional dancer with no more interest in her than in any other student in the class. But as he led her through some baby salsa moves, she couldn't help but feel that he saw her as someone special. Rio looked at her and, she could have sworn, almost smiled.

Well, I couldn't swear under oath, but it really did look like a smile.

The class was watching intently as he led her through her steps: a back step with the right foot, together for two counts, then forward with the left, to his rhythmic "quick-quick slow, quick-quick slow." Suzanna was jubilant. She felt so alluring and so *Latin* that it was all she could do not to turn into a mysterious, smoldering mass of gelatin right there on the dance floor.

"Let's try that to music," Rio said, as he nodded to a sullen-looking young man standing in the corner of the room manning an iPod.

Suddenly, a snappy salsa beat pulsed through the room. Rio took Suzanna's hand and led her through what, until seconds ago, would have seemed to her like impossible moves. And yet her feet, in all their dance-shoe glory, were stepping lightly over the polished wood. There *was* something special between them! She could feel it! Rio couldn't seem to take his eyes off her. She held her breath as they finished their intimate yet completely exposed dance. He spun her playfully around, for all to see. Then he pulled her close and dipped her. She closed her eyes, wanting the moment to go on forever.

"When you dance"—he breathed hot Latin breath into her ear— "you need to stand up straight." He released her. "No hunching."

No hunching? Suzanna stood alone in the middle of the room as Rio walked away. Could there be a less romantic condemnation in all the history of dance?

Suzanna returned to her place in line, flushed from equal parts exhilaration and humiliation. She furtively checked out the other people in the class. Most appeared to be in their early- to mid-thirties— about her age—but there were a few who were in their twenties and one or two in their forties. She wondered briefly when it was that she started noticing people's ages. When she was a teenager and in her twenties, she seemed to be more interested in people's weight.

When did I start worrying about being old instead of fat?

One man, who seemed to be in his late thirties, stood next to Suzanna. He was wearing well-worn jeans, a cotton button-down shirt in a buttery yellow, and leather shoes. The shoes didn't really work with the jeans, but the shirt had saved him. She guessed he noticed her giving him the once-over, because he suddenly introduced himself as Andy, and she wondered if he'd heard Rio admonish her posture. She reminded herself that she was there to have fun and she introduced herself with a smile. Andy informed Suzanna that he had been coming to class for about two months.

"You must be getting pretty good, then."

He shrugged.

"I guess I'm better than I was," he said, with an endearing, lopsided grin. "But I don't think I'm good enough to go to a salsa club yet."

"Oh, you should go to one," Suzanna said in her best I'm-a-really-easygoing-person voice. "I'll bet it's fun."

"Well, I don't know . . . when you get to be our age . . ."

Suzanna returned the sentiment with a comradely shrug, but she found herself feeling annoyed and defensive. She looked at the two of them in the mirror and gauged him to be . . . at least . . . *five* years older than she was. She simmered.

Is there some unwritten rule that people over thirty aren't allowed in salsa clubs?

Mercifully, Rio was ready to move on. Suzanna stood up straight and returned her attention to the front of the room. The class was now facing—naturally—a wall of mirrors. Rio faced the mirror as well. When addressing the class, he made eye contact through the reflection.

"Dancing is not just about footwork," he said.

If Suzanna had had a notepad, she would have written this down. It sounded so profound coming from his full lips. He continued, telling the class that dancing was about attitude.

"You must convey the attitude of the dance. The waltz," he said, "is a romance. Salsa—is a challenge."

He spun around and put his hand out to one of the women in the front row. The woman, Suzanna suspected, was one of those people who had danced before. She had raven hair tied up in a casual chignon, and cheekbones like cut glass. Physically, she was the perfect complement to Rio, which grieved Suzanna like a small death. The woman looked casual, comfortable, and damn near perfect. She was also, Suzanna noted, wearing well-worn black dance shoes. Well, she might have had some practice and been around a block or two, but she obviously got no shoe guidance from Dante's Dancewear. The woman practically glowed when she puts her hand in Rio's.

Simpering cow.

The gloomy iPod master, who looked like he was on the verge of unconsciousness but never missed a cue, put on a stronger, fast salsa that thundered out of the speakers. Rio and his partner started to dance, she stepping back, he stepping toward her, quick-quick slow, quick-quick slow. He looked her right in the eye as he twisted his hips toward her and then away. This routine made Suzanna's interlude with Rio look like an Olympic athlete taking pity on a palsy sufferer. Suzanna's euphoria crashed, but she gamely tried to concentrate on the lesson at hand.

"Challenge me," he said to the woman. "Come *at* me, Lauren."

Lauren? Nobody with black hair is named Lauren.

Suzanna found herself jealous over the fact that Rio knew the woman's name.

Maybe she's his sister, Suzanna could practically hear Fernando hissing in her ear.

Suzanna chided herself. It was an annoying fact of her life that even when they were not with her, she could practically feel her roommates' reactions to things she did. She started to flush, knowing that Fernando would think she was being a huge loser right now.

Lauren tilted her body slightly forward in a more aggressive stance. As she twisted and curled toward him, she seemed literally to be heating up. A pink tinge appeared in her cheeks and a tiny sexual spark glistened in her eyes.

Suzanna bit her lip.

I have a lot to learn.

CHAPTER 4

Most afternoons, when business had wound down, Suzanna rode her bike on the scenic bike path just beyond the boardwalk. The path hugged the curves of the Pacific shoreline like a pair of Spanx. She always rode as fast as she could—it cleared out the cobwebs and calmed her. She usually thought about the business or about how annoyed she was with her two friends. But now that she was taking dance lessons, she realized she had something positive to think about on her rides.

Maybe salsa is just what I need. Maybe everything is going to work out.

She pedaled back to the Bun and tucked the bike into the little storage shed at the side of the building. She stuck her head in the door of the tea shop and waved to Harriet (known as Harri), a fellow student of Eric's who was working part-time as a waitress. Suzanna really felt like she'd hit the big time two years ago, when she realized the stores were becoming too much for just the three of them to handle. Eric was already in the thick of his business degree and he had found Harri, who, if Suzanna's calculations were correct, would probably graduate in another twenty years. Harri seemed content to be part of the Bun family—as content as Suzanna used to feel. Suzanna wondered if the contentment would rub off on her if she hung around Harri.

She'd have to ask Harri to join her for a cup of tea.

Suzanna caught sight of Fernando dishing with a group of ladies who were sitting at the best table in the house. The ladies, as usual, were fawning all over him. He deserved it, Suzanna thought. She'd been trying to think of positive things to say to herself about her friends lately. Fernando made everyone feel so special. She glanced back at Harri, who gave a thumbs-up. This was their signal that the restaurant was running smoothly and Suzanna could, as Fernando so annoyingly put it, "toddle along." Suzanna walked across the floor to the bookstore. Fernando might always have a grasp on the tea side of things, but Eric usually had a predicament that could use an opinion or another set of hands.

She stopped dead in her tracks and hid behind the door, hoping no one saw her, sort of like a cop in a police drama. Eric was standing at the counter, handing over a stack of books to Suzanna's older sister, Erinn Wolf. When Suzanna had first entertained the idea of buying the old building, it was Erinn who provided the money. She had made it happen. And Suzanna hadn't even asked.

Erinn had been a Broadway wunderkind in the eighties and had made a bucket of money. Her hits had dried up by the mid-nineties, but she still managed to pull in a decent wage with lecture tours and other obscure, intellectually based pursuits. By the time Suzanna needed money for the building, Erinn didn't appear to be working much, but she insisted on financing her sister.

Suzanna was hesitant. She hated to admit it, but she didn't even really know her sister. They had not been close as children—not unusual given a ten-year age difference—and Suzanna had only been nine when Erinn left for New York. Naturally awkward, Suzanna didn't find it easy connecting with Erinn, but found that sharing the excitement of her dream gave them both something to talk about on their sporadic long-distance phone calls. One day Erinn had demanded to know just why she wasn't being asked to invest in her little sister's great adventure. Suzanna couldn't think of a nice way to tell her that it was because she, Suzanna, didn't think Erinn could really afford it, considering the long years between hits.

Their mother said that Erinn wasn't really good with people and that she was looking to get closer to her sister in the only way she knew how.

"Taking the money would be a kindness," their mother said.

Well, then.

Suzanna always felt guilty that she wasn't able to repay Erinn. Her sister, bless her, did not consider the money a loan. It was a gift. But Suzanna always felt shabby about not paying her back.

Erinn had finally given up on New York—or, more specifically, New York had given up on Erinn—and moved to Santa Monica, just north of Venice. She bought a beautiful old home on über-upscale Ocean Avenue and never mentioned anything about her personal or professional life. And she never mentioned money, although Suzanna could tell her sister had started to economize. Just the other day, Suzanna noticed her sister had asked for a to-go bag at the tearoom, something she had never done before.

Suzanna knew that Erinn was certainly not in dire financial straits . . . and yet.

But still . . .

If hiding dancing lessons from the boys wasn't bad enough, how could she look her sister in the eye and say, "I'm splurging on dance lessons because I'm hot for the instructor when I should be throwing some money your way"?

Clearly, Erinn had to be added to the list of people who would never hear about Suzanna's new passion.

From the doorway, Suzanna watched the exchange between Eric and Erinn. She soothed her guilty conscience a bit by reminding herself that she wasn't witnessing an exchange, but a perk—Erinn's perk. Because Erinn had been the Bun's initial financier, Suzanna had decided that Erinn could take her money back in trade. Her sister never paid for books. And she did love books. Everyone in the area knew that Erinn was a playwright who hadn't had a hit in years. Playwrights and failed TV and movie people—the town was littered with them.

Erinn always told a joke about two eighty-year-old homeless guys who were sitting on the beach, reading *Variety*. One homeless guy says to the other, "I don't know who any of these new people are." And the other one says, "What does 'CGI' mean?" The two look at each other for a minute and the first man says, "We've got to get out of this crazy business."

Suzanna didn't find this at all funny, but her sister always said, "Well, at least I'm failing gracefully."

Erinn may have been without a hit for many years (and across two coasts), but she was always researching new story ideas. Erinn was in her early forties but she looked even older. She lived alone in her big house along with a large, ugly cat. Suzanna studied her sister from the doorway and her heart went out to her. Erinn looked tired and . . . lonely. Whenever Suzanna fantasized about getting a little space between herself and the guys, she thought of her sister. Would she end up like that? A woman who had family a few miles down the road but was still so completely alone? Suzanna shivered.

"Hi, Erinn," Suzanna said, gathering up her guilt as she entered the bookstore.

"Suzanna."

Suzanna waited, and suppressed a smile. Erinn had a disconcerting habit of just saying your name—with no follow-up. She'd done it ever since they were kids. Suzanna, Eric, and Fernando had been mimicking this unnerving habit for years.

"Eric," Suzanna would say, if they were passing in the hall.

"Fernando," Eric would say to Fernando.

"Suzanna."

Suzanna was happily lost in the memory when she realized Eric was speaking to her.

"Erinn is working on a new play about the Spanish Armada," he said.

"Really?" Suzanna said, genuinely surprised. "Have you told Mom?"

Have you told Mom? was always a good stalling tactic for Suzanna when she wasn't quite sure what to say to Erinn. It was amazing how well this simple sentence worked for almost any occasion.

The Wolf women came from intellectual stock. Their mother was a history professor and their late father had been an English professor. The brains had clearly not been evenly divided when it came to the offspring. Of the two girls, Erinn was definitely the egghead. When Suzanna was very little, she would be amazed when Erinn would come home from school with straight As, even though Suzanna never saw her study. Because she was so much younger, Suzanna assumed that she herself would be getting astounding grades as she got older, equating good grades with age rather than a

DNA crap-shoot. When she got to the age when she could see that this was not about to happen, she asked her mother about it.

"I'm not as smart as Erinn, am I?" she had asked.

Her mother, who was creating a historical timeline at the time, looked up at her younger daughter and studied her. Suzanna had the feeling the answer was not going to be good.

"No, dear, you aren't," her mother said. "But you should thank your lucky stars. Your sister is too smart. It's going to be very, very hard for her to ever be happy."

"So," Suzanna said, trying to digest this, "I should be happy that I can be happy."

"Exactly!"

Over the years, Suzanna had shared this story with many people. Some felt that her mother had done her a terrible disservice by implying that Suzanna could get away with not striving because she had been given a get-out-of-jail-free card—a "you're not as smart as Erinn" pass from her mother. But Suzanna didn't feel that way at all. She was grateful to her mother for being so honest. She felt a huge burden lift off of her. She wasn't as smart as her sister, and she should stop trying to be—and she should figure out how to be herself.

Figuring out how to be herself was taking a little longer than anyone expected, but Suzanna had never resented her mother's take on things.

And let's face it, I'll never be interested in anything as dirt-dull as a play about the Spanish Armada.

Suzanna tuned back in to the conversation.

"The Spanish Armada, huh?" she said. "That should be, um, interesting."

"Of course it will be interesting. I wouldn't write it if it weren't going to be interesting."

"I really don't know much about the Spanish Armada," Suzanna said.

"Exactly!" Erinn said. "But once you've seen my play, you will know everything there is to know—from the Spanish perspective, of course."

"Of course."

Eric added a final book to the stack in Erinn's arms. Suzanna held the door open for her.

"I'm sure your play will teach us a lot," Eric said.

Erinn turned and looked up at him.

"I cannot teach anybody anything. I can only make them think."

"Nicely put," Eric said, smiling at her.

"Thank you. I will send Socrates your compliments."

"Bye," Suzanna said.

"Suzanna," Erinn said—but then, surprisingly, she continued. "Walk with me."

Suzanna saw Eric's eyebrows shoot up as she dutifully followed her sister out to her car.

"Have you ever heard of Peter Pan syndrome?" Erinn asked.

"Well, no. Should I?"

"I think you have it."

"You think I have Peter Pan syndrome? That's ridiculous."

"You don't even know what it is."

"I don't need to know what it is. It sounds ridiculous."

"Don't be so swift to judge," Erinn said. "It's a psychological condition that manifests itself in the inability to grow up. It is usually applied to men, but in your case, I think the medical community would make an exception."

"I'm so relieved," Suzanna said. Judging by her sister's expression, Erinn didn't understand that this was sarcasm.

"Remember when you—and your *roommates*—went back to Napa for your tenth high school reunion a few years ago? You were the only three who hadn't any sort of real profession or gotten married or had kids. And nothing has changed. You are stagnant."

"We have a real profession!"

"You don't need to be defensive. This is just an observation. You just don't seem . . . very mature for thirty-three."

"I'm only thirty-two. And besides, if this applies to Fernando and Eric, too, why are you taking it out on me?"

"Because I love you," Erinn said matter-of-factly, and got in her car. "I suppose that's why."

Suzanna was speechless as she watched Erinn drive away.

Well, a torrid affair will be just the grown-up thing, then, won't it?

Suzanna walked back up the steps, closed the door, and looked around the shop. In the age of Kindles and audio books, she was always surprised that they managed to stay in business. Her thoughts were interrupted by the sound of keys turning in the lock of the tea shop.

"It's about time you got back," Fernando said, locking up the tearoom with a resounding *clunk*. "I've been trying to talk to you all week!"

Fernando, who closed the tearoom an hour before Eric closed the bookstore, rushed across the room. He was at loose ends, having just broken up with his gym-rat trainer boyfriend. The affair had left him brokenhearted (and broke, since the boyfriend had "borrowed" several grand from Fernando as a down payment on a gym). Suzanna had been relieved when this particular affair flamed out. Fernando spent every spare moment at the gym, and at five-feet-seven, he had probably worked his body a little too hard. In Suzanna's eyes, his head had started looking startlingly small atop his massive shoulders. While Suzanna felt bad about the breakup, she was glad that Fernando would be giving his workouts a rest. The only problem was, now he was spending all his time coming up with new ideas for the tearoom.

Now what?

"We need to add a swing to the porch in front of the tearoom," Fernando said.

"We can't afford it," Suzanna said, feeling entirely justified, since she just opted out of private dance lessons for the sake of economy.

Fernando followed her around the store as she straightened up the shelves.

"Seriously, Suzanna, I am so sick of the same old, same old."

Join the club!

"Sorry, sweetie," Suzanna said, "but same old, same old is pretty much what you're stuck with when you run a tea shop."

Suzanna climbed the sliding ladder—one of her favorite things about the old-fashioned bookstore—without a word and Eric seemed to magically appear with a armload of books to be reshelved. Fernando pushed the ladder along the wall and Eric handed Suzanna the books one at a time. Suzanna smiled down at her two cohorts.

Look at us! We're like a finely tuned machine.

"How much could it cost to buy a swing?" Fernando asked as he slid the ladder expertly along its track.

"You're just bored," Eric said. "A swing won't help. Plus, it will be an insurance liability."

Eric stretched and handed a book up to Suzanna. He winked at her as she reached for the book. It always unnerved her that he had such an easy wink.

Why can't I have an easy wink?

With much effort, Suzanna had gotten over her lifelong crush on Eric. There was a time when that wink would have sent her soaring, sometimes with hope, other times with despair. But having a crush on your childhood friend turned high school buddy turned business partner, just got exhausting—and the days of wistful longing for Eric were over. She returned the book to its place on the top shelf with an emphatic shove. Usually, this thought vaguely depressed her, but now, with the fabulous dance instructor in the works, she actually found herself taking pleasure in it.

"That's easy for you to say," Fernando said to Eric, giving the ladder a small tug. "Suzanna listens to you!"

"I do not," Suzanna grabbed the ladder for balance as she looked down at the top of Fernando's head. "I mean, no more than I listen to you."

"Oh, really? Then why can Eric have a book club when I can't have a swing?"

"Not again," Suzanna said, jumping down from the ladder.

She turned to Eric for support, but he just smiled his "you're on your own, sister" smile, scooped up another pile of books, and picked his way through the haphazard stacks of books and periodicals toward the back of the nook. Fernando crossed his arms in a well-rehearsed huff.

"First of all, a book club doesn't cost any money," Suzanna said. "And second, if I recall, the book club was *your* idea."

"That's because I'm supportive," Fernando said.

Suzanna tried not to roll her eyes. If memory served, Fernando had actually come up with the book club idea for the tearoom. He had just read a book by Michael Cunningham called *Land's End*, about Provincetown in Cape Cod, and he wanted to share it with the world.

If you made any sort of "I'm an outsider" comment to Fernando, he was off and running. Suzanna tried to gently point out that you couldn't form a club of outsiders . . . it was an oxymoron. The whole point of being an outsider was aloneness. Did Johnny Depp run around starting book clubs? *He* understood the allure and mystique of being the Outsider. The Stranger. The Silent One.

Oh, if only Fernando understood how to be the Silent One.

"You start signing up outsiders and you're just going to look like a bunch of losers," Eric had said.

But Fernando was not to be dissuaded. He had been in a fever and Suzanna had finally given her consent. Fernando bullied all his ladies (including Harri and Erinn) into attending the book club meeting in the tearoom. Eric took pity on the group and was able to get them a substantial discount on a bulk order, and the session came to order with each participant clutching her own new copy of *Land's End*.

Fernando's flirtation with the book club idea lasted less than one meeting. Instead of discussing *Land's End*, the ladies wanted to discuss the more famous of Cunningham's tomes, *The Hours*, a lovely book which was turned into a movie starring Nicole Kidman wearing a prosthetic nose.

"All the old bats wanted to talk about was how *brave* Nicole Kidman was to wear a big fat ugly nose," Fernando said, as he reported the end to his book club. However, the ladies who attended the book club loved it and badgered Eric to keep things going. Now there were monthly meetings in the nook. Fernando alternately insisted on taking credit for the idea or used it as leverage that Eric had something exciting going on and he didn't.

Suzanna's cell phone rang, mercifully cutting off Fernando's swing bid. She looked down at the screen, which was signaling that her friend Carla Caridi was calling from Napa. Suzanna furrowed her brow, hoping that it looked to Fernando like she had a very important business call to take. She indicated that she would take the call in the office and Fernando rolled his eyes. As Suzanna headed to the office, he called after her.

"Say hi to Carla for me."

Rats!

Suzanna closed the office door as she clicked on the phone.

"Carla, hey!"

"Hey! How's the beach?"

"Coastal."

"As usual."

Suzanna smiled. Carla always had a comeback—the story of their lives.

It always amazed Suzanna that people in Los Angeles seemed to change friends every ten minutes, and here she was, still tied to all three of her childhood cronies. Until high school, when Suzanna, Fernando—and sometimes Eric—became attached at the hip, Carla had been Suzanna's constant childhood companion. Suzanna's parents had moved to Napa from New York City when Erinn was nine, before Suzanna was born. Suzanna couldn't remember a time without Carla. Carla was as much a part of her life as her own family. Good thing, too, or Suzanna would have dumped her a million times.

Suzanna and Carla's relationship had had some pretty breathtaking ups and downs over the years, but since they really were almost family, they always managed to patch things up. Carla was always ready to jump in with an insightful insult any time Suzanna had had it with either of the boys.

"Boys treating you like the jewel you are?" Carla asked.

"More like cubic zirconium, but yeah, things are fine."

The two women caught up on friends, family, and jobs. Carla might have stayed in Napa where her family owned a winery, but she had gone on to study architecture. She lived on the East Coast after college, got married, then divorced—and returned to Napa. She not only had become somewhat of a big muckety-muck in architectural design around the wine country, she also helped run her family's winery with her father.

Carla always was an overachiever.

Luckily for Suzanna (and Erinn), Carla's family's winery was right next door to the Wolf residence. Carla made it a point to check on Suzanna's mom every week, now that Suzanna's father had passed away. This eased Suzanna's guilt about not seeing more of her mother—and anything that eased guilt was a good thing.

Suzanna had resolved to tell no one about her big secret, but Carla's voice, which was like a magic carpet ride back to the past, always broke down her defenses.

"I'm taking dance lessons."

"Dance lessons. That sounds fun. We've had some dangerous frost up here . . . how's the weather in L. A. ?"

"The weather is fine . . . like it always is . . . ." Suzanna said. "Aren't you amazed that I'm going to take dance lessons?"

"Well, I'm sure Fernando is pretty coordinated . . . but I'm surprised Eric would agree to dance lessons," Carla laughed. "I mean, he can barely put one foot in front of the other sometimes."

"It's not for the three of us. It's only me."

Dead silence.

Suzanna rejoiced—inwardly. Now she had Carla's attention.

"Really?" Carla asked.

Suzanna could tell Carla was measuring her words. "You're going to do something without Fernando and Eric? Is everything OK there? Do you need me to fly down?"

"No . . . Everything is great. I just want a little breathing room."

"Why?"

"What do you mean, 'why'? You're always telling me I should be a little more independent and now you're criticizing me."

"I am not criticizing you. This just isn't like you, that's all."

"Well, it's like me now."

"Okay, whatever," Carla said.

"Fine."

"Isn't Fernando jealous? I think he would love dance lessons."

"I . . . I . . ."

"Oh my God, Suzanna, you haven't told them!"

"I just told you—I need a little breathing room. I don't need their permission to breathe and I don't need their permission to take dance lessons."

"I'm not arguing with you."

"Did Eric ask *my* permission to go to business school?"

"How should I know?" Carla replied.

"Well, he didn't. Did Fernando ask my permission to invest in a run-down gymnasium?"

"I'm going with no—just a wild guess."

"You're damn right he didn't."

"Look, don't get all defensive about the dance lessons. I think it's great."

"You do?"

"I do. Suzanna, you're almost thirty-three and this is probably the first decision you've made on your own. This is very mature of you—except for the lying part."

"I'm not lying. I'm just evading."

"OK, this is very mature of you—except for the evading part. Better?"

"Well . . . thanks," Suzanna said. "Look, I gotta run. Smooch."

"Smooch."

Suzanna heard Carla's phone click off and she stared at her iPhone as if it were going to impart some sort of techno-wisdom. She had almost told Carla why she was taking dance lessons, but decided against it. Carla was a little on the practical side, if truth be told, and Suzanna was pretty sure she would fail to see the charm in the car–bicycle encounter. Carla thought dance lessons were a mature thing to do.

Why muddy the waters?

CHAPTER 5

After getting off the phone with Carla, Suzanna spent a half hour tidying up the office before dinner. She stared in irritation at a pile of receipts sitting on her desk. Now that he was within sight of his business degree, Eric was constantly revolutionizing Suzanna's bill-paying system. He had started her out slowly, with a software program called Quicken. But as soon as she'd gotten the hang of that, he'd fallen in love with another program that caught his eye, which he then threw over for something even more financially glamorous.

I should have known. He has the same fickle attitude with operating systems as he does with women.

Currently, everything related to expenses and bill-paying was meticulously entered in a computer program called QuickBooks. Eric was very patiently teaching Suzanna how to handle each program, but it always came down to her having to spend an awful lot of time entering numbers into the computer. Suzanna grabbed a handful of receipts and started typing.

The bills could be paid in the time I spend doing this!

As she entered the last bill into the Mac, she glanced at the clock. It was after seven. She'd better start thinking about dinner. Suzanna looked around the office, trying to think of something else to do. She had a habit of keeping an eagle eye on her business, so when she wanted to stall for time, "catching up" was never much of an option. She shut down the computer, locked the office, and headed home.

She walked out into the small yard behind the bookstore and tea-room and headed up the backstairs to the second story. A great feature that she took advantage of more and more frequently was that there were two sets of stairs leading up to their living space. One set of rickety wooden steps snaked up the back of the building, while another ran right through the center hall that divided the tearoom. Eric, Fernando, and she lived together in what they referred to as the Huge Apartment. The door at the top of the stairs opened directly into the kitchen. Suzanna stepped inside and smiled. She loved this room, and every time she walked into it, her spirits immediately lifted.

The room was oddly shaped, something it had in common with all the rooms in the tea shop/bookstore/apartment compound. The kitchen was a perfect square, which made it look massive, but a large percentage of the square footage had been wasted floor space until Eric had built a large workstation, now center stage on the black-and-white-tiled floor.

Fernando was at the stove, and Suzanna braced herself for a complaint. Fernando had redesigned the kitchen at the Bun about two years ago, and had been campaigning ever since to redo the upstairs kitchen as well. But Suzanna loved the kitchen just the way it was. If the vintage stove was finicky, so be it. If Fernando was cooking something that needed precise heat, he could always work in the Bun kitchen.

"I'm starving," Suzanna said, relieved to find it wasn't her turn to make dinner. "What are we having?"

"Salad, peanut soup, and fresh bread."

Suzanna felt her throat constrict. She and Eric tended toward the shepherd's pies and angel-hair-with-tomatoes-and-garlic-variety dinners. Suzanna had often wondered why Fernando refused to cook normal dinners like everybody else.

"Oh?" Suzanna said. "That sounds. . . peanuts, huh?"

"I know! I found the recipe online. It's an African dish. Slaves apparently brought it to the American South. They still serve it all over Virginia, according to the article I read. Try it," Fernando said, nodding toward the pot.

Suzanna often relied on bread to cut the weirdness of many of Fernando's creations, but when she eyed the bread maker, it was still ticking away. She clearly was going to have to go cold turkey on this one. She grabbed a spoon and tentatively tried the soup. She often chided herself for not being more adventurous—after all, she owned a restaurant—but she usually gave herself a pass on this particular flaw. She had other things to worry about.

"Wow!" she said. "This is good."

"I know! I'm thinking about putting it on the menu."

Suzanna's whole mood shifted. She thought the tea shop customers would really enjoy this new treat and it would get him off her back about the swing. Win–win!

"I'll call it 'Slave Soup,'" he said.

Suzanna's good humor tanked.

"You can't put 'Slave Soup' on the menu."

"Sure I can . . . I'm part Cherokee."

"Sure he can," Eric echoed, coming in to join the conversation. "It could be a post-racial-era statement."

Fernando snorted.

Suzanna stared at the boys. Were they joking?

It was obvious that none of them harbored any prejudices. After all, they were two men (one gay) and a woman, living together with not a hint of sexual tension—unless you counted Suzanna's tamped-down feelings for Eric, which she didn't. And Eric, who was firmly heterosexual, didn't even have a type. He dated casually, as far as Suzanna could tell, and the women he went out with were all over the map—tall, short, curvy, thin, and of every race and religion. He could have been the poster boy for Benetton. Even so, the boys made politically incorrect jokes that she never would have dared to utter.

Eric took a quick look at the stove and countertop. Determining that they would need soup bowls, bread plates, and flatware, he started to set the table, which was tucked into a corner of the room. The table was built into one of the walls and sat three, not the conventional four. When they had first seen the apartment, they had all happily taken that to be a sign that they were meant to be together. Nowadays, to Suzanna, it seemed more like a commandment carved in stone.

The three of them sat down to eat dinner. Suzanna poured wine and Fernando passed around a wire basket with a checkered napkin placed over the sweet-smelling warm bread. Suzanna took the basket and inhaled the fragrance of the bread—one of her all-time favorites—before she opened the napkin. Only when her nostrils had had their fill did she reach in and pull out a slice of warm bread.

It was lavender.

"Isn't it gorgeous?" asked Fernando.

"What is this?" Suzanna asked.

"Bread," he replied.

Suzanna looked at Eric.

"It is bread," he said.

"Did you know about this?" Suzanna asked Eric.

"Was I in charge of dinner?"

"It came to me while I was making tea sandwiches for the billionth time," Fernando said. "I thought, 'What if I dyed some of the bread a nice mountain laurel?'"

"Oh!" Eric said. "Mountain laurel bread . . . like the walls! Very cool."

Suzanna could feel her eyes welling up with tears. As far as she was concerned, the boys were being totally passive-aggressive. They always said that the walls were lavender but only referred to the color as mountain laurel because Suzanna insisted on it.

"This is about the swing, isn't it?" Suzanna asked.

"No, Suzanna, it's about my spirit being drained of any creativity."

Suzanna turned to Eric.

"Are you going to help me out here?"

Eric swallowed his soup, put down his spoon, and looked at Fernando.

"I know what you mean. I felt my spirit dying, too. That's why I decided on business school. Just the creative outlet my soul was looking for."

The boys howled and high-fived. Suzanna stood up and threw down her napkin.

"I have had it with you two!"

The boys looked startled.

"Hey, Suzanna, chill out," Eric said. "It was just a joke."

Suzanna picked up a slice of purple bread and thrust it under Eric's nose.

"Oh?" she said. "Does this look like a joke to you?"

"No," he replied. "It looks like a science experiment."

"Hey!" Fernando looked at Eric. "I thought you were on my side."

"I'm not on anybody's side! What the hell, you guys. Come on. Calm down."

"I will not calm down," Suzanna said, still holding the bread. "Forget it—I'm not hungry."

She threw the bread on the table.

"And for your information, the walls are mountain laurel and this bread is lavender."

Suzanna stalked out of the room and headed down the hall toward her room. She stopped, turned around, and stalked back to the kitchen. When she got to the doorway, she waited until the boys noticed she was standing there. They looked at her and waited.

"And I don't want to hear that I'm probably just having my period," she said, and turned on her heel.

As she walked down the hall again, she heard the boys speaking in low voices.

"God, heterosexual women can be so Gothic sometimes."

"Well, you got to admit, this bread looks pretty gross," Eric said.

Suzanna's anger subsided a tiny bit as she walked into her room. Eric had at least defended her.

The next morning Suzanna, feeling a little sheepish at her outburst, decided she should give Fernando a hand in the Bun's kitchen. She slipped in quietly. Fernando was already hard at work mixing shredded chicken, homemade mayonnaise, and curry powder. He looked at her sullenly and pulled several mountain laurel loaves out of the oven. They stared at each other. Suzanna didn't have the energy to fight.

"You're in charge of the kitchen, Fernando."

"Thank you. Well, if I can't have a swing . . ."

"Let's just leave it, OK?"

"OK."

Fernando seemed to be satisfied and the rest of the morning went smoothly.

Suzanna looked around the kitchen. Her practiced eye told her that today they were doing cucumber, curried chicken, and egg salad. They started making the finger sandwiches in what she hoped was companionable silence but was in fact abject terror that her clientele was going to think they were being served some penicillin-laced delight.

Suzanna flitted between the two establishments as sort of an overseer, but always made sure to be on hand for the afternoon tea rush, serving as the hostess. Her nerves were on edge as Harri carried out the first tray of mountain laurel finger sandwiches. Harri shot Suzanna a confused look.

Oh, no! A panic swell.

Suzanna clutched the little podium that stood at the entrance to the tearoom, but it was no use. Her heels lifted off the ground. She tried to concentrate. Sometimes, if she could focus, she could keep her big toe on the ground, but the sight of the triple-tiered tray full of crustless purple finger sandwiches was too much for her. She felt herself floating perpendicular to the podium.

Well, at least I'm not on the ceiling.

Even though her ears were clogged, and every sound seemed far, far away, Suzanna managed to hear a squeal from table twelve.

Maybe I should let go of the podium. It might be safer on the ceiling.

But the squeal turned out to be one of delight. The Red Hat Society—women of a certain age who wore red hats and purple dresses to their weekly tea at the large circular table—called Fernando out and were showering him with applause and kisses. They *loved* the purple sandwiches.

Pop! Suzanna's feet were back on the ground. She shook her head and realized that Harri was standing beside her. Suzanna was always stunned when Fernando's crazy ideas and fits of pique met with approval from the customers. He marched to his own drummer and people seemed to get in line to join his band.

"I sometimes wish I could just soak up his vision," Harri said. "I mean, I just don't understand how you could be working away in a kitchen and suddenly think, 'You know what these sandwiches need? Some red and blue dye . . . . just mix them together and add to the dough until it's a nice . . . mountain laurel and I'm good to go.'"

The rest of the afternoon rush passed pleasantly. Eric stopped in to make sure Fernando and Suzanna weren't plotting each other's demise, and Suzanna had to sheepishly admit that Fernando had a winner on his hands—everyone seemed to love the bread. They were chatting when Phyllis, a tiny firecracker of eighty and one of their regular customers in both the tearoom and the bookstore, started past them on her walker.

"Hey, Phyllis, what did you think of the new sandwiches?" Eric asked, knowing that of all the customers, Phyllis was sure to hate them.

Phyllis was as old and bitter as the day was long.

"I don't know what you were thinking," she said. "Why don't you just leave well enough alone?"

Suzanna thought instantly of her dance instructor and pushed him out of her mind.

Phyllis never had a good word to say about anything that was served at the Rollicking Bun. Suzanna used to worry that she would stop coming to the tearoom—granted, it would be a much more pleasant environment without her, but she spent a lot of money there. Last year, Phyllis had had a hip replacement and wasn't around for a few months, and Suzanna was surprised to find that she really did miss her. Phyllis was frailer since her surgery, and used a walker. She never stopped complaining, but she never stopped coming in, either.

Phyllis turned her remarkably keen eyes on Eric.

"Did you get that book I called about?"

Eric and Suzanna exchanged a look over the old woman's head. Phyllis would never say the name of a book she had asked for. She wanted to make sure Eric remembered on his own. Eric called it "proving his love."

"Yes, I did. *The Beggar Maid*, right?"

Phyllis beamed.

"That's right."

"I put away a copy just for you."

Phyllis headed across the hallway toward the bookstore. Eric tried to take her elbow, but she slapped him away.

"I can manage," she said. "I'll go look around the store."

Eric and Suzanna watched her go.

"What a day!" Suzanna said.

"See? All's right with the world," Eric said. "Now, if Phyllis had liked those sandwiches, then you'd have something to think about."

Suzanna leaned her elbows on the podium.

"I'm exhausted."

"You need to have more faith in us."

"Oh, right! Did you have faith in those sandwiches?"

"I didn't have to . . . . I run the bookstore," he said, kissing her on the top of her head. "Just relax, Suzanna. How many times do I have to tell you that? Things always work out."

Suzanna knew that the kiss was just friendly. She had trained her heart to not leap when he did that, but it was still an act of will not to react. She watched him go back to the bookstore.

Eric was right about a lot of stuff, but he wasn't right all the time. Everything didn't always work out.

CHAPTER 6

Suzanna had been taking dance lessons for several weeks, and every bone in her body screamed. In tempo—but it still screamed. She had no idea dance classes would be so draining. Of course, the mental exertion of trying to learn dance steps while fantasizing about her instructor probably added to her exhaustion. Suzanna knew in her aching bones that if she could just master some of the movements, she'd have a shot at her teacher. As it was, that infernal Lauren still appeared to be teacher's pet.

Keeping her salsa secret proved to be easier than she had thought it would be. The boys went about their business and she went about hers. The only real problem she faced was practice. With the guys living and working side by side, she really couldn't focus on practicing between classes. As it was, every morning, while Suzanna brushed her teeth with a two-minute-timer Sonicare toothbrush, she focused on various instructions. She also practiced her steps when she was grocery shopping, banking, or any time she found herself in any kind of line. Besides getting her ready for the next class, these impromptu practice sessions made her feel as if she were getting closer to Rio.

Business was good, both in the bookstore and the tearoom. There was a bit of a spike in business when the regulars and marijuana users found out, through word of mouth and tweets, that Fernando was serving lavender sandwiches, and everyone wanted to see for themselves. Personally, Suzanna was hoping the curiosity factor would soon wear thin; she was sick of Fernando's gloating face every time a customer raved about his innovation.

One afternoon, while the afternoon-tea crowd was ebbing, Suzanna gathered up the day's receipts and was about to head into the back office, when the door of the tearoom opened. Although the sun was in her eyes, Suzanna could decipher the silhouettes of a man and a woman entering.

Damn! Latecomers.

Suzanna sighed and neatly stacked the receipts on the podium. She put on her best welcome-to-our-cozy-corner-of-the-world smile and grabbed some menus. As the door closed and her eyes adjusted to the light, her smile froze.

It was Rio and Lauren.

Suzanna's palms started to sweat. She grabbed the menus, but they started to slip out of her wet palms. She fumbled, but retrieved the menus before Rio or Lauren noticed the slipup—or her. Suzanna looked around the room in a panic. Because the afternoon rush was over, Harri was off duty and Fernando was busy cleaning up in the kitchen. She was on her own. Appearing as casual as possible—or at least trying not to float to the ceiling—Suzanna sauntered over to them, making sure she was not hunching.

"Table for two?"

"Yes, thank you," Rio said.

"Follow me."

Suzanna led them to the best table in the house. Maybe she couldn't impress these two with her dancing, but she could show off her establishment to the best of her ability! As she put the menus on the table, she could see Rio had his hand on the small of Lauren's back, ushering her toward a seat. They were both dressed casually, in jeans, so Suzanna knew they hadn't come from the dance studio. Suzanna smiled brightly, but not too brightly.

I'm playing it cool, pretending I don't know them.

They, too, seemed to be playing it cool. Either that, or they didn't recognize her from class.

Neither of them looked at Suzanna as they glanced over the selections. Suzanna was torn as to what to do next. She didn't want to risk turning them over to Fernando, in case it suddenly dawned on them who she was and they start discussing class (although this was seeming less and less likely as the seconds ticked by). But if she took their orders and they did suddenly mentally engage, she'd look like an idiot for not saying anything.

The decision was made for her, when Fernando, who had radar for new faces, came out of the kitchen.

"Hello, there!" Fernando said. "Welcome to the Rollicking Bun!"

Suzanna slunk away, realizing that she was not in jeopardy of being recognized.

"First time here?" Fernando asked.

Suzanna stopped, mid-slink. Was it their first time here? She strained to hear their reply, but she could detect only a murmur. She went back to the podium and tried to busy herself so that she could be where the action was but remain out of sight.

She listened while Fernando explained the various choices, which were:

CREAM TEA: Tea, scones (orange and raisin), jam, and cream

LIGHT TEA: Tea, scones and sweets (mini raspberry cheesecakes and chocolate-dipped strawberries)

FULL TEA: Tea, sandwiches (on mountain laurel bread!) scones, and sweets.

"We'll have the cream tea," Lauren said.

"Two cream teas, it is," Fernando said, as he flipped their menus expertly to the back page where the tea selections were found. The Bun had a dizzying array of loose teas, and Fernando knew all of them by heart.

When Suzanna, Eric, and Fernando first got to Los Angeles, the three of them went to a Mexican restaurant where there were no menus. Instead, an old waiter would recite the selections. The waiter was entranced by his own descriptions as he led them through their choices. There was a beef tamale that "is a tribute to the corn fields of Mexico," a tostada whose "lettuce is wet with the tears of the migrant workers," and a chicken mole "whose white meat tastes like it was born in the sauce." The food lived up to the hype and the three of them went back again and again. One day, they realized that the descriptions were always the same, and the magic started to wear thin.

One night, Eric joined them late and when the old waiter came over, Eric said absently, "Just give me the chicken that tastes like it was born in the sauce."

They never went back after that, but Fernando embraced some of that old waiter's theatrics, because he loved to show off his teas.

"What tea do you recommend?" Rio asked.

"Well, we have several excellent teas . . . our Jasmine Blossom Green is very popular, our herbal is Peach and we're featuring a wonderful white. White tea is the rarest of all teas . . . and ours has some lovely nutty overtones."

Suzanna's mouth dropped open in shock. She couldn't believe that Fernando was pulling out the white tea! That was their private stash! And why? Rio was obviously straight—it was written all over his disdainful face. But it was clear that, even given his sexual orientation, Rio had managed to cast his spell over Fernando.

Suzanna lost track of the conversation when Fernando lowered his voice to what he always thought was a sexy growl, but Suzanna thought made him sound like a gay James Cagney. She quickly grabbed a dust cloth and started swiping at teapots not far from Rio and Lauren so she could hear better. She knew she was taking her chances, but the thought of missing out on any utterance of Rio's was too much.

Apparently she hadn't missed anything, because when she tuned back into the conversation, it was still about tea.

"The Japanese Cherry is very special, too," Fernando said.

"Do you have Earl Grey?" Lauren asked.

Suzanna tried not to snort out loud as Fernando's face fell. He had offered her a pearl and she had asked for the discarded oyster shell.

"Earl Grey, it is," Fernando said.

He spun on his heel and returned to the kitchen. Suzanna tried to keep an ear to the ground in order to catch pieces of Rio and Lauren's conversation, but she didn't hear anything worthwhile—nothing to help her determine the nature of their relationship. Actually, the only thing of any note that Lauren said was, "Oh, look, the sandwiches match the walls."

Finally Rio and Lauren left. Rio gave Suzanna a quick nod, which made her heart lurch. As much as she wanted to convince herself that his nod meant something, in all honesty it looked like the sort of nod everybody gave her when they were leaving the place. Only a little less friendly.

After she finally managed to close the tea shop, Suzanna peered into the bookstore. Eric was helping a gorgeous woman load up on books from the dollar section. He followed her to the door and Suzanna stood with him as they watched the woman walk down the path. It was hard not to be mesmerized by the lettering on the butt of her sweat pants. It read SASSY and the Ss moved in rhythm to her steps, one S going up and one down with each contraction of her buttocks.

Eric took his eyes off the girl's ass and turned to Suzanna.

"Hey!" he said. "Are you OK?"

Suzanna could feel tears welling up inside her. Damn Rio! She thought perhaps she was being too hard on her old friends and that maybe she'd confide in Eric. They used to share all their secrets. Maybe it was better that way after all.

Suzanna noticed that Eric was wearing a new T-shirt. It read THE BEST MAN FOR THE JOB MIGHT BE A WOMAN. She wiped at her eye.

"Nice T-shirt."

"Yeah," he said. "It helps me get laid."

Suzanna bounded into the hallway between the tea shop and the bookstore and ran upstairs to the Huge Apartment. She could hear Eric calling up the stairs, "That was a joke!" as she slammed the door.

I will not cry. I will not cry. I will not cry.

She cried so hard that she couldn't breathe. After an hour or so of self-inflicted misery she got up, washed her face, and headed down to the office to input the day's receipts—her goal before she was sideswiped by Rio and Lauren. She wasn't sure if she was more annoyed with Lauren and Rio or with Eric for insisting on all this financial planning and updating that was taking up more and more of her time. Hell, she wasn't getting the business degree!

She clomped down the stairs and passed Fernando and Eric in the kitchen. She pretended she didn't see them and, mercifully, they pretended they didn't see her.

Putting aside her irritation at having to follow yet another of Eric's computer programs, she threw herself into the project with complete concentration. Drowning herself in work had always been a lifesaver for Suzanna and she could feel her feeling of hopelessness lifting. She somehow managed to toss all her emotions aside when there was a stack of bills to be paid or major decisions to be made. Hours could go by without her even realizing it—a merciful skill, she had to say. It had saved her time and time again.

Once all the receipts were entered, bills were paid, and food and supplies orders placed, Suzanna stretched. She looked at the clock. She had been at it for almost three hours. She smiled. Three hours when she didn't think about men! She shut off the computer and headed back up the stairs. As soon as she hit the first step, she could smell the aroma of gingerbread coming from the kitchen. Suzanna inhaled deeply. Her mouth watering, she headed up to the kitchen.

Maybe this is a peace offering?

Suzanna thought back to Fernando's lavender loaves.

This gingerbread had better be brown!

As Suzanna climbed the stairs, it occurred to her that everything Eric worked on—books and computers—was quiet. Everything Fernando did, on the other hand, was noisy. He was always banging around either the tea shop kitchen or the Huge Apartment kitchen, whipping up new things

Suzanna followed the wonderful aroma into the kitchen, where Fernando stuck a warm confection under her nose. Suzanna inhaled. Heaven! But mysterious. Suzanna examined the tray in Fernando's hands. Mercifully, it was the right color, but it didn't really look like gingerbread . . . it looked like fudge.

From the look on his face, Suzanna could tell this was exactly the response he was looking for.

"OK, I give up!" Suzanna said.

"It's medieval gingerbread," he said, plunking the tray on the counter and sprawling on the large upholstered chair that sat incongruously in the corner of the kitchen.

"What's wrong with regular gingerbread?" Suzanna asked, poking at the medieval-thing-on-a-plate.

"*Boring* . . . I know you think we have to stick with the tried and true Englishness of our tea shop, and I am looking for something interesting to do, you know, so that I don't blow my brains out, and I found this recipe on the Internet. It's from *The Canterbury Tales*. You don't get much more English than that!"

Suzanna ignored his tirade and took a bite.

It did not taste like gingerbread, but it was amazing. Fernando and Suzanna had been tasting recipes together for so long that he didn't even need to ask. By the rapt look on her face, he *knew* he had a winner. He jumped up and down on the chair like a gay Tom Cruise and told Suzanna that he had had to translate a recipe from the fifteenth century, which was full of terms he didn't know, such as "throw thereon and strew thereon," but he finally figured it out and came up with his recipe.

"I've tried making it with several different honeys," he said, "because the honey really flavors the gingerbread, and I think jasmine honey will work the best for the shop . . . it will taste great with tea."

Suzanna readily agreed that they should add this astounding new item to the menu, but she remained braced. She knew that the gingerbread sample was just a bribe. These late-night chats always came with an agenda and she waited until he decided to let her in on the latest inner workings of his brain.

"I have a new idea for the tearoom," he said.

"You've already served purple bread and now you're introducing medieval gingerbread, for God's sake. Isn't that enough?"

"No, it isn't," he said.

"Fernando, how many times do I have to tell you: tearooms, by their very nature, don't constantly need new ideas. The whole point is to be stodgy. Our tearoom is a haven."

"For the stodgy."

"No . . . it's comfort for the huddled masses."

God, I sound pretentious. I sound like Erinn!

Luckily for Suzanna, Fernando was quite used to her pretensions, and the preposterous vision of Los Angeles's huddled masses lining up for afternoon tea didn't cause him to even bat an eye. She knew that Fernando would just keep throwing ideas at her until she caved in out of exhaustion. The gingerbread had weakened her resolve, but she tried to remain strong.

"Okay," she said, "what's your idea?"

Fernando jumped up and started pulling paperwork from under the dinner plates. The sales pitch was ON!

CHAPTER 7

"Eric!" Fernando called out as he started laying his papers on the kitchen table. Suzanna's eyes widened in alarm.

Eric is in on this?

"I thought we'd redecorate," Fernando said. "We'll paint the tearoom cream—no more of that pastel we've got going on. The room is just too damn twee."

Suzanna felt stung.

"It is *not* twee. That's a horrible thing to say."

They had known each other so long, their negotiating skills were well honed. When Suzanna started to whine, Fernando became a disdainful adult.

"May I continue?" Fernando asked.

Suzanna gripped the edge of the table and nodded.

"Think, Suzanna—the walls will be cream! Cream, get it? Cream in a tearoom? It's so obvious, I don't know why we didn't think of it before."

"We never thought of it before because we probably thought cream walls would look. . . white."

"Cream is not white, Suzanna."

"OK, beige, then."

Fernando ignored her and called for Eric again. Clearly, he wasn't going to go into this without backup. Eric stuck his head in the room and Fernando nodded him in. As he sat, Suzanna looked at Eric, who was wearing his glasses instead of his contacts. This look always surprised Suzanna. With his glasses on, and the first hint of gray showing in his five o'clock shadow, Suzanna thought again about how long they had all known each other and how intricately their lives had been linked.

And clearly we can't make a decision about redecorating without a group vote.

Fernando started spreading out paint chips on the table—chips in various shades of white and beige. He threw a stack to Eric, who also started laying them out. So they were in this together! The paint chips seemed to take over the entire surface of the kitchen table, looking like a monochromatic game of solitaire.

Apparently, we're talking every conceivable hue of cream and Cremora known to man.

Fernando looked at the paint chips lovingly and glanced at Suzanna.

"What do you think so far?" he asked.

"I don't see why you're so hot for a white or beige . . . if you're going the theme route, why don't we just paint the walls a 'tea' variable."

"Such as?"

Suzanna took a deep breath. Fernando was just being obstinate. How many conversations had they had over the years about the fascinating variety of colors tea came in? Tea came in all sorts of colors, from black to brown to green to red to orange.

"I'm just saying that we could do the tea theme and still have some color," Suzanna said.

Fernando glowered. Suzanna pinched off another piece of gingerbread, which, she hated to admit, was working its magic.

"OK, so, cream walls . . ." she said between mouthfuls.

She met Eric's eyes when she said it, and Eric gave her one of his killer smiles. She waited for that feeling in the pit of her stomach when he gave her that look, but for some reason, it didn't materialize. Why not?

Rio!

They both returned their attention to Fernando, who was rolling out a blueprint sort of thing that had been done on some fancy computer program. Since Suzanna knew that Fernando had next to no computer skills, she gave Eric an accusatory glare. He raised his hands in surrender, a gesture that said "I had nothing to do with this."

Suzanna tried to take in all the details. It wasn't easy, because Fernando was talking a mile a minute, pointing out feature after feature before Suzanna could get scared and say no. According to the plan, besides the walls being cream, the tea shop would feature an entirely neutral color scheme. She thought about Rio and Lauren ordering Earl Grey and Fernando—the traitor—offering their precious white, and she pictured the different shades and tones of tea. There had to be a way to sneak in some color. No need to fight that particular battle now.

Tea really was endlessly fascinating.

But so was Rio.

Suzanna had stopped listening, but when the room went silent, she tried to recall where they were and vaguely remembered Fernando mentioning tablecloths. Taking a stab in the dark, Suzanna said:

"Maybe the tablecloths could be a nice café au lait."

Fernando looked as if Suzanna had stabbed him.

"That's a coffee color," he sniffed. "The tablecloths will be Darjeeling."

All in all, Suzanna liked the design. She had to admit this new layout had a very interesting look to it, and while it was very different in tone from her sweet little tea shop, the new look was very clean, elegant, and comfortable all at the same time.

Plus, this will distract the boys and I can spend more time dancing without getting caught.

"I like it," Suzanna said. "I really do . . . but do you think it might put off our regulars? I mean, this new look is very . . . sophisticated."

"Our clientele is very loyal to us," Fernando said.

Suzanna had to agree. Their customers had stuck with them through faddish coffee houses and martini bars. Fernando assured Suzanna that this new version of the shop would retain the interest of the loyals—it would still be very warm and accessible while appealing to a whole new audience.

"Well, it's intriguing, Fernando," Suzanna said. "But I'm not sure we can afford it."

Suzanna caught the boys exchanging a look.

Aha! So Eric was not as innocent as he pretended!

Suzanna waited. Eric cleared his throat and pulled a sheet of paper from the stack on the table. It was full of graphs that looked to Suzanna like a mountain climber's route.

"We can afford it," Eric said. "I've run the numbers. The kitchen is fine and can keep running throughout the remodel. We only need to close the dining room for two months."

Two months! That's forever!

"I know you're thinking two months is forever." Eric looked at Suzanna. "But if we transfer everything from the back office up here to the apartment, consolidate some of the book sections and use the side yard, we can keep the tearoom going in the book nook. It will be smaller and we probably won't be able to accommodate walk-ins, but it's a workable plan."

"I'll want to run these numbers myself," Suzanna said.

The boys nodded, but all of them knew that Suzanna couldn't crunch numbers any better than Fernando. That was Eric's department.

Suzanna looked over the elaborate blueprint asking questions about detailed design and finance. They had an answer for everything. Suzanna wasn't sure if she was just predictable and they had anticipated all her questions, or if they had really thought this thing through as thoroughly as it appeared they had. Suzanna hated to admit that it looked like they had researched every possible angle before approaching her.

In the old days, if any one of them had even the hint of an idea, the three of them would be dissecting it together. Their relationship was changing—and it was probably all her doing. After all, wasn't she the one pulling away?

Be careful what you wish for.

Suzanna might need some space from the boys, but she wasn't ready to think the boys might do just fine without her. If this remodel was going to happen, she was going to be an integral part of things! She stared at the design. Rio kept flashing through her mind, but she swept him aside.

Suzanna arched her eyebrows at Fernando.

"You did this?"

"Why do you look so surprised?" Fernando said, looking insulted.

"I'm sorry, Fernando," Suzanna said. "I just didn't know you could draw blueprints."

"I can't," Fernando said, without a trace of irony. "I told Carla what I wanted to do and she drew them up . . . but it was my idea!"

"I can't believe you'd bother Carla with this!"

"She said you'd love it," Fernando said. "Does she know you, or what?"

"And is she planning on coming down here and helping with this?" Suzanna asked.

"Well, as a matter of fact, she is coming down," Fernando said. "Eric asked her if she knew of any good contractors in our area who didn't cost a fortune . . ."

Fernando looked so smug Suzanna could hardly stand it.

"She said she wants this done right," Eric said, "and it would be fun to hang out with us for a while."

I'll bet.

Suzanna put her head in her hands. She knew that she should be happy that her only real female friend—a very well-respected architect—had drawn up such magnificent plans and was offering to oversee the renovation. But she wasn't happy. She wasn't happy at all. Although it seemed several lifetimes ago, Suzanna never really got over the fact that in their sophomore year of high school, Carla stole Eric's heart . . . and body . . . away from her. Eric and Carla were both single right now. What if, all these years later, their romance rekindled?

But now Suzanna had Rio to focus on.

"OK," Suzanna said. "Let's do it."

CHAPTER 8

From her second-story bedroom, Suzanna looked out her window. It was just past dawn, and the boardwalk was still silent. She was drinking a new tea she was thinking about trying out in the shop, a blood orange herbal. When she first opened the tea shop, she had to rely on Fernando to decipher teas for her, but she'd gotten the hang of it over the years. This new tea was sweet and naturally decaffeinated . . . it might be a good choice to introduce to older kids at the weekend afternoon teas. She made a note to discuss this possibility with Fernando and Harri. It might also be a nice selection for those misguided people who dismissed teas as "bitter."

While she thinking about the blood orange tea, she noticed a truck pulling up in front of the building. Her lazy morning attitude was replaced by a supercharged jolt when Carla jumped out of the truck and looked up at the sign that proudly stated: THE ROLLICKING BUN: HOME OF THE EPIC SCONE. Suzanna quickly realized that Carla was not taking in the sign so much as taking in the whole structure. She had been on Suzanna's turf for exactly four seconds and was apparently already in work mode!

Suzanna studied her as Carla studied the building. Carla's hair was still dark and long, although it was caught up in a few erratically placed clips. At thirty-three, she looked great—even better than she had at twenty-three. How did that work? She had the figure of a woman who was always on the go, rather than a starved gym-rat—or, for that matter, a slinky dancer like Lauren. Suzanna smiled to herself as she watched Carla unload a large toolbox. No wonder she was in such good shape! Clearly, this was the body of a hands-on architect!

Suzanna rapped on the window and Carla looked up. She took off her sunglasses and the brilliant green eyes flashed so brightly that Suzanna could see their color from the second story.

Carla beamed up at her. Suzanna raised her hand in greeting, but found herself paralyzed mid-wave. Eric had obviously seen the truck, too, and he was bounding down the stairs, still pulling on a shirt. Suzanna watched, fingers still frozen in the air. She watched as he scooped Carla up in a bear hug. Suzanna tried to take another sip of tea, but couldn't swallow. Eric was actually squeezing Carla's butt cheeks and they were both laughing. The two of them were joined by Fernando, who was wearing gold paisley pajamas. He threw himself at Carla and Eric and the three of them leaped around in a tangle of limbs. Finally, they stopped and looked back up at Suzanna.

Suzanna realized she had to go downstairs. She grabbed a robe on the way to the stairway. She plastered a grin on her face as she walked down the steps and into the front yard.

"Hi, hi, hi!" Suzanna said.

Carla squealed and hugged her as the guys looked on.

"I know it's early, but I called Eric about an hour ago and he said to just head on down!" Carla said.

Suzanna kept her smile in place.

"Oh, you could have called me!"

"I know," Carla said. "You're sweet. But Eric and I have been talking about the remodel so much, it just seemed natural to call him."

"Really? I would have thought since we're remodeling the tearoom, you would have been talking to Fernando."

Fernando had grabbed Carla's suitcase and Eric picked up the tool kit and they all headed back upstairs.

"Oh, well, Eric and I have been going over the finances. That's the big bugaboo, you know. The design part is easy."

They all headed up the stairs.

"Well, we're glad you got here safely," Suzanna said, trying to shake off the image of Eric grabbing Carla's ass.

"Uh, I am so happy to be here," Carla said. "I was so burnt out up north. As soon as we finished the harvest, I told Eric I was coming down."

Suzanna pictured Carla stomping grapes, gypsy skirts raised high, the ruffles gently grazing the crest of her lace bikini undies. As she danced through the grapes, Carla sent grape-stained kisses through the phone to Eric.

Suzanna discarded this scenario immediately. And not just because Carla wouldn't be caught dead in bikini undies (not to mention a gypsy skirt). She chided herself for falling victim to such a hackneyed image. Stomping feet and squishing grapes were mostly fodder for fantasy—and an unhygienic fantasy at that.

"I can't wait to see everything," Carla said in the darkness of the stairwell. "Can we just dump the bags and go look at the tearoom?"

"You three go look," Suzanna said. "I'll make breakfast."

"But it's your place," Carla said. "Don't you want to come see?"

"You guys are the ones with all the ideas!" Suzanna said. "Go ahead!"

Eric, Carla, and Fernando headed back down the stairs. Fernando was still in his pajamas, Eric at least had buttoned his shirt. Suzanna started banging around the kitchen, angry with herself for being so passive, and angry at her friends for not begging her to go downstairs with them.

She started to scramble a dozen eggs and turned on her iPod to some hot salsa music. She started dancing around the kitchen and her spirits immediately lifted.

Quick-quick slow. Quick-quick slow.

She heard someone enter the room and quickly shut off the music. She turned from the iPod and saw Eric standing there watching her. His eyes met hers. She could see a sadness as old as time and felt she could sense his very soul. Her heart leaped with naked, otherworldly, unspoken bonding. Perhaps seeing her dance had unleashed a passion he had not realized was there. Suzanna realized she was turning red.

"You've got mold, Beet," he said sorrowfully.

You have no idea.

"I guess you mean the building has mold?" Suzanna asked. "This isn't a personal observation or anything?"

She tried to carry off her little joke, but found she couldn't quite meet Eric's eyes. As she turned back to the eggs, Carla and Fernando came tromping up the stairs.

"I had forgotten what a gorgeous place this is—mold notwithstanding," Carla said.

"Is the mold a dealbreaker?" Suzanna asked, secretly hoping it was. Carla could return to Napa and the three of them could go on with their irritating lives.

"Oh, no. We can handle that. And I'm just bursting with ideas."

Suzanna softened during breakfast. It was like old times, with laughs and good-natured insults flying around the room like superheroes.

"And how are the lessons going?" Carla asked Suzanna.

Eric and Fernando turned to Suzanna with twin quizzical expressions. Suzanna could see the dismay in Carla's eyes reflecting her own. Thankfully, Carla—always a quick thinker—jumped back in.

"Didn't you tell me Erinn was going to teach you Italian?"

"Oh, well . . . you know Erinn. Always talking," Suzanna said. "In whatever language."

That wasn't exactly a lie, was it?

Suzanna grabbed Carla's bag.

"There's plenty of space in my room," she said. "Come on."

"Are you sure?" Carla asked. "I mean, the remodel is going to take some time. I can get a hotel."

"Oh my God—are you kidding me?" Suzanna sounded like a highschooler, but a sincere one. "This is going to be awesome!"

Carla threw her arm around Suzanna in a way that took her back to those safe childhood days. The boys got to work cleaning up the breakfast dishes as Suzanna and Carla trudged down the hall.

They caught up on all the news from Napa as she unpacked. Thanks to Carla's determination, her family's winery was always looking for new and interesting ways to make a visit more appealing to tourists, and her design skills had made the place a premier destination. But she also never lost sight of the fact that "the wine's the thing," and in recent years the Caridi Winery had won some big medals for numerous wines. They were especially renowned for their merlot.

"Remember when that movie, *Sideways*, came out?" Carla asked.

Suzanna nodded absently, struggling with the instructions on an air mattress. One of her customers had had a garage sale and Suzanna bought the air mattress for five dollars "just in case." That was three years ago. She was so happy when she remembered it; it made her feel like a willing and casual hostess.

It isn't that I'm not a willing and casual hostess, I'm just out of practice.

"Napa Valley was holding its breath after that guy makes fun of women for drinking merlot . . ."

Suzanna looked up from the instructions.

"Napa Valley was holding its breath?" Suzanna asked, trying to suppress a smirk.

Carla shot her a look.

"God, you sound just like your snooty sister," she said.

Carla was never a big fan of Erinn's.

Suzanna shrugged and plugged the mattress cord into the outlet. It stunned her how fast the two of them could start bickering.

"All I meant was, the idea of Napa Valley holding its breath is a pretty hilarious statement, don't you think?"

"OK . . . what would *you* have said?"

"Something like . . . 'All the winemakers in Napa were concerned that there would be a merlot backlash.' "

"Your parents and sister would be proud that you're guarding the English language so diligently."

"It means the same thing, and is a pretty good sentence in its own right."

"Bite me," Carla said, throwing a pillow at Suzanna. "How's that for a pretty good sentence?"

It turned out that there had been no merlot backlash after all, but of course, this news now came as an anticlimax.

While it was fun having all her childhood friends around, once again Suzanna felt afraid passion might be rekindled between Eric and Carla. She had to admit that she would begrudge the recoupling of her two friends while insisting to herself that she had made peace with the idea that Eric would never see her as anything more than just a pal.

When she had first bought the Bun and was working day and night to get the place in some sort of shape, Suzanna had developed a huge crush on one of her workmen, a smoldering Latino not unlike Rio. His name was Alamar. She and Fernando both thought that he was just the hottest thing ever. Luckily for Suzanna, he played for her team—exclusively.

Suzanna tried to remember if Eric had been jealous of her attention toward Alamar, but she didn't think so. For one thing, Eric had a girlfriend at the time, and he was a really loyal, faithful boyfriend. Since Suzanna's amorous laser beam was focused on Alamar at the time, she really admired Eric's devotion. Fernando, on the other hand, kept trying to find a chink in his armor. One day Eric was moving a ladder and Fernando was in his way. Eric said, "Move it, gorgeous"— and Fernando was off in a fantasy. Suzanna couldn't count the number of times she'd told Fernando that Eric wasn't gay, but Fernando was adamant.

"No straight guy has ever called me 'gorgeous' and not slept with me."

Well, much to Fernando's disappointment, Eric didn't sleep with him.

Short flashes of painting walls with Eric, buying cheap antique trinkets to add to either the book nook side or the tea shop side, making out with Alamar in the kitchen—the memories all sort of ran together. Those were fun days. Suzanna was firm with herself. She'd been as frisky as any of them. She needed to stop worrying about Carla and Eric. That was crazy. That was the past. Rio was the future.

Although . . . the past repeats itself. After all, I still have a massive crush on a hot Latino.

Carla was wasting no time getting the tearoom ready for the remodel. Suzanna, after repeating and repeating her "I don't care what happens with Eric and Carla" mantra, came upon them, heads together over the dining room table.

"Suzanna!" Carla said. Suzanna scrutinized her, but Suzanna knew she wasn't acting guilty or uneasy. "Eric and I have been going over the schedule . . . and I think we can get everything done by your birthday."

"That's less than two months away."

"It'll be tight, but I really think we can do it," Carla said.

"Hey, Beet," Eric said. "We need to find a carpenter."

"Carla, you must know carpenters," Suzanna said.

"You can't afford my guys."

"I'll see what I can do," Suzanna said. "I'll check on eBay."

"Check craigslist," Eric said.

"You check craigslist," Suzanna retorted.

"Is it my tearoom?" Eric said. "I've got the bookstore all day and classes every evening. . . ."

"Kids, kids, no fighting," Carla said, laughing.

"Speaking of classes," Suzanna said to Eric, looking at her watch, "you better go. It's already seven-thirty."

Eric jumped up, kissed both women on the tops of their heads, grabbed a backpack full of books, and headed out to his finance class. Once she was sure the coast was clear, Suzanna stood up. Carla broke out in a huge, conspiratorial smile.

"Salsa?" Carla asked.

"Salsa," Suzanna said, grabbing her purse and heading out the door.

Every week before dance class, she promised herself that she would try some sort of flirtatious move in order to hit on Rio. After all, Alamar had adored her. But once she got to class, all her fantasies crumbled. She could see that half the female students had the same MO.

Suzanna would look disdainfully at the other women—how sad they were. After all, he taught dance for a living. Clearly he had no interest in them, any of them. Suzanna would catch a glimpse of herself in her low-cut wrap top and perfectly fitted dance pants and think:

I am so pathetic I can barely stand myself!

Rio showed the class a new step and they tried it out as a group first. Then they went into dance rotation. When Suzanna first started dancing, dance rotation made her a little nervous, but rotating proved interesting. Even though she was busy trying not to make a fool of herself, there were moments here and there when she actually learned something about her dance partner.

Andy snagged her blouse during a spin.

"Sorry my hands are so rough," he said. "Occupational hazard."

Suzanna was about to politely ask what his occupation was, but it took almost the whole class period for her to rotate back to him, and then the question seemed forced.

She'd started to recognize several of the regulars in class. Besides Lauren and Andy, there were Sandy and Alexia, a pair of sisters in their early twenties who could have been cast as a pair of mysterious Swedish spies should the need arise. They were very nice, but Suzanna was a tiny bit jealous that they seemed to improve at an accelerated rate. During one of their dance rotations, Suzanna was again dancing with Andy and she mentioned how good they seemed to be getting, while he and she were, well, progressing a little more slowly.

"They go to the salsa clubs every weekend," he said, "so they get in a lot more practice. Maybe we should go sometime."

With that, Rio called "change partners"—and she was left wondering if she had just been asked out on a date.

"Try to keep your upper body still," Rio said to the class. "Like so . . ."

He started to move to the music; his shoulders were barely moving, but his hips were a tornado of activity. One of the great pleasures of this class was that it was not only perfectly acceptable to be staring at their teacher's glorious crotch, it was actually encouraged.

Lauren was also watching Rio. She was looking perfect, as usual. Her dark hair had a gorgeous blue cast to it. You could only see it when the light from the disco ball hit it just right. Understated. Elegant. She made Suzanna feel lumpy and clumsy whenever she danced by her, Lauren's hair catching the glint of the ball whose light was streaking picturesquely across the studio.

Suzanna actually thought about tripping her one day.

She just brings out the worst in me.

As much as she obsessed over the beautiful, taut dancer, Suzanna realized she was a complete nonentity to Lauren. She felt as if she were back in high school again with all her insecurities bubbling to the surface.

"Are you having problems with the step?" Rio asked.

Suzanna blushed, realizing that her mind had wandered.

"No, I . . . no."

"Please concentrate."

Suzanna was relieved when he returned his attention to the class. She rotated back to Andy.

"He's tough," Andy said.

Suzanna, embarrassed, tried to change the subject.

"So . . . occupational hazard. What do you do?"

"I'm a carpenter."

PART TWO

NAPA VALLEY

CHAPTER 9

Although she was nervous about the remodel, Suzanna took comfort in the fact that everything seemed well thought out and planned. She put great store in plans. Suzanna's parents, Martin and Virginia Wolf, had not always been planners. Months before Suzanna was born, they bought and converted a rundown old barn in Napa, California, into a cavernous home. Determined to get the new house finished before the baby arrived, Suzanna's mother was so intent on installing some salvaged wainscoting that she ignored her labor pains until it was too late, and Suzanna was born at home. Her father used to say you could sum up Suzanna's early life by saying she was born in a manger and raised by Wolfs.

Haha.

Both of Suzanna's parents were born in the early 1940s. They were among the very first baby boomers, and life had taken them through a fairly exhausting roller-coaster ride of cultural mores. The 1950s saw them cowering under school desks, waiting for the Big One to go off while the 1960s had them bearing witness to the deaths of the Kennedys and Dr. Martin Luther King, protesting the Vietnam war, and fighting for women's rights.

They met as students at a protest rally at Temple University in Philadelphia, but after awhile they got pretty burned out, what with trying to save the world. They got their college degrees and a marriage license. They put the ills of the world on the back burner, moved to New York City, and started their own lives. Erinn was born in New York, but by the time Virginia was pregnant with Suzanna, the Wolfs had decided that New York was no place to raise a family. They moved to California with their twin professorships—he, English, she, history—with no great plan other than to teach and raise their children. Except for the occasional renovation to the barn–house, the senior Wolfs' lives didn't change much in thirty-some years—until Martin died in a car accident. He had been crossing Route 29 and was smacked down by a drunken tourist's rental car.

"Poor Father," Erinn said to her sister after Virginia called with the sad news. "He would have hated that he died a cliché."

Erinn and Suzanna made it a point to visit their widowed mother often. The eight-hour drive from Santa Monica to Napa gave Suzanna and Erinn a chance to get to know each other a little better. By the time they made the return trip, they were often ready to kill each other.

Suzanna had to admit that her mother was doing alarmingly well. Suzanna knew her mother had loved her father, but she seemed to have blossomed these last few years.

"It's amazing what life holds in store," her mother said to her visiting daughters. She was looking in the mirror and arranging her new hairstyle. "I never thought what life might be like without your father. I miss him terribly, but I'm discovering all kinds of new things about myself."

Erinn and Suzanna looked at each other in alarm. They were not the sort of family that discussed intimate details—and the younger Wolfs had no interest in hearing about what these new discoveries might be. A haircut—OK. They could talk about that. But anything more confidential than that and the conversation would come to a screeching halt.

Suzanna sometimes wished that the women in her family were a little more open with each other. The fact that her mother—her *mother*—was ready to experience life in an entirely different way, really made Suzanna think.

"I don't want to wait until my husband dies before I find myself," Suzanna had said to Erinn on a ride back to Southern California.

"Don't you think you should find a husband?" Erinn said. "Before you kill him off?"

Suzanna turned up the radio. Erinn wasn't sensitive about not being married, but Suzanna was getting touchy, as much as she hated to admit it.

Virginia used to say that Martin and she had enough haphazard knowledge to get them through life... in the sixteenth century. Thank God she had a sense of humor. It wasn't easy going through life named Virginia Wolf, especially if you were a college professor. One of Suzanna's earliest memories was of her mother coming into the house and saying to Martin, "If one more student tells me, 'I'm not afraid of you, Virginia Wolf,' I'm going to scream."

Virginia was a professional woman all her life, and she had flirted with the idea of keeping her maiden name. There was some professional pressure to do so. But she always insisted that it was important that a nuclear family all share the same name. That might have been true, but Suzanna always suspected that it might have had something to do with the fact that her maiden name was Fudgett, and anything had to be better than that.

When Suzanna was in fourth grade, a new kid joined the class. Her name was Candi Cane. The other kids just laughed their heads off when the teacher introduced her, but Suzanna burst into tears of empathy. She could just envision the poor girl coming home every night for the rest of her life wearing the look she knew all too well from her mother.

Suzanna befriended the poor girl, who turned out to be kind of a jerk. Carla was in the class, too, and Suzanna had hoped to share the misery, but Carla was always one of the cool kids, so trying to saddle her with Candi Cane was not in the cards. Suzanna stood steadfastly by Candi through the rest of the school year—on principle—and was thrilled to find out at the beginning of fifth grade that Candi's father had been transferred to the Midwest.

For as long as Suzanna could remember, Carla had been in her life. Suzanna's father used to think it was hilarious to introduce the Caridis as "our closest friends" since Carla and her family lived next door at a winery. Carla's father used to brag that his grandfather came to Napa in the 1900s and the family had been in the wine business ever since. The fact that his grandfather shut the winery during Prohibition and it remained shuttered until 1972 didn't seem to faze him.

Although insanely busy with her architecture practice, Carla still helped run the bustling winery alongside her father. She was loyal to a fault.

When she wasn't stealing boyfriends.

Suzanna could still remember the first time they'd met.

Or she thought she remembered. The two of them had relived it so many times that it almost seemed like a movie they had seen. They were both pretty sure they had their story straight, even though they still argued about some of the details.

They were about five years old and the Caridis were having an open house after installing some new oak barrels at the winery. The Wolfs were invited. Erinn was fifteen and bowed out. Suzanna's parents went—and dragged along a grouchy Suzanna, who, even at five, knew that an open house at a winery was not a place for a little kid to have a good time.

But then she met Carla—also having a lousy time, even though it was her family's winery. The two girls eyed each other for awhile: two five-year-olds take a while to warm to each other, no matter what adults think.

Suzanna was a shy kid, but Carla seemed to have the genetic material of a Vegas showgirl. She craved admiration and basked in the attention of the adults. But adulation will hold a five-year-old's attention for only so long, and Carla eventually turned her high beams on Suzanna, who had the habit of sucking her thumb when she was nervous. Erinn would call her "Suckagawea" to shame her, but basically, their folks were the kind of parents who thought she'd grow out of it when she was good and ready.

Suzanna and Carla stared at each other in the Caridi's huge front hall.

"Only babies suck their thumbs," Carla said.

"Nu-uh," Suzanna said. "I suck my thumb and I'm not a baby."

Mercifully, Carla seemed to accept this logic and asked Suzanna if she wanted to go see the new wine barrels before the adults did. Anything that even remotely hinted of getting ahead of the grownups sounded tantalizing, so she went.

The wine barrels were taller than the girls; pale yellow in color and lying in two neat rows. When describing this scene in later years, Suzanna would tell people that the wine kegs looked like they were waiting for a waltz to begin. This always annoyed Fernando, who would butt in and say there was no way a five-year-old would think that. Eric would take her side and say it was just poetic license. Either way, to Suzanna's five-year-old eyes, those wine barrels were cool.

Carla said they should each climb up on an end barrel and jump the whole line.

"Let's race!"

Racing atop the wine barrels was thrilling—Suzanna felt like she was flying. Carla, however, was flying faster (Suzanna suspected she had a lot more practice), and she was about four barrels ahead.

Suddenly, Carla jumped down. As soon as her little feet hit the ground, the grown-ups appeared at the door. Suzanna always cringed when she thought back to the expressions on the faces of the grown-ups standing in the doorway as they changed from mild interest and curiosity in the new oak wine kegs to horror as they beheld the airborne Suzanna happily jumping from one barrel to the next. Carla, feet firmly planted on winery floor, was innocently batting big green eyes at the adults. Suzanna stopped racing only when she heard her father's voice.

"Suzanna! Get down from there! What do you think you're doing?"

Suzanna looked down startled. Her father was clearly using his young-lady-this-is–inappropriate-behavior voice, but Suzanna honestly had no idea what she was doing wrong.

Mr. Caridi got into the stern-parent act.

"Carla, you know better than this! Why didn't you stop her?"

"She's a guest, Poppi."

Eric (who wouldn't come into the picture for another eight years, but was certainly conversant in this oral history of the Carla and Suzanna friendship) always wondered why Suzanna found this story so charming. Shouldn't she have been angry?

The first time Eric said this, Suzanna tried to look back with an impartial eye. She wasn't angry with Carla. Instead, she thought, "Wow, this kid is *good*. She'll go places in the world, or at least in kindergarten, and I'll be right there beside her."

Call it survival instinct, but Suzanna could tell that having Carla Caridi on your side of the sandbox would rock.

CHAPTER 10

Eric Cooper moved into the snug Napa neighborhood when they were all thirteen. The Cooper Vineyard was about four wineries down the lane from the Caridis', and four wineries and a meadow from the Wolf barn–house. Napa in the seventies and early eighties was a small, small town, so if somebody your age hit town, everybody knew about it. Suzanna and Carla rode their bikes past the Cooper Vineyards every day that summer until they caught a glimpse of him. When they finally saw him walking down the lane, they were thrilled to find out he was really cute—and one of the few boys who was a reasonable height at that age. Eric was loved by all. Cool kids loved him, dorky kids loved him, even grown-ups loved him. He was one of those kids who was completely comfortable talking with adults. Suzanna's parents, for example, were dazzled by him. The first time she brought him home—Carla had managed through some incredibly quick thinking to snag him as a partner on a three-way science project—Suzanna's father was working on a lesson plan on haiku, that Japanese seventeen-syllable, three-line poetry thing.

Eric got into a discussion with him about it and, on the spot, made up a haiku:

The sea tumbles near
Go back, mighty, mighty wave!
How to dry my shoes?

Her parents had burst into applause. Suzanna was thrilled that her family was impressed, but also jealous of the adulation her parents slathered on the boy. Erinn was off in New York City by this time, but Suzanna could hear her father bragging about Eric whenever he and Erinn talked on the phone.

"I'll tell you, Erinn. He's the smartest thing in Napa Valley now that you're gone."

Suzanna tried not to bristle. After all, Eric was amazing and smart and inquisitive. How could they *not* love him? Her parents loved knowledge—or more specifically, her parents loved thinking. Suzanna felt as if she was always letting them down. After Erinn—and now Eric—with their shiny intellects, she didn't have a prayer.

During a teenage parental bitchfest, Suzanna complained to Eric that her father came into the room one evening when she was sitting in front of the television. He shot her a sorrowful look.

"Could you at least *look* like you're thinking?" he'd asked.

Suzanna rolled her eyes as she relayed her predicament to Eric.

"Now, every time my dad goes by, I try to think some important thought, and it's ruining my TV shows."

"What do you think about?" Eric asked.

"What?"

"What important thoughts have you come up with?"

"I don't know . . . the usual . . . Was Napoleon really as bad as everyone thought? Would anyone ever discover who Jack the Ripper was?" Suzanna said.

She was lying. Under pressure to think, she usually came up with something like, "Why does my mom always open her mouth every time she puts on mascara?"

Eric nodded. Suzanna knew he wouldn't have any trouble coming up with a profound thought when put on the spot.

"I'm running out of things to think about," Suzanna confessed.

"Well, that's easy. He didn't ask you to really be thinking, he asked you to *look* like you were thinking. How hard is that?"

At that moment, Suzanna realized that she was in love with her neighbor. He really was a genius! And using his gift for evil, not for good.

She put Eric's plan into action, and while she was clumsy at first, she did soon get the hang of just looking as if she were thinking. She would hear her father's boots on the floorboards, and one of her eyebrows would arch intelligently. As he walked by, they would give each other an erudite nod. He'd go on his way, and Suzanna would go back to watching *The Wonder Years* without missing a punch line.

Eric's family was new to the wine industry and their focus, in those first years, was on the business. They weren't negligent of their son, but they had other things to worry about. Eric was a good kid, so his parents simply left him to his own devices.

By the time she, Carla, and Eric started high school, Suzanna had no complaints when he started hanging around her house after school. Her parents considered him a good example for their daughter now that big sister Erinn was in New York and there was no straight-A sibling in whose scholastic footsteps Suzanna could follow. Suzanna tired to ignore the envy she sometimes felt when her parents were blathering on and on over Eric's wonderfulness. Wasn't not measuring up to Erinn's wonderfulness enough?

Because Suzanna's father was an English professor, it went without saying that the English language was big at the Wolf house. They had a special place in their collective heart for the palindrome, a word or sentence that reads the same forward as it does backward. "Able was I ere I saw Elba" was the premier example, although naturally, as a kid, Suzanna preferred "As I pee, sir, I see Pisa!"

One time, in the tenth grade, Suzanna and her class were studying palindromes. The teacher, a bearded young man with a sense of humor, offered a good example: "A Toyota. Race fast, safe car. A Toyota." Suzanna ran home and passed it off as her own. Her parents actually gasped in appreciation. She practically melted from their praise.

Take that, Eric.

Suzanna did have some complaints, however, when Carla suddenly felt drawn to the household whenever she saw Eric's bike in Suzanna's front yard.

Science project or no science project, if Eric's bike was in the driveway, you could count on Carla showing up.

Suzanna and Carla were best friends by proximity and a gruesome "blood bond" in which they sealed their fate with a ceremony (involving a very sketchy-looking rusted nail, if Suzanna recalled) when they were ten. Both girls took their blood bond seriously, but by the time they were fifteen, they knew instinctively that when it came to boys, all bets were off.

May the best adolescent win.

And Carla won. She stole Eric from Suzanna. That is, Carla stole Eric, according to Suzanna. According to Carla, Eric was a free agent.

After many years (and enough wine) Suzanna would admit that Carla didn't technically steal Eric from her because he wasn't technically her boyfriend. But he was her boyfriend in her mind—and at fifteen, that should have counted for something. And after many years (and a little more wine), Carla would admit she wasn't completely innocent—she did know that Suzanna loved him.

Suzanna never admitted that she saw it coming. She just had no idea how to prevent it. She wasn't as smart as her sister or as pretty as her neighbor. What was a girl to do, except roll with the emotional punches? To add insult to injury, she found out about them in her own kitchen. The three of them were working on yet another science project, determining what noxious weeds were spreading through the valley. Eric was especially fixated on the *Arundo donax*, a cane-like grass that was displacing native plants and wildlife, causing flooding and erosion. Because it was flammable, he argued, it would make a great visual for their classroom project—nothing like fire to get that teenage blood flowing!

Suzanna left the room to get some samples, which were growing in the backyard. She had a nagging feeling that she shouldn't leave Eric and Carla alone in the kitchen too long, so she grabbed a tray of the *donax* and started back into the kitchen as fast as she could.

But not fast enough.

At first she wasn't sure what she was seeing—she thought they were just bent over their books or something. But no. As hard as she tried to ignore it, there was no denying it: her best friend and her boyfriend-in-her-mind were making out!

Suzanna was too embarrassed to tell her parents, but too distraught to go it alone, so she called her sister in New York. While she did her best, Erinn was a huge hit by this time and didn't have the focus or patience to discuss teenage angst. But she did listen to Suzanna pour out her heart.

"So you were growing *donax* in the backyard?" Erinn asked.

Suzanna stopped sniffling. Unhappy as she was, she could still recognize a non sequitur when she heard it.

"Yes," Suzanna said.

"Dear God, Suzanna," Erinn said, "you were actually growing harmful weeds in our yard? Didn't it occur to any of you that you're surrounded by precious grape-growing vines? Have the three of you lost your minds?"

Suzanna couldn't think of anything to say and hung up the phone.

Maybe it had something to do with growing up in a small town . . . there weren't a whole lot of people to be friends with. Or maybe Carla and Suzanna were just destined to remain friends. But somehow, they got through it. Although Eric and Carla dated through junior year and Suzanna did meet Fernando shortly after the monster make-out reveal, Carla, Eric, and Suzanna managed to keep it together. And they got As on all their science projects throughout high school.

Deep inside, when all was said and done, Suzanna never completely trusted Eric or Carla again.

But then again, after all was said and done, Suzanna never completely trusted anyone again.

After Carla and Eric hooked up, Suzanna was at loose ends for the rest of the year. Carla and Eric still invited Suzanna to go everywhere with them, but she declined as often as possible, and without letting it look as if she was a sore loser. She tried to give the impression that everything was fine, but there was definitely some sort of internal shift. Although she kept her grades up, she was no longer interested in school or making new friends. Not that making new friends was much of an option. Suzanna never really did get the hang of being popular.

Suzanna begged her parents to let her live in New York City with Erinn. She argued, constantly and aggressively, that she could finish out the rest of high school with her older sister in a more sophisticated setting. Unfortunately, since her parents were college professors and were very aware of exactly how sophisticated New York City was, they said no.

Suzanna's recollection of the rest of the semester remained hazy. She only remembered being horribly adrift and lonely. Until she met Fernando. He was a transfer student—and a godsend. One day, when Suzanna was having a particularly intense moment of self-loathing, she passed by a reflective window between classes and stared at herself in dismay. She started tugging at her hair (like all teenage girls, she assumed if she got her hair right, she'd get her life right.) and as she pulled and twisted, she said, to no one in particular,

"God, I hate my hair."

And a voice replied softly in her ear, "You don't hate your hair . . . you hate yourself. Your poor hair is just taking all the blame."

Suzanna spun around (both hands still clamping clumps of curls) and there was Fernando. Even though he was only sixteen, he already had his hot little taut body going for him. Suzanna was stunned. She couldn't believe such a cute guy was talking to her. But when she looked around and saw that there wasn't anybody else around, she realized he had to be talking to her. One minute, he was leaning against a pole, appraising her, and the next, he took her hair, twisted it into some sort of Gibson-Girl-on-steroids bun, and disappeared into the crowd just as the bell rang.

Suzanna was speechless when kids in her American Literature class complimented her on her new look. It took her a few minutes to realize they were sincere.

Suzanna kept her eyes open and would spot Fernando from time to time in the gym, shooting hoops by himself, or getting into his father's truck after school. The next time she actually spoke to him, she was standing in the art-department classroom by herself before some sort of awards ceremony, freaking out, quietly and alone, about her dress. She had bought it at a great little boutique and thought it was perfect, but now, in the harsh glare of high school, she could see that it was wrong, so wrong. It was dorky. She was dorky. Luckily, she was wearing her Gibson Girl up-do, so she knew that at least her hair looked good.

Fernando popped in silently again and gave her the once-over.

"Honey, that dress looks like something Bob Mackie would design after a stroke." He shook his head. "Next time, take me shopping with you . . ."

And with that, he grabbed a pair of scissors, cut off her sleeves, widened the neckline, and pulled the whole thing off one shoulder. He spun her around so she could see herself in the reflection of the classroom mirror. Suzanna had to admit it—she looked pretty good. While she stood blinking in gratitude, Fernando was rummaging around in the pastels. He picked up a charcoal, licked it, and rimmed her eyes.

"See?" he said. "You can be fabulous. You just need to work it."

"Thanks," she replied.

"I'm Fernando," he said, as he continued his overhaul.

"And I'm—"

"Late for the ceremony," he said, pushing her out the door.

After that, she'd see him around, and they started to become friends. He was a loner, like she was, but in his case, it was by choice. Apparently, Fernando was a magnet for people and if he wasn't careful, his life could instantly overflow with hangers-on. But for some reason, he took a liking to—or pity on—Suzanna, and they became inseparable.

Suzanna really liked him, but there was also some satisfaction that she was getting even with Carla and Eric, even if only in her own mind. They, of course couldn't have cared less, lost in their own world as they were. If anything, they were probably relieved that Suzanna now had somebody to hang out with. In any case, it didn't hurt to be seen everywhere with an incredibly handsome guy.

Fernando told her right off the bat that he was gay, so there wouldn't be any "weirdness," as he put it. Suzanna was disappointed, of course, but even though she hated to admit to stereotypical thinking, she kind of guessed he was gay when he told her that she could be "fabulous if she would just get that stick out of her ass."

Every time Suzanna was scared of looking a little too flashy, Fernando would nudge her to go for it. But because this was real life, she didn't suddenly shoot right to the top of the list with the popular kids just because she suddenly had a secret stylist.

CHAPTER 11

Suzanna cried herself to sleep at night once Eric and Carla were considered a couple by all their friends. The pain was compound. She'd not only lost Eric, the object of her desire, she'd also lost Carla, her best friend. But the possible biggest torment of all was worrying that Carla would tell Eric all about the teenage fantasies Suzanna had spun and share them in excruciating detail. During her campaign to move to New York, Suzanna poured out her heart to Erinn about her fear that the two of them were laughing at her.

"They aren't laughing at you," Erinn said. "They're busy."

Erinn shared their mother's talent for clear-eyed advice, no matter how much it smarted.

Throughout their friendship, Carla had always been the visionary. When she received a large trampoline for Christmas the year the girls turned twelve, Carla begged her father to put it in the side yard, so she could look at it from her window. Mr. and Mrs. Caridi never woke up to the fact (literally and figuratively)that Carla's bedroom was on the second story and that they had bought their daughter a late-night escape route.

It wasn't that Carla didn't love the trampoline for what it was— the girls would bounce on the trampoline for hours on end—it was just that Carla always managed to envision everything to its fullest potential. She would catapult herself out her bedroom window, drop onto the trampoline, and soundlessly bounce into the grass. Then she'd make her way over to the Wolf barn–house, where she would let herself into the kitchen (nobody locked their doors in Napa in those days) and sneak through the living room and down the hall to Suzanna's room. When Suzanna's mother had designed the house, she left the organic footprint of the barn in place. The girls' bedrooms were old horse stalls with thick walls at the far end of the structure. Once Carla was past the living room, where overhead the senior Wolfs were sleeping in the loft, she was in the clear.

It hadn't immediately occurred to Suzanna that Carla would curtail her nighttime visits when Eric became her main focus. It was as if her entire world went down a rabbit hole. The girls remained civil and publicly social (neither was into catty revenge or painful drama) but things were certainly not the same. Suzanna tried not to wonder if Carla was hurling herself out of her room and making her way to the Cooper winery every night. Luckily, her new friendship with Fernando was opening up new worlds—they cooked, they sewed, they conquered. Fernando made it his mission to keep Suzanna's mind off Eric and Carla, going to great lengths to keep her distracted. Anything he was doing, he included her.

One Saturday, he invited her to his house and Suzanna enthusiastically pedaled over on her bike. Fernando lived with his father. His mother had moved back to Mexico when Fernando was a baby. Suzanna was flabbergasted when Fernando told her this nugget in his matter-of-fact way. But Fernando made no bones about it. His father, Armando Cruz, worked for a large winery but had aspirations to be a vintner himself one day. He owned a small plot of land where he grew the obscure merlot grape, confident that merlot would catch on with the California palate. Mr. Cruz was way ahead of his time.

The road to Fernando's was mercifully flat, but the weather was hot and the fields were heady with the scent of ripening grapes. She was wobbly when she got off her bike and pushed it up his rutted driveway.

Suzanna dropped her bike in the backyard and entered a kitchen that smelled more like grapes than the wineries did. She looked at Fernando quizzically, but he was intensely focused on a bubbling pot. There were grapes being boiled, grapes piled a foot high on the counter, and grapes draining through colanders in the double sink.

"What's all this?" Suzanna asked.

Stir, stir, stir.

"Pop didn't give these guys his seal of approval for wine," he replied, pointing to the heap of grapes on the counter. "I thought I'd make jelly and sell it—put the money toward my college fund."

"That's a good idea," Suzanna said, mentally calculating how many jars of jelly one would have to sell in order to even buy the books required for college.

Every once in awhile, Suzanna felt guilty about the fact that college was a given for the kids of the wealthier families in the valley. Now that she and all her friends were juniors in high school, college was on everyone's minds. Although Suzanna's parents weren't rich, they, too, had made college a priority and had saved their entire lives for their girls' tuition.

Back when Erinn was in high school, she'd been offered scholarships—of course—to all the important universities and had settled on NYU. But her playwriting career took off almost as soon as she hit New York City, and she was so busy making headlines and money that she quit sophomore year. Even though Erinn and Suzanna's parents were academics, they were understanding about Erinn leaving school. Erinn could always go back to college if the fantastic life of the young playwright didn't pan out.

Suzanna pinched a grape and popped it in her mouth. She winced.

"Ick," she said. "This grape tastes gross."

"Don't worry about it. I can make anything taste good."

Suzanna looked at all the grapes, the jars and pots, and was alarmed at exactly how much grape jelly he was undertaking to make.

"You know," Suzanna said, "you really aren't supposed to make grape jelly in large batches. You're only supposed to make about six cups at a time or it won't gel."

Fernando looked frustrated as he surveyed the countertops full of grapes.

"How the hell do you know that?"

"Mom and I make jelly every year," she said.

"Well, crap!" he said, and then looked to Suzanna for help. "Now what?"

Suzanna stuck her hands under the faucet and washed up.

"We'll work fast and see what we can save."

"Hurry! My future is in these jars!"

They washed, crushed, sieved and measured grapes, sterilized jars, and measured sugar and pectin.

"This seems pretty runny," Fernando said as he gently stirred the jelly.

"Let me check."

Suzanna knew they were racing against the clock. She'd put a metal tablespoon in a glass of ice water and now that they'd arrived at the gelling stage, she pulled it out, scooped up a little of the hoped-for jelly, and let it cool to room temperature on the spoon.

"If it thickens up, we've got our jelly. If it's too runny, we'll need to mix in a little more pectin," Suzanna told Fernando, who was watching the jelly, willing it to thicken.

Miraculously, they pulled it off. They poured the sticky grape jelly into little jars, sealed them, and plunged them into their boiling water bath.

While they were washing up, Suzanna licked one of the spoons.

"This is delicious!"

"I know!" he said. "Thanks for the help."

"No problem. It was fun."

Fernando put his sticky fingers on her shoulder.

"We're a pretty good team," he said.

That night, Suzanna was so worn out, she was practically asleep the minute she hit the pillow. She hit the pillow softly, arranging her curls per Fernando's instruction on how to avoid bed head.

It was a toss-up as to which caused Suzanna more anguish that year, the Eric–Carla situation, or worrying about college. It was pretty much a no-brainer that she would be accepted to decent universities. Maybe not Princeton. Or Yale. Or Harvard. Or Georgetown. Or any of the universities that had been begging for her sister ten years earlier. But she had more than a fighting chance at a fair portion of the academic world. Although she had only vague recollections of Erinn applying to colleges, she did remember that her parents took more than a passing interest in the procedure. They lost none of their concern with their second child and lovingly filled Suzanna's room with pamphlets from various schools.

Suzanna gave Fernando some of the leaflets that stressed financial aid, hoping he wouldn't feel left out. As he grimly pointed out, his grape jelly sales wouldn't get him across the bridge to San Francisco.

"It will be just like *American Graffiti*," Fernando said, thumbing though the pamphlets. "Some of us will go off to college without a blip and some of us will stay home and rot."

"Yeah," Suzanna replied, keeping up the *American Graffiti* imagery, "and some of us will be total jerks and drag the other guys down."

Because of her irrational guilt over Fernando not having her options, Suzanna dragged her feet with the whole college process. Her parents were doing their best to let her make her own decision—God knows they'd seen enough disgruntled college kids between them to last a lifetime. It amused Suzanna, in a benign passive-aggressive way, watching her parents trying not to guide her, when she could tell they were going to burst into flames if she didn't start taking her future seriously. She knew they just hated it when they acted like conventional parents, and she wanted to make them happy, but she also wanted Fernando to be happy. She felt she owed him more.

Suzanna's mother's nerves got the better of her and she suddenly whisked Suzanna off to Philadelphia to see Temple University, hoping it would inspire her to commit. Even though her parents often talked about their clear-eyed "protest days," they were also pretty sentimental about their alma mater. It was May, and Suzanna was overwhelmed by the beauty of the East Coast springtime. It was gorgeous!

Suzanna's mother knew what she was doing. She knew from experience that it is really hard to make a decision about how you want to spend the next four years of your life when you are surrounded by flowers—flowers on the ground, flowers in window boxes, flowers in the *trees!* Of course, anyone in his or her right mind would want to go to school in the East! A person would be crazy not to want to go to school in the East! It's one of God's cosmic jokes to seduce young people with East Coast springs and falls, then—let them move there, and *whammo!* Here come winter and summer! SURPRISE!

Springtime aside, Suzanna fell in love with the campus—and got caught up in the prospect of having a college agenda. The day was a whirl of buildings with the words Journalism, English, History, and Chemistry emblazoned importantly on them.

Suzanna found it interesting to see her mother out of context. She seemed younger here in her college town, without the mantle of her own professorship (although, Suzanna noted, she used it when she needed it, as they went from laureled hall to laureled hall and saluted old professors of hers). It occurred to Suzanna, while they were eating lunch at an old Philadelphia haunt called City Tavern, that she never thought about her mother or father as having a life before parenthood. She just sort of pictured her parents as two flat balloons suddenly filling with air when Erinn was born—and helium the moment she arrived. This concept startled her, and she almost choked on her chowder.

"Temple seems pretty cool," she said. "I can picture you and Dad here."

Her mother was having a second glass of California wine . . . it was strange seeing all the familiar labels from the Napa neighborhood in such an unfamiliar landscape. Virginia actually looked a little flushed, which never happened at home. All that wine—it was practically in the air at home—and Suzanna realized she had never seen her mother even remotely tipsy before.

"We had some wonderful times here. It seems like only yesterday."

She ordered a third glass of wine, and held it up to the sunlight. She squinted at it knowingly.

"I almost married somebody else," she said suddenly.

Suzanna tried to take this in.

"There was this guy . . . and he was in a band . . ."

Shoot me now. Not a guy in a band!

Her mother was clearly on a roll here, a blitzkrieg down memory lane. She continued, "Yeah . . . he was really into his music. He would talk about music day and night. When we'd be having coffee with friends, he'd be drumming on his thigh . . . and he was a bass player. All he thought about was music, music, music. I was very young and mistook his passion for . . . for . . . well, let's just say he was extremely focused on himself—and his needs."

Needs?

Suzanna did not want to be discussing anyone's needs with her mother—except her own.

"You'll find out, sweetheart, that just because you're in love with someone, it doesn't mean you should marry him," her mother said.

Suzanna was overwhelmed. They just came to Philadelphia to look at a college and she was getting bombarded with stuff she *did not want to know.* She needed to get the conversation back on safe ground . . . get it back to herself, where it belonged.

"So what happened?" Suzanna asked. "When did Dad enter the picture?"

"Well, I met your father at a rally for something or other—some save-the-world ordeal. Isn't it funny how something can seem so important at the time and you don't even remember it later?"

"Hilarious."

'Well, obviously I was a sucker for passion on one level or another . . . one guy with his music, and your father with his social conscience. But as I got to know your father, I could see the difference. Your father's passions were other-directed—he was such a good man. And that's who you marry, Suzanna. You marry the good man."

I'm eighteen and can't even get a date, but thanks, Mom.

"And besides," said her mother, with a strange look—if it wasn't on her dear mother's face, she would have described the look as leering—"and besides," she continued, cheeks blazing. "Your father was so damn cute."

Suzanna could feel a panic swell coming on, which . . . panicked her. Panic swells were still a fairly new phenomenon. But because she was sitting at a table, she managed to stay in her seat by gripping the chair as tightly as she could. She concentrated on getting things back under control.

"Well, are you happy with how things turned out?"

She wondered if she really wanted to know the answer. She waited while her mother looked at the historic street outside the window. Her very own cobblestoned time machine. Her eyes seem to mist over as she searched for an answer.

"Honey." She took Suzanna's hand and let out a pitiful sigh. "Sometimes I just get so sick of the Virginia Wolf jokes."

Suzanna loved Temple and could see herself on the East Coast. Just as she tried to visualize keeping her feet on the ground during a panic swell, she now tried to visualize herself walking the hallowed grounds of some stone-clad, ivy-covered university. But she continued to stall, and junior year evaporated without Suzanna taking any overt action to get into college.

One summer night between junior and senior year, Suzanna was positioning one last strawberry blonde curl when she heard her bedroom door open. The sound was so familiar it didn't occur to her to be scared. But standing there was a scary sight: Carla, tears and mascara streaming down her cheeks. Suzanna sat up and opened her arms. Carla let out a muffled wail and launched herself into Suzanna's embrace. The girls fell asleep without ever talking, but Suzanna knew Carla well enough to know that the relationship that had broken her own heart had now broken Carla's.

In her mind, they were even. They never discussed the breakup.

CHAPTER 12

Fernando had his heart set on some sort of art school. He he didn't really care if it was design or cooking or hair and makeup as long as it screamed I AM AN ARTIST. Unfortunately, his father couldn't see past the financial obstacles and pretty much told Fernando that if college was going to happen, Fernando was on his own.

Suzanna's parents were happy to discuss college options with him, and Martin Wolf offered to take Suzanna and Fernando on a tour of a northwestern college, Cornish College of the Arts in Seattle. Fernando was thrilled with the opportunity and grateful to Suzanna's parents, whom he called "Professor Wolf" and "Mrs. Professor" or "Mrs. P."

It was pouring rain in Washington state as they followed a young tour guide around the soggy campus. The guide said that the programs were designed to provide all students with a general foundation of academic skills.

"As opposed to those other college campuses," Martin Wolf whispered to his daughter.

After a tour of the campus and the city, Fernando persuaded Suzanna's father to take them on the ferry out to Vashon Island. This, actually, had been Fernando and Suzanna's secret agenda. When the thought of going their separate ways unnerved them, Suzanna and Fernando often fantasized about going to college—together. One of the charms of Cornish was that it was within striking distance of

Vashon Island, where the two of them envisioned living a remote life and taking the ferry back and forth to school.

Suzanna and Fernando were great fans of Betty MacDonald, an American author who wrote about life on Vashon Island. Suzanna had been listlessly trolling her mother's library one afternoon and came across *The Egg and I,* the autobiographical account of Betty MacDonald's life as a young wife on a chicken ranch in the 1920s. Suzanna loved the book and insisted that Fernando read it. He said he didn't really see what she liked so much, but then Suzanna passed on Betty's next venture, *The Plague and I.* Fernando was hooked on the lighthearted account of her time in a tuberculosis sanatorium. Then MacDonald wrote *Onions in the Stew*—and this was about Vashon Island. Ever since they had read that, Suzanna and Fernando had been dying to visit.

The ferry trip to the island was everything they dreamed it would be. Suzanna's heart beat faster as the island came into view out of the fog. They jumped off the rocking boat and had lunch in a drafty café. After an hour of poking around town, Suzanna and Fernando felt their collective dream fade.

As Fernando recounted to Suzanna's mother when they got back, "Your husband was cool taking us up to Washington. But Vashon Island was boring as shit."

Mrs. Professor laughed and told Fernando to watch his language.

"Seriously, Mrs. P . . . can you imagine a place that makes Napa look like it has a pulse?"

Senior year sped by. Suzanna was still up in the air about college. She excused it by telling herself that she was going to concentrate on getting her grades up rather than focus on college. She hung out with Fernando, and then Eric and Carla in varying degrees. When Carla and Eric broke up, Carla moved on to an entirely new group of friends, although she did do science projects with Suzanna and Eric from time to time. Their cumulative knowledge really did give them an edge and they somehow managed to put all personal feelings aside to capture those elusive few remaining good grades.

Eric, through some unspoken agreement, seemed to retain the rights to the friendship with Suzanna and, by extension, Fernando, and the three of them did almost everything together.

Suzanna and Carla sometimes hung out together on the weekends, but, as a pair, they didn't play well with others.

Although there had been nothing romantic between Carla and Eric for almost a year, there was certainly no indication that Eric now returned Suzanna's admiration. And Suzanna still saw Carla as a threat to the any-minute-now romance that might spring up between Eric and herself.

Suzanna was studying in her room and looked up to see Carla running down the lane toward the barn–house. She was whooping, and waving something in the air. Suzanna closed her book and raced out to meet her friend. Carla bounced around in a circle while Suzanna read the letter that Carla had been waving. It was an acceptance letter from Howard University in Washington, D. C. Suzanna grabbed Carla by the wrists and they leaped in a circle, squealing with relief. For Suzanna, the relief was twofold. First, that her friend had, deservedly, gotten into an amazing school. Second, since Eric had set his sights on Berkeley, which was almost a local school, the fact that Carla would be three thousand miles away was a huge blessing. Fernando had confessed to Suzanna that he, too, wanted to get into Berkeley, but Suzanna knew that would never happen.

"Well, I can dream, can't I?" Fernando said resolutely.

Letters of acceptance (and rejection) were making the rounds at the school. Suzanna noticed that the news of Carla's acceptance letter brought back the look of panic to her parents' eyes. Suzanna was studying a map of the San Francisco area, hoping a college might reveal itself to her as the perfect place—one that would satisfy her parents and be near Eric and Fernando—when the phone rang. It was Eric, and he wanted to see her right away. She headed out to meet him on the road between their houses. It was a path they'd been taking since childhood. She would leave her house and Eric would leave his and they'd head down opposite ends of their little dirt lane toward each other. The way the road was laid out, both of them would have to crest a little hill, when they could see the other one. When they were kids, as soon as the other was in sight, they'd start to run.

But they had grown, and while Suzanna's instinct was still to run toward him the moment she saw him, he was now way too cool for any of that. They sauntered toward each other at a maddeningly slow pace until they were walking side by side. By this time, Eric and Carla had been broken up for almost a year—an eternity, by high school standards. Suzanna no longer braced herself for their reconciliation. She'd moved on to the next stage, that of periodically getting her hopes up that the lightning bolt of love would strike Eric right on the spot and he would realize the object of all his desires was standing right in front of him . . . or at least beside him on a dusty little road in Napa.

"What's up?" Suzanna said in the casual tone Fernando had drilled into her.

"Check it out," he replied, handing her a letter.

Suzanna opened it and saw that it was an acceptance letter from Boston College.

She felt her throat tighten. Eric was going away?

"I thought you were going to Berkeley."

He shrugged.

"Well, I didn't get in," he said. "But I'm going to Boston! Is that cool or what?"

Suzanna's eyes started to well with tears and she tried to swallow. He'd talked so much about Berkeley that she hadn't even considered him going away. He looked down the road.

"I can't wait to get out of this place," he said.

Suzanna watched Eric head back toward his house as she blinked back tears.

She felt her feet lifting off the ground. But Eric stopped and turned around. She felt her feet settle back on the ground. She stared at him. They were about ten feet apart. He made no move toward her, but just kept looking at her.

"You want to go to the prom with me?" he asked.

Suzanna felt her brain seize.

"Go to the prom?" she asked, her mouth moving as if filled with marbles. "With you?"

She tried to concentrate, but it was no use. The question came as such a shock and, coming on the heels of the news that Eric would be going to the opposite coast, she had no defenses. She started to float again.

No! Not now! Not now!

Eric, with his easygoing way, just continued the conversation as if everything was normal.

"Yeah. I mean, I'm not seeing anybody and you're not seeing anybody . . . are you?"

Luckily, her belt got caught in the low-hanging branch of a

sycamore, and she tried to sound as casual as possible while dangling among the leaves.

"No . . . I'm not seeing anybody."

"So, we're on, then?"

"Yeah, sure. We're on."

Eric smiled at her, turned around again, and headed home. Suzanna looked at the sky. How long would she be hanging up here in midair? She had to get home and tell her mother that she was going to the prom with Eric. Maybe she didn't have a future—or even a college—all mapped out, but she had a date to the prom. And that date was with Eric! It was like a dream come true. She worried—and wondered—about how Carla was going to feel about this.

Pop! With unsteady ankles, Suzanna was back on the ground, already dreaming of the prom. Her parents tried to hide their obvious elation. Suzanna suspected that they saw Eric as her salvation. The dive from deliverance to prom date was a pretty big one, but at this point, her parents were pretty much grasping at straws.

After informing her parents about the prom news, she raced up to her bedroom to call Carla. She stared at the phone for a few minutes. Carla and Eric really did seem to be over their junior-year romance. Carla had gone on to a steady relationship with Scott, the senior-class president, and Suzanna had no good reason to think she might not be happy with Suzanna's news.

But still . . .

Suzanna steeled herself, called Carla, and broke her big news.

"That's fantastic!" Carla said. "I had a feeling he might ask you."

Suzanna tried to punch down the demon that was leapfrogging through her head, whispering that the two of them had been discussing her. She reprimanded herself—she was not going to let herself spoil this moment. Eric had asked her to the prom and that was all that mattered.

She had a hard time sleeping that night, counting the hours until she got to school and saw Eric. She didn't spot him until lunchtime. He had already grabbed a table and was deep in conversation with Fernando. Suzanna came over and joined them, wondering if the invitation to the prom had upped her status in his eyes. Apparently not; their relationship appeared to be exactly the same.

"Fernando isn't going to the prom," Eric said. "Did you know that?"

Suzanna did know that. Fernando had said that if he couldn't attend the prom with his boyfriend, then he wouldn't go at all.

"But you don't have a boyfriend," Suzanna said.

"That isn't the point."

Since Suzanna couldn't figure out what the point was, she dropped it.

"That sucks, man," Eric said.

"So, you guys are going to the prom together," Fernando said, eyes blazing at Suzanna.

Suzanna reddened as she realized she had forgotten to tell Fernando this earth-shattering news. She knew she would not be forgiven easily and would have to kiss up for weeks for her transgression.

"Oh! Yeah! We are," Suzanna tried to sound casual.

"He's making a statement, Beet," Eric said.

"I know," Suzanna said, trying in vain to control her flush.

"Well, I think the three of us should go together," Eric said. "That's at least part of a statement."

Fernando might have been angry with Suzanna, but he dearly loved his best friend and could read the panic in her eyes as her dream crumbled.

"No, that's OK," Fernando said, grabbing Suzanna's wrist lest she float away. "I don't really care about the prom, anyway."

Suzanna could have cried, she was so overcome by his loyalty. Why was it that Fernando could understand every nuance of her psyche and Eric wouldn't see undying love if it hit him like an anvil?

"No, seriously, we should go together," Eric said. "We've done everything together this year. We should go to the prom together, too."

"Well, what about our science projects?" Suzanna asked.

"What about them?" Eric asked.

"We didn't do those together . . . We did them with Carla."

"You're right," Eric said, just as Carla and Scott were walking by. He turned to them.

"Hey, Scotty, Carla. Suzanna, Fernando, and I are all going to the prom together. You guys in?"

Carla looked surprised and tried to do a mind-meld with Suzanna, but Scott and Eric were already slapping high-fives. It was a done deal. The five of them would be the first—and to date, the only—double-and-a-half date at the Napa Valley High School prom.

Carla and Suzanna decided to go dress shopping in San Francisco. Fernando insisted on coming. Suzanna balked, saying that this was a "girl's day," but Fernando would not be dissuaded.

"You can't pick out a dress without me," he said." You'll go into all those stores, get overwhelmed, and forget what your taste is. Face it, Suzanna, you need me."

Suzanna (and Carla) knew she couldn't argue, and off they went in the Caridi family car to the big city across the bay. On the highway, they passed a sign that read UNIVERSITY OF CALIFORNIA, BERKELEY. Suzanna averted her eyes as the iconic bell tower on the Berkeley campus came into view. Although Suzanna had advised him against applying, Fernando sent in an application anyway.

"They can't say 'yes' unless I apply," he had said.

Suzanna pointed out that, even if by some miracle they accepted him, how did he plan on paying for it?

"That's what we call a 'fun' problem."

When his thanks-but-no-thanks letter came, Suzanna wondered how and why he always put himself in the path to get hurt. It was as if he had absolutely no fear of rejection.

"It's not that," he had said. "I just know you can't succeed unless you try. You know, like Jack Nicholson in *One Flew Over the Cuckoo's Nest* . . . when he tries to rip the sink out of the wall. Remember?"

"Yes . . . he can't rip it out. He fails."

"Sure, he fails . . . but he says, 'At least I tried.'"

Suzanna noticed that Fernando also turned away from the campus as they drove by and wondered if Berkeley held as many dashed dreams as it did students.

Fernando helped Suzanna select her dress. He had been right, of course. Within half an hour, Suzanna had lost all confidence in herself and just gave herself over to him.

Fernando outdid himself. He found a spectacular white strapless dress with huge polka dots splattered all over it. To add to the mayhem, the dress also had a red taffeta bodice and three tiers of red taffeta ruffles on the skirt. He zipped Suzanna into it, spun her around and said to her:

"Oh. My. God. You look like an explosion in a ruffle factory."

To the saleswoman, he said:

"We'll take it."

Carla wanted no input, and picked a sleek black halter dress. Fernando itched to jazz up her ensemble, but Carla knew what she wanted.

Always did. Always would.

Napa Valley kids were among the first to start taking limousines on prom nights. The five friends climbed into the back of a stretch and went to all their parents' houses for pictures—except for the Cruz house. Fernando's father said he had to work and wouldn't be around. Carla had smuggled a couple of bottles of wine out and the friends toasted each other in the back of the limo. Scott did not have as much experience around wine as the other four, and got drunk, much to everyone's amusement.

The dance started out well, although, as much as Suzanna wanted to have a picture taken just with Eric, Suzanna was disappointed that the five of them had their official picture taken together. Suzanna danced with Eric and Fernando, and they all dealt uncomfortably with Scott's drunken and unsophisticated lust for Carla. While they were dancing, he would try to grope her breasts. Carla would slap his hands away, first playfully, and then a little more aggressively. Suzanna was dancing with Eric and could see him following the action with his eyes. Suzanna realized she was jealous of Carla getting Eric's attention, even though she realized she was being horrible—if only internally.

As the evening progressed, Scott got bolder. He and Carla were sitting out a dance; Carla had suggested that perhaps they should take a minute to sober up. Suzanna was dancing with Fernando and Eric was off talking to some of their friends, when Scott started to walk his fingers, like the "eensy-weensy spider," up Carla's thigh, in front of everybody. Carla seemed frozen. Half the kids stopped dancing and their eyes were glued to Scott's fingers as they advanced up Carla's leg.

Suddenly, the situation was resolved.

One minute, Scott's hand was creeping up Carla's skirt and the next, he was splayed out on the floor, rented tux and all, clutching his face and howling. Suzanna's first confused reaction was how stupid he looked, with his satin bow tie tilted at a less than jaunty angle and his yowling red face. When she was able to tune into the scene lucidly, she saw Carla crying in Eric's arms. Eric, Carla's knight in shining armor, had decked Scott. Fernando squeezed Suzanna's shoulder in sympathy. Eric helped Carla step over Scott and they walked over to Fernando and Suzanna. Eric looked at Suzanna.

"Come on, Beet, let's all go home."

CHAPTER 13

Suzanna was in a funk for a week after the prom. She knew she should have been proud of Eric for coming to Carla's rescue—and she was—but mostly she felt deflated. She tried to be mad at Carla, but she just couldn't muster the imagination it would take to make this Carla's fault. There was just no way she was ever going to be an object of desire as far as Eric was concerned. She knew it. For the weeks leading up to the event, thinking about the prom had been a welcome relief from the tension of thinking about colleges. But after the fact, it was back to wondering what her future was going to hold. All she knew was that it was a future without Eric. Even if Eric were staying in town, which he wasn't.

College seemed more and more like a dreamland the fact that it appeared that Fernando was staying at his father's place for the fore-seeable future made it impossible to whine to him about her dilemma. As she predicted, the jelly fund left him far short of a college endowment, even if he had had a college to which he could apply it.

Suzanna knew she had let too much time go by—and the dream of fall admissions had slipped away—but she was sure she could salvage the situation if she could make up her mind and at least declare a school for the following spring. Although her parents never pressured her, Suzanna knew how much the Professors Wolf wanted to be able to hold their heads up at her graduation and say, "Well, Suzanna just wants to take a semester off to clear her head and then she'll be starting [insert college name, *any* college name here] for the spring semester."

But she just seemed to be immobile. She couldn't picture leaving the security of Napa, and particularly Fernando.

Fernando was the one who finally broke the stalemate. As they walked home from school after a hard day of listening to the other seniors discussing their futures, Fernando said: "I'm moving to Los Angeles."

Suzanna was surprised by the calm delivery of this statement. Normally, Fernando was overly dramatic about the most minute detail, yet here he was with earthshaking news and he just said it as if it was the most natural thing in the world. Suzanna decided to just go with the flow.

"Really?"she said. "What did your dad say?"

"Not much. He really can't afford to send me anyplace, so I guess as long as I'm not costing anything, he's okay. He's probably relieved that I've got a plan."

"What's your plan?"

"I just told you—I'm moving to Los Angeles."

"What are you going to do when you get there?"

"Get a job."

"Doing what?"

"I don't know. Something fun."

"Something fun. That's your plan."

"Hey, it's more than you've got."

The reality of that statement took Suzanna's breath away.

"What if I went to Los Angeles with you?"

Fernando stopped walking and looked at her. Suzanna couldn't believe she'd said it. Her parents wouldn't be very happy, but—one never knew. Maybe they'd be relieved that she'd finally made up her mind about something.

"Well," Fernando said, "Then you'd have a plan, too."

The Professors Wolf tried not to be judgmental. They really did. And Suzanna did say that she was going to go to Los Angeles just long enough to find some sort of life interest. When her parents were frosty with her, she pulled out the big guns:

"Erinn went to New York and she didn't finish college. And look at her. She couldn't be a bigger success story if she tried."

She knew she wasn't fighting fair. Even though Erinn was wildly successful with her Broadway career, Suzanna was aware that her parents were severely disappointed that she hadn't stayed in school.

She was fighting dirty, but at least this argument shut them up.

The last few weeks of classes went by fairly smoothly. She found that many of the kids actually seemed to be jealous of the fact that Fernando and Suzanna got to take a break from school. Suzanna felt giddy to be getting out of school. Graduation day had gone perfectly, marred only by the printed program that listed all the kids and their colleges, with the glaring exception of Fernando Cruz and Suzanna Wolf. Suzanna noticed that when her parents came backstage to congratulate her, they didn't bring a program with them. As she hugged her parents, she thought:

I'll make this up to you, I promise.

But like many important things rattling around in Suzanna's head, she never got around to actually saying it.

Four days before they were to leave for L.A., Fernando and Suzanna were frantically packing up Suzanna's belongings. Boxes filled her room. In one corner, boxes of stuff to give to charity. In another corner, boxes that would accompany her south. The content of the boxes for charity kept shifting. Desperate as she was to get rid of as much as she could—she felt that would give them a clean slate—Fernando had other ideas.

"Honey, we already have so much emotional baggage, a few more boxes won't hurt . . . and shoulder pads are going to make a comeback. Mark my words," he said.

And suddenly, a box marked "charity" would appear in the "to L. A." stack.

"I am so sick of this," Suzanna said, throwing down the packing tape.

"Come on, Moan-a. Chin up."

Her father called down to them and asked Suzanna to come upstairs. Suzanna and Fernando exchanged a long-suffering teenage look. The last thing either of them wanted to endure was another bittersweet exchange with her parents. Even though they were both nervous and a little sad about leaving, they were both guiltily excited—an emotion they were trying to hide from their assorted adults.

"Lately, I feel like a terminal cancer patient," Fernando said. "Every time my dad looks at me, he gets misty-eyed."

"I know. It's unnerving," Suzanna said, moving one last box back to the charity pile. She headed down, Fernando at her heels. "Come on, let's get it over with."

True to form, Suzanna's parents were standing at the top of the steps with *that look.* Fernando and Suzanna eyed at each other, and her father said in a strangled voice, "Come outside."

"I bet they bought us a dog," whispered Fernando.

"But the new apartment won't let us have dogs," Suzanna said, although she was pretty excited about having a dog, too.

Once outside, they stood rooted to the ground.

"That's not a dog," said Fernando.

And it wasn't. It was a car! A red 1979 Land Cruiser and, although it looked suspiciously like a mail truck, Suzanna thought it was the coolest car ever! She was so overwhelmed, she spent a minute wiping her eyes and beating herself up for not being cool in front of Fernando. Which was ridiculous, because the sight of the car brought a full-on bout of gasping sobs from Fernando, who was now wrapped in Virginia's arms.

When Suzanna was finally able to focus on the car, she noticed an alarming protrusion between the two seats.

"It's a stick shift," Martin said, "but you have plenty of time to learn to drive it before you leave."

I have four days!

"Let's take it for a ride," Martin said, climbing into the passenger seat.

Suzanna settled into the driver's seat as her mother helped a still-sobbing Fernando into the back.

"OK, the first thing you do is put the key in the ignition . . ."

Somehow, she did manage to learn how to drive the five-speed. When she offered to teach Fernando to drive it, he gave her a disdainful look. His father may not have had enough money to send his son to college, but he had taught him to drive all sorts of farm equipment when Fernando was child.

"I could drive that thing with my eyes closed," he said.

"Please don't."

Finally, it was time to leave. Fernando had said goodbye to his father, who matched Fernando's grape jelly fund, much to Fernando's surprise. Mr. Cruz drove Fernando over to the barn–house, tipped his hat, and drove off. Fernando stared after the truck until it disappeared in a cloud of dust, and then put his one bag on the ground. He had turned his mind resolutely toward the future.

Suzanna's father had had a trailer hitch installed and rented a U-Haul trailer to lug all their worldly goods to Southern California. After endless battles with Fernando, Suzanna finally had her trip organized. She was bringing her music collection (records and tapes of soulful or pissed-off singers like k. d. lang, Melissa Etheridge, Bonnie Raitt, and Sophie B. Hawkins), clothes (lots of black denim and her own wimped-out version of grunge), and some furniture: a bed for her, a bed for Fernando, two hand-painted dressers designed and executed by Fernando, a bookcase, a huge table and four unusual chairs (Fernando had grabbed four discarded 30-gallon wine barrels from the side of the road—only Napa Valley would have wine barrels set along the road instead of the random mattress or lamp—and had taken a saw and upholstery stuffing to them. They now were extremely comfortable but odd-looking high-backed chairs), a rocking chair, and a new futon.

Why her parents decided she also needed a futon when she was already bringing a bed, was a mystery to her. Fernando suspected they wanted to make sure that if she had an overnight guest of the opposite sex, they could at least feel that they gave her every opportunity to send him to the sofa.

Suzanna got in the overstuffed Land Cruiser's driver's seat and looked at her parents. Her mother had been crying, but Suzanna could tell she had resolved to be strong for her daughter's sake. She sniffled a bit and gave Suzanna a watery smile.

"Bye, guys," Suzanna said, trying to keep Goat Girl silent. (Fernando always called Suzanna "Goat Girl" when she was trying not to cry. Goat Girl has that quivery voice with a sort of a bleat in it: "Byyyyyyye, guuuuuys.")

Suzanna tried to steady her voice. "Thanks for the Toyota! Really. I love it."

Her mother's fortitude was about to give way.

"A Toyota. Race fast, safe car. A Toyota! Boo-hoo-hoooo-hooo."

Great.

Well, at least that made it easier to pull away.

They were silent as Suzanna drove over to the Caridis' winery. She lurched up the dirt road—she was still getting the hang of the stick shift—through the eucalyptus trees and thought that a final drive up a picturesque private road leading to an even more picturesque winery really symbolized the end of her childhood—possibly more than leaving her parents in a spray of gravel. This *was* Napa!

Her car farted and died in front of the house.

Carla zoomed out the front door with a duffel bag. Since she was not leaving for D. C. for another month and was getting antsy, she was going to drive down the coast with her friends and then fly home. Fernando wasn't thrilled that Carla was horning in on their big adventure, but since Suzanna had the car and her parents were pretty much financing this whole thing, she got to throw her weight around a little bit.

"Oh, so this week we like Carla," Fernando had said.

"We always like Carla," Suzanna said. "Even when we hate her. She's like family."

Fernando had gotten out of the car to rearrange some boxes in the back, and when he was ready to get back in, Carla had commandeered the front seat. Fernando got stormily into the back.

"Let's go, let's go, let's go!" Carla said.

Suzanna started the car and they headed down the road.

"Can you stop at the drugstore?" Carla said as they passed through downtown. "I need to get some gum."

Fernando sighed heavily as Suzanna swung into a parking space.

"I'll be right back," Carla said as she hopped out of the Land Cruiser.

As soon as Carla was out of the car, Fernando crawled back into the front passenger seat.

"Two can play at this game," he said, his butt still in the air.

Suzanna tried to set the radio buttons while they waited. Suddenly, there was a huge *thud!* On the hood, which spooked Suzanna and Fernando so severely they practically cracked heads. There, in the glare of downtown's sunshine, stood Eric, smiling sheepishly. The loud thud had been caused by his oversized backpack, which he had plunked down on the hood.

"Want some company?" he asked, as he climbed into the back seat with his bag.

At that moment, Carla came bounding out of the drugstore. She jumped into the back of the Cruiser.

"Surprise! Surprise!" she said. "I invited Eric."

Suzanna exchanged a horrified look with Fernando. What would her parents think? What, for that matter, did she think? And why had Fernando gotten back into the passenger seat? Carla and Eric were now in the back seat together. Eric caught her eye in the rearview mirror.

"It's cool, isn't it?"

"It's cool," Suzanna said, starting the engine.

The car stalled about seven times before they finally headed down the highway to Los Angeles. Once they were underway, the car never stalled again. Fernando took that as a sign that all was going to be well . . . and Suzanna was desperate to believe him.

They stopped for the night at that masterpiece of kitsch, the Madonna Inn in San Luis Obispo.

"Michelangelo could not have built anything more beautiful," Fernando said, gazing up at the cake-frosting turrets.

"I think you mean Da Vinci," Suzanna said. "Michelangelo didn't design buildings."

"God, you sound like your sister," Carla said.

"No she doesn't," Eric said, while he pumped gas into the Land Cruiser at the Madonna filling station.

Suzanna flushed modestly as Eric defended her to Carla.

"Erinn would have been right," Eric continued. "Suzanna is wrong. Michelangelo designed lots of buildings—like the mortuary chapel for the Medici family in Florence."

"Wow. Now you sound like her mom!" Carla said.

Suzanna's cheeks started to blaze. Eric looked at her.

"Sorry, Beet, but it's true."

"I just meant Michelangelo wouldn't have designed the Madonna Inn, that's all," Suzanna said—although that wasn't what she meant at all. She was showing off and it backfired, but she wasn't about to admit that.

The four of them walked into the lobby of the hotel. It was truly a design trainwreck. The Inn looks like a wedding cake on steroids, the lobby like a detonation at Santa's Workshop. The Madonna Inn wasn't exactly on their student budget, but with the unexpected infusion of Eric's money, the group thought they might as well splurge.

They decided on a plan. The girls would go to the front desk and request a room. Then, if the gods were smiling on them and they actually got a room, the boys would sneak in.

It was summer and the Madonna Inn was a destination with locals and tourists alike, so they approached the front desk, hoping for the best. They had their fingers crossed that they might at least find a vacancy in one of the less intense rooms . . . maybe the Fabulous Fifties room or the rather unnerving What's Left—a room retched from odds and ends left over from the rest of the rooms.

But the Inn had a tour cancel out and they managed to snag the Caveman Room. With its cave like atmosphere (in this case, considered a good thing), the room had solid rock floors, walls, ceilings— and even a rock shower. The girls got the key and went up first. They boys showed up a few minutes later. They all loved the room, Fernando genuinely and the other three in a we're-laughing-at-you-not-with-you kind of way.

Carla bounced on the bed as soon as they hit the room.

"Well, at least the bed isn't made of rock," she said.

"This is just too fabulous," Suzanna said, running her hands over the rock walls.

"You're sounding Hollywood already," Carla laughed.

"I can't believe that a whole tour cancelled. That sucks for the hotel," Suzanna said.

"But it's good to be us!" Eric said. "We're just damn lucky."

"Yeah," Fernando said. "But it's the kind of luck you feel guilty about."

"What?" Suzanna asked. She wasn't feeling guilty in the least.

"You know. Sort of like when you're in a traffic jam and there is a hideous accident and even though somebody is probably dead, you're actually relieved that you're in the front of the line and won't have to wait long."

Suzanna nodded her head. Now she did feel guilty.

For not feeling guilty.

They went downstairs to the dining room, which, in July, had a Christmas tree set up.

"Listen to this," Suzanna said, reading the menu, "they have something called Pink Shrimp Dolce Vita! 'Dolce vita' for whom? Certainly not the pink shrimp."

Eric snickered appreciatively—something Suzanna always loved about him. He always understood even the most obscure reference. Suzanna and Eric each ordered the shrimp.

"So the shrimp would not have given up their *vita* in vain," Eric said.

Carla ordered pasta primavera and Fernando ordered spaghetti and meatballs.

"So, Eric," Carla said as they dove into their food. "Boston is only a seven-hour train ride to D. C. I hope you plan on coming down once in a while."

"Or you could come up north," Eric said.

"Maybe I will. In case I need to escape."

"You haven't even started and you're already looking to escape?" Fernando asked.

"Well . . . I'm afraid I'll be lonely."

Suzanna could tell she was not the only one taken by surprise by this admission. Carla always seemed to be ready to try anything.

"I'm just really scared," Carla continued. "What if everybody hates me? What if I wasn't cut out to be an architecture major?"

"You'll figure it out," Suzanna said. "It's college, not prison."

"You're one to talk," Carla said.

Suzanna reddened, but realized that Carla only meant that she and Fernando had chosen a path—together—that did not include prison.

College.

"Everything is going to change," Eric said. "But it'll all be good."

"What if I can't find a boyfriend, and I'm the only single person left on campus?" Carla said, as if she hadn't even heard Eric.

"Are you kidding me?" Suzanna asked, incredulous. "With your body? And that great head of hair? Those D. C. boys won't know what hit them."

"Well," said Carla, a little indignantly, "I think it takes more than a great head of hair to fit in . . ."

"Yes," Eric said. "The great body is going to help, too."

Carla turned her watery smile to Eric. He squeezed her hand. Suzanna put her fork down. She suddenly had no appetite.

The Land Cruiser arrived in Los Angeles without further incident. The kids called Napa to check in with parents. Suzanna's mother and father apparently hadn't gotten wind of the fact that Eric had been a stowaway, so Suzanna breathed a sigh of relief when she hung up the phone. She was fully aware that she probably had just dodged a bullet.

With Eric riding shotgun and working as navigator, Suzanna threaded her way through the streets of Los Angeles. They were on their way to Palms to pick up a set of keys from their new landlady. Los Angeles was gigantic and keeping track of the directions was tough, even for Eric, who was usually pretty good with a map.

Los Angeles seemed to be terrified by its own vastness, giving itself other names every couple miles: Palms, Balboa Lake, West Adams, Baldwin Hills. It was almost impossible to take in.

Finally, the Land Cruiser pulled up in front of a tiny adobe house on an aptly palm-tree-lined street in Palms. Since Suzanna's parents were paying for the apartment, Suzanna left her new roommate—and Carla and Eric—in the Toyota when she went to fetch the keys.

"Hi, Mrs. Larson. I'm Suzanna Wolf."

"Where's your mother?" asked Mrs. Larson, suspiciously eyeing the U-Haul.

"Ummm . . . . she's home . . . in Napa. I'm renting the apartment. I mean. My parents are going to pay for it and everything . . . . I'm just going to be staying here . . . remember?" Suzanna gripped the door-frame so that she wouldn't start floating. This woman was making her very nervous.

Mrs. Larson handed Suzanna the keys and walked down to the car. She continued to give the car's possessions and passengers her stink-eyed squint. She indicated Carla and asked about her in a stage whisper.

"She's my friend . . . she's driven down with me to keep me company. She's going home tomorrow."

"Well, she'd better be," said Mrs. Larson. "Two boys, two girls, I don't want any funny stuff."

"She said two *boys* and two *girls* . . . she thinks we're two gay couples," Fernando hissed in Suzanna's ear as she got back in the car. "And she doesn't like it. She's homophobic—she's a bigot!"

"Unless somebody is wearing a sweatshirt that says 'I love gay people,' you think everybody is homophobic," Eric said. " 'Two boys and two girls' could mean anything."

Suzanna pulled away as fast as she could without seeming rude. Luckily, the apartment was several miles from Mrs. Larson's prying eyes. It was a one-bedroom on the Venice boardwalk, three flights up, and it suddenly seemed much smaller than it had when they first rented it. Looking at it with a bulging U-Haul breathing down their necks, it now revealed itself as a single room with a large closet.

Carla was staring out the window at the beach. It was a gorgeous day and the sun was glinting off the ocean like some kind of advertisement.

"Can you believe you're going to live here?" Carla asked without taking her eyes off the water.

"No," Suzanna said honestly, with a slight tightening in her chest. "I can't."

They managed to get everything from the U-Haul up the stairs and into the apartment. Considering how few possessions they had, it was surprising how long it took them to unload. By evening, they were famished. The four of them decided to go to a tiny Mexican restaurant they had heard about, and they stepped out onto the Venice boardwalk.

During the day, the boardwalk was full of benign, colorful characters who somehow turned into scary, long-toothed creatures when the sun went down. Suzanna and Carla found themselves walking closer and closer to the guys.

"Don't look at me, sweetheart," Fernando said to Suzanna. "One of these creeps makes a move and I'll scream like a girl."

Within a few weeks, they had figured out which parts of the boardwalk to give a wide berth. They hung out at a teashop called the Flying Geese Tea Shoppe and Fernando spent a lot of time there, soaking up the atmosphere and insisting that he was going to work there one day. "I love that place," he said. "But that name has got to *go*."

The Mexican restaurant, called the Baja Cantina, was loud, crowded, and fun. The locals were friendly and all four of the Napa contingent danced until the early hours, when the bar finally closed. Carla had met a cute guy and said she'd find her way home. Ditto for Fernando.

Suzanna and Eric decided to go for a walk along what was left of the Venice canals, a newly gentrified area that glowed romantically in what was left of the moonlight. Suzanna tried not to get her hopes up as they stood shoulder to shoulder on one of the curved wooden bridges that spanned the canals. She could see their reflections quivering in the water.

Suzanna's senses were on high alert. What if they did get romantic? How could you resist getting romantic on this bridge in the moonlight? She worried that if she passed out right now, she'd topple into the canal and either break her neck and die or just get covered in mud and humiliation. She decided that she had to stay conscious, no matter where this evening took her.

"I read something interesting about these canals," Eric said.

"What did you read?" Suzanna said.

"That the city wanted to clean up the area, but the ducks kept eating the vegetation. So the city fathers came and checked out the ducks and decided—conveniently—that the ducks were diseased and would have to be put down."

"That's terrible," Suzanna said, hopes of romantic kisses evaporating like the diseased ducks.

"Yeah," Eric said. "And when the vegetation was all grown in, they brought in new ducks."

"Huh," Suzanna said as a duck quacked underneath them. She had no idea what to make of this story, but she was pretty sure it wasn't Eric's attempt at seduction.

"Hey," Eric said, walking across the bridge. "There's a little boat here."

Suzanna followed him. There was a tiny blue rowboat tied to a moldy bollard sunk deep in the canal.

"I'm sure it belongs to one of these houses," Suzanna said.

"We'll bring it back," Eric said as he untied the rope. "Get in . . . it's got oars and everything!"

Suzanna was terrified, but she would have impaled herself for another five minutes with Eric, so she got into the boat. Eric pushed off and they rowed silently around the canals. Suzanna was so happy, she couldn't speak.

"Hey, listen" Eric said, when they had rowed to a silent part of the canals. "I've been thinking . . ."

Suzanna tried to clamp down on her thoughts.

Don't get your hopes up. Don't get your hopes up. Don't get your hopes up.

"Oh?"

"Yeah . . . I'm thinking of not going back to Napa."

Suzanna lit up.

"You mean you'll stay here until it's time to go to Boston?"

"No," Eric said, looking into the water. "I mean . . . I'd like to stay here for the year. I don't want to go to school yet."

Suzanna could barely make out his features in the dark.

"What will your parents say?"

"They'll have a shit-fit."

Suzanna was surprised. Eric didn't usually swear.

"I'll just tell them I'm not ready," he said. "Look, I know you guys are going to be tight for space, but as soon as we get jobs, we can move someplace bigger. What do you think?"

Suzanna realized that if she said yes, he'd probably kiss her.

"I'll have to ask Fernando," she said.

Suzanna drove Carla to the airport the next morning, put her on a plane back to Napa, and prepared to settle into a life in Southern California with Fernando—and now Eric.

PART THREE

DOWNTOWN

CHAPTER 14

Suzanna had missed two dance lessons in a row. The remodel of the tearoom was taking all her time, concentration and money. Eric had been right: with a reconfiguration of the nook, they were able to keep both establishments running. But because Eric and Fernando had jobs to do during the busiest parts of the day, Suzanna and Carla were now moving increasingly heavy pieces of furniture on their own. Suzanna missed the rush of salsa dancing. Her thighs were starting to wobble again, which put her in a bad mood. Not to mention that the experience was proving to be stressful, chaotic, and exhausting. She told Carla as much.

"I know it's a pain in the ass," Carla said. "But if you'd hire a carpenter, we'd be able to move things along a lot faster. And we could stop hauling stuff ourselves."

Suzanna and Carla had dragged a small rectangular table through the hallway toward the opened-up space in the book nook that was to serve as a scaled-down tearoom. Suzanna stopped in her tracks and wiped perspiration from her forehead. Carla put down her end of the table.

"I sort of have a guy I could ask to help us," Suzanna said.

"I don't want a 'sort of' guy. I want a real carpenter."

"He is a real carpenter."

Carla smacked the table with her fist and then showed Suzanna the blisters caused by two weeks of manual labor.

"You mean, you and I don't have to be doing the heavy lifting?"

Suzanna looked panic-stricken into both the nook and the tearoom to make sure no one was listening to them.

"Keep your voice down."

"Why are you hiding him?" Carla asked, although she did lower her voice. "Is he an ax murderer?"

"Of course not."

"I mean, at this point, I don't really care . . . as long as he's also good with saws and hammers."

"He's not an ax murderer," Suzanna said, lifting the table again. "He's a dancer."

"A dancing carpenter," Carla said as they wedged the table into a corner. "Only in L. A."

"He's a guy from salsa class. His name is Andy. He showed me his portfolio and he's pretty good."

"Then why isn't he here?"

"Because I've been too busy to get back to dance class and ask him."

Carla tried to steady the table, but the old wooden floor wasn't level and the table tilted. Eric, who had just carried a heavy bag of books to the car of one of their loyal customers, bounded back into the store just as Suzanna was trying to shore up the drunken table legs. She kept packets of Sweet 'N Low in her pockets for just that purpose.

"What are you doing, Suzanna?" Eric asked.

Suzanna looked up from her crouch.

"I'm using these sweeteners to steady the table."

Eric went behind the counter, rummaged around in a drawer, and came back with several small wedges. He held them out to Suzanna.

"Here," he said. "Use these."

Suzanna stared at them and held them up for Carla to see.

"These are fantastic!" Suzanna said. "What are they?"

"I level the bookcases with them," Eric said. "Just a little something I invented."

"Eric, you are amazing!" Suzanna said.

"Oh, for God's sake, Suzanna!" Carla said. "He didn't invent them. They're called shims."

"No they aren't," Suzanna said, defending Eric's good name. "A shim is what people stab other people with in prison."

"That's a shank," Carla said.

Suzanna looked to Eric and back to Carla. Carla was looking annoyed and Eric had a maddeningly blank face.

"You're lying," Suzanna said to Eric, who was kneeling next to her and leveling the table legs.

He picked up the Sweet'N Low packets and shook them at her.

"This is not cost-effective," he said, tossing the packets into the trashcan and heading back to work. "You got the front?"

Suzanna nodded. "You got the front" was shorthand for "If you can manage the store, I'll be working in the office."

Suzanna turned to Carla.

"You're an architect from Napa Valley," Suzanna said. "How can it be that you know shims from shanks?"

"How can it be that you own a business in Los Angeles and don't?"

The women checked the other tables, straightening corners and checking for stability. When you were serving hot tea all day long, you couldn't be too careful.

"This looks pretty good," Suzanna said, although she had her doubts.

"Don't change the subject. Go to the dance studio right now and bring me back that man."

"He doesn't just hang around the dance studio all day."

"Well . . . did you get a phone number? An e-mail address?" Carla asked.

"I don't have any contact information, no."

"You know something? I don't think you really want me to hire this guy."

"Maybe I don't."

"Why?"

"Because I'm not sure I want to have somebody from dance class here. Suppose he tells the guys about my lessons?"

"Suppose he does?"

"It's just getting too complicated. First I wasn't telling Eric and Fernando, and then I wasn't telling Erinn. If I confess now, it will seem like I've been trying to keep it from them."

"You have been trying to keep it from them."

"I know. But I can't have Andy blow my cover. I'll tell everybody in my own good time."

Carla struggled to move a sideboard into the alcove with her shoulder. When that didn't work, she sat on the floor and tried to move it by propping her back against it and trying to leverage it with her feet braced against the wall. The sideboard budged, and Carla managed to get the behemoth to the doorway, where all progress stalled. She corralled Suzanna and the two women tried to lift it. The sideboard groaned but did not leave the floor. Carla looked at Suzanna.

"Well, you need to get him here before the two of us kill ourselves. You can either ask him not to mention dancing or just leave it alone and hope for the best."

"What would you do?"

"I think hiding dance lessons is completely stupid in the first place."

"But if you didn't think it was stupid, then what would you do?"

"If he's like most of the carpenters I know, he'll be too busy trying to out-testosterone Eric to get into a conversation about dance," Carla said. "A straight guy isn't going to waltz in here—no pun intended— and start talking about his salsa lessons, believe me."

"OK," Suzanna said. "I'll ask him to stop by. If you like him, you hire him."

She studied Carla, who seemed determined to move the sideboard through sheer force of will.

"Soon," Carla said, still shoving the sideboard and getting nowhere. It would have to wait until the patrons moved out and Fernando and Eric could move it. She stopped struggling, breathless. "Ask him soon."

Suzanna felt a surge of panic at officially closing the tearoom side of the Bun, but she and Carla—with occasional help from Eric, Fernando, and Harri—did manage to get a section of the book nook open for afternoon tea without missing a beat. The place—minus the sideboard—really did look snug and inviting. Suzanna and Carla stood in the doorway of the nook, admiring their handiwork. Erinn had brought them an armload of miniature roses from her garden and Fernando had created centerpieces of roses in tiny, mismatched English china vases for the five small tables.

"Well, I'll leave you to the tea," Carla said. "I'd better go start the demolition while you have your mind occupied."

Suzanna, who usually flushed when things were tense, suddenly turned pale. Carla looked at her in alarm.

"Suzanna! What's wrong?"

Suzanna couldn't find her voice. She felt as if she were going to pass out. Carla smacked her hard on the back, and Suzanna started to breathe again.

"Rio," she whispered. "It's Rio."

"What? Who? Rio, the dance instructor? Where? Here?"

"Yes," Suzanna said, gripping Carla's arm. "Harri's bringing him in."

She pulled at Carla, who seemed rooted to the spot. "Let's go! I don't want him to see me."

"Are you nuts? You can't hide in your own store . . . especially when half of it is closed. Besides, I'm not going anywhere! I want to see this."

Suzanna ducked behind Carla and busied herself at the miniscule newsstand as Harri led Rio into the new nook-cum-tearoom.

"Maybe he's coming to see why you haven't been to class in a couple weeks," Carla whispered.

"Shhhh."

Rio nodded to Carla as he slipped around her in the tight space. He didn't seem to notice Suzanna.

"Oh my God, Suzanna. He is so hot."

"Would you please be quiet?"

"Hmm. Harri seems pretty into him. You may have competition."

Suzanna peered over Carla's shoulder and watched as Harri led Rio to one of the tables. Harri was using her wholesome looks for all they were worth.

"She can be such a slut," Suzanna said.

Carla snorted. Rio and Harri looked in their direction, but both women hurriedly thrust their noses into magazines.

Harri smiled impishly as she put down a menu. But instead of looking at it immediately, Rio opened his book. Suzanna felt this was clearly a signal that he wanted to be left alone, but Harri continued to stand there. Suzanna and Carla stayed at the front of the store and kept up the pretense that they were absorbed in their magazines.

They strained to hear Harri.

"What are you reading?" Harri asked.

Rio smiled faintly and held up his book. From where Suzanna was standing, she couldn't make out what it was, but she saw Harri studying it carefully.

"What language is it written in?" she asked.

"Spanish," replied Rio, who didn't seem at all annoyed by her.

"Oh, are you Spanish?"

"No," he replied, "I'm Costa Rican."

Suzanna and Carla rolled their eyes at each other over the tops of their magazines as Harri went into an energetic fit about how much she adored Costa Rica.

"She's good!" Carla whispered. "I have a feeling that if he'd said 'Colombia' or 'Belize' or 'Mexico,' she would have been just as enthusiastic."

"The thing I love best about Costa Rica is the weather. . . it's so interesting," Harri said. "I mean, the whole country is completely within the tropics, but it has at least a dozen climatic zones and is markedly diverse in local microclimates."

Okay, maybe she does love Costa Rica.

"My name is Harriet, by the way, but everybody calls me Harri."

"I am Rio."

"Wow . . . great name," she said.

"It means 'river' in Spanish," he said.

"Really? That is so cool."

Oh, please! She's a college student! She's slinging around words like "microclimates" and doesn't know rio *means "river" in Spanish?*

Suzanna and Carla watched in amazement as Rio reached into his pocket and pulled out his cell phone.

If he gets her phone number, I'm firing her right now.

But he seemed to just be showing Harri something on the phone. He flicked the screen time and time again . . . Was he showing her pictures? Harri simpered and put her hand to her heart and touched his shoulder. What was going on?

Harri finally took his order—white tea and shepherd's pie—and headed into the kitchen. She shot Carla and Suzanna a look as she scooted around them, leaned in, and made panting sounds.

"She flirts like she just got out of prison," Carla said. "OK, enough sightseeing. I've got to get to work. But now I see why you want to keep this one to yourself!"

"Would you please be quiet? He has ears, you know."

"I do know. I noticed them framing that yummy ponytail."

"You are not helping!"

"Just my professional opinion!" Carla said. "As an architect, I'd say he has not one design flaw."

Suzanna cringed. She was afraid Rio might hear them. She also found herself feeling a little proprietary. This was one man she didn't plan on sharing with Carla—or Harri. Rio was her fantasy man!

"And get me that carpenter!" Carla said. "If the dance instructor is anything to go by, I can't wait!"

"Andy isn't hot," Suzanna said in a whisper. "He's office cute."

"Office cute" was a term Carla had picked up when she first started working in a big architecture firm and was describing some of the guys who worked there. "Office cute" was the guy in accounting you didn't notice at first. Then, one day, when you were all standing around the cappuccino maker, he'd make a funny little joke and walk away. You'd say to the woman next to you, "You know, I never noticed before, but Kevin in accounting is pretty cute."

Suzanna always thought Kevin Spacey was the perfect prototype for office cute.

"It's been so long since I've had a date, I'll settle for office cute," Carla said. "Especially office cute with a tape measure."

Carla followed Harri back to the off-limits teashop, where Fernando still manned the kitchen. Suzanna watched Rio as he cracked open his book again. She came out from behind her magazine and started to tidy up the newsstand. She tried to convince herself that perhaps he did know this was her place and he was just playing hard to get. After all, he didn't seem like a guy who would frequent a tearoom, and she'd never seen him in here before she started dance lessons. But if that were the case, he'd taken hard-to-get into the stratosphere. His eyes never left his book as he ate his shepherd's pie. The only bright spot for Suzanna was that he didn't seem to have any interest in Harri, either—and she flapped to his side every few minutes to see if everything was all right.

Suzanna looked up from the newsstand as Fernando suddenly appeared in the doorway to the nook.

"Fernando, what are you doing here? Get back in the kitchen," Suzanna said.

"Oh, quiet down, Moan-a. Harri's in the kitchen . . . She says the hot Latin guy is here."

A muffled banging could be heard in the tearoom. Suzanna hoped it was Carla pulling out the wainscoting rather than Harri pulling down pots and pans. Rio looked up at the sound and Fernando waved. He said something to Rio in Spanish that Suzanna couldn't understand.

Rio nodded, took a few more bites of shepherd's pie and a long sip of tea and then stood up. Suzanna froze as he walked toward Fernando. What was going on?

Fernando picked up one end of the sideboard and Rio took the other. Suzanna watched in fascination as the men moved the sideboard into the nook and tucked it neatly into its designated spot.

Fernando and Rio exchanged a few more words in Spanish. Rio grabbed his book off the table, tossed down a tip, and left. Fernando stared after him with a little sigh. Suzanna came out from behind the newsstand.

"What was that about?" Suzanna asked.

"I said I'd comp him if he'd help me move the sideboard."

Suzanna flared.

"Are you crazy? What if he'd hurt his back?"

"Well, it was worth the risk to see those biceps flex," Fernando said.

"We could have been sued!"

"Moan-a, you got to go for it once in awhile . . . you know?"

Well, she did know. And she wasn't telling.

Fernando turned back toward the kitchen on the other side of the building.

"That wasn't cost-effective, by the way," Suzanna called after him.

Suzanna was still fuming when Harri came over. The two women stared into the street, trying to conjure the vision of Rio. It was as if they had awoken from an erotic, mutual dream and were trying to hang on to it.

"So . . . Harri," Suzanna said. "I saw you talking to that guy. Looks like he might be a player. What do you think?"

"No way," Harri said. "He has pictures of his mother on his phone."

Suzanna tried not to react . . . she wasn't even sure what to make of it. But a man with pictures of his mother on his phone had to be a good guy . . . Didn't he?

"Besides," Harri said, "I wanted to bite that ponytail holder right out of his hair."

CHAPTER 15

Soon after Carla's demand that she produce Andy, Suzanna steeled herself to return to dance class. She was in a heat waiting to see Rio again, but she was worried that she would be far, far behind the other students after almost three weeks away. But if she didn't stop procrastinating, Carla would probably stalk off the project in protest! Carla had managed to get the entire tearoom cleared of the wainscoting and old shelves practically by herself, but she couldn't wait for help any longer. Eric and Fernando did what they could—when they could—but Carla was very clear that she needed more muscle on a more consistent basis.

Suzanna found a parking space right outside the dance studio, which she always took as a good omen. She looked in to see the regulars filtering in, putting on dance shoes, practicing stretches and talking in small groups. Lauren watched herself intently in the mirror, perfecting her already perfect technique. Suzanna sat in her Smart Car, hoping to catch Andy before he went in, and was looking down the street so intently that when someone knocked on her window, she jumped. It was Andy, smiling in at her. She rolled down her window.

"Hey," she said. "I was waiting for you."

"I thought you'd taken a powder," Andy said. "We've missed you."

Suzanna got out of the car, collected her dance shoes, and set the alarm on her car.

"I had work stuff."

"I wish I had work stuff," he said, offering her quarters for the parking meter.

"That's just what I want to talk to you about," Suzanna said, grateful for the easy opening.

As they walked into class, Suzanna gave Andy instructions on how to get to her establishment. She was flattered that he knew the place. He'd never been to afternoon tea, he said, but he'd been in the bookstore a few times.

Suzanna looked over her shoulder to see Rio entering the class. The unearthly quiet that filled the room whenever Rio entered the room settled over the studio. Andy gave Suzanna a little thumbs-up, and they turned their concentration to class.

Rio called for a rotation and Suzanna found herself in the arms of a very weird guy. He was medium height with an alarming belly that protruded over his belt. He was wearing a cowboy-esque plaid shirt—with snaps—and had sparse but unruly hair that stuck up like he'd been the victim of a static-electricity prank. He followed Rio's instructions well enough, but as soon as Rio stopped talking, the guy started dancing to some tune in his head . . . and the tune was usually something that had nothing to do with salsa. When you were partnered with this man, you were suddenly doing West Coast swing or the foxtrot. If he wasn't creepy, or if he had been a better dancer, this might be interesting, but he wasn't and it wasn't.

The class was a little short on men, and Rio was in the rotation. Suzanna kept an eye on the rotation process and counted down . . . three men until Rio. Two men until Rio, one man until Rio . . . Rio! She had rotated into Rio's arms at last. She put her palm in his and put her other hand on his right arm.

"Class, pay attention!" he said, and all eyes were on them. "We have learned that when we dance, we start in closed position, yes?"

Everyone in the class soberly nodded yes, adjusting their own closed positions—the man and lady standing in front of each other, slightly offset to the left, with the lady's arm on top of the man's. Suzanna made eye contact briefly with Andy, who was partnered with Lauren. He gave her another little thumbs-up.

"You all look sloppy," Rio said is a stern voice. "Closed position has four contact points . . ."

He released Suzanna from their frame and she was left standing with her arms hanging limply at her sides. Instinctively, she stole a quick look at her watch.

"Are you bored?" Rio asked.

Suzanna reddened.

"No . . . I . . . oh, did I look at my watch? That's just a nervous habit."

Rio went back to addressing the class. Suzanna needed to fend off a panic swell, so she tried to concentrate on something else . . . like how awkward she felt standing in front of the class with nothing to do with her hands.

If only these yoga pants had pockets.

Suzanna couldn't decide if she would look thinner if she crossed her arms, or if that would make her look closed off . . . She had just finished reading an article on body language and, apparently, standing with your arms folded was not an inviting look. Luckily, by the time she decided that perhaps she might be best served by just putting a hand jauntily on one hip, Rio looked at her and put out his hand.

"Let's begin again."

He took her right hand in his left and they clasped hands, palm to palm. Suzanna moved her left arm up onto his shoulder and he all but shook her off.

"Wait for me," he said.

He offered his hand and they clasped palms again. He put his right hand on her back, while addressing the class.

"Notice that I am connecting with the lady's back. I am using a cupped hand . . ."

God, oh God!

Rio had cupped his hand around Suzanna's back fat, that awful place she obsessed about where the skin flopped over the bra band. She could feel the untoned skin wobbling in his left palm as he demonstrated to the class that the man does not spread his fingers across the lady's back, but keeps his thumb and fingers together. Suzanna now prayed for a panic swell, but they never happened if someone was grounding her.

Contact point three was a blur, because her mind had seized. All she knew was that contact point three had something to do with settling her arm from the armpit to the elbow onto the part of his arm that was connected to her back fat.

"Placement for contact point four is very important." He turned his head to the class, making sure everyone was paying attention. "This is where the lady's left hand and forearm are placed on the man's upper arm."

Suzanna started to put her hand into place, but he intercepted her palm.

"The lady's hand should rest somewhere between the man's deltoid and his bicep," he said, taking her hand and running it smoothly over his upper arm.

Suzanna had no idea what a deltoid was or where to find one . . . but she was certainly enjoying the quest.

Concentrating on the whole closed-position thing was really tough on her it didn't matter whether her hand was on his bicep, deltoid, or shoulder, she would get distracted. Rio might be telling her that she needed to straighten her leg, or balance on her big toe, or dance on the inside edge of her foot; it didn't matter, because all she could think about was his muscle tone—which, by the way, was excellent.

One thing Suzanna had learned in dance class was that almost all men have great shoulder muscles. They might look fat or scrawny, but when they were spinning you around and you could feel their shoulder muscles expanding and contracting under your fingertips, well . . . it was just pretty damn distracting.

"There is another connection point," Rio continued. "We don't worry about this in salsa, but I am going to tell you anyway, because you may find the information useful . . ."

Wow, Rio is on a roll. These are the most words I've ever heard him speak.

Everybody in class perked up.

"In smooth or international style dancing, there is body contact," he said, letting go of her to address the class.

Suzanna stood frozen. She looked down at her watch. As soon as she did it, she realized her mistake and hoped to heaven that Rio hadn't seen.

She looked in the mirror—and he was glaring at her. He put out his hand. She offered her palm, but he shook his head.

"Give it to me," he said.

Suzanna could hear people gasp and giggle. She knew a panic swell was imminent and actually welcomed it, but before she lifted off, Rio grabbed her wrist. He pulled the watch off her arm and put it in his pocket.

"You will never be a good dancer if you don't pay attention."

Suzanna nodded, willing herself not to cry.

"The lady's center is in contact with the man's ribcage, like so," he continued, pulling her tight against his body. "The connection begins at the upper thigh and continues up the torsos."

He was holding her so tightly that she could feel his breath going in and out. While trying to forget about the humiliating watch incident, Suzanna also tried not to key into the feeling of his ribs moving against her. It was so pathetically thrilling, she was afraid she was going to keel over—a poor man's Marie Osmond. She snuck a peek at Lauren, just to see if she was remotely jealous, but Lauren just looked exquisite in her boredom. Suzanna registered that she had her arms folded across her perfect chest.

She does look closed off.

She also noticed that Lauren's breasts look awkward, sort of squashed together. Suzanna wondered if they were real. Carla would know. Fernando would know. Eric would know. Why couldn't she tell fake breasts when she saw them? She looked at her naked wrist, which was sitting daintily on Rio's shoulder, realized what she was doing, and jerked her eyes back toward Rio. Mercifully, he hadn't noticed this time.

Rio continued to explain why the woman and man had to be connected like this, but she couldn't even hear him. She could hardly breathe as her hormones ricocheted around the studio. She admonished herself and told herself to focus. Dancing was serious business and she was acting like it was the female's equivalent of getting a lap dance.

They took a break and several of the dance students headed to the water cooler. One of the women asked Suzanna if the watch had been expensive.

"Kind of," Suzanna said. "But I'm sure he's going to give it back."

The woman shrugged dolefully.

As she sipped from the ridiculously tiny cup, she overheard the funny-haired cowboy hitting on Lauren. He leaned into her like a caricature of a used-car salesman. She couldn't hear what he was saying, but the body language was unmistakable. His belly rested on Lauren's arm; her face was a mask. Suzanna gulped her water as quickly as she could so she could get a refill. That way, she might be able to catch some of their dialogue. She stepped lightly toward the cooler and could just make out Lauren's words.

"I'm sure that would be lovely," she said, "but I only go out with really good dancers."

And with that, she headed back to class.

Suzanna still hated her, but man, that was good!

Class resumed, and Suzanna remained Rio's partner for an extended period of time. Usually, this was her idea of heaven, but he seemed frustrated with her.

"You are sliding back on your left foot," he said.

She tried the move again, only to have him "tut-tut" her.

She willed her feet to dance correctly. Even though the watch thing had thrown her, everyone else seemed to have moved on. She needed to get over herself, as Fernando would have said. Since taking up salsa, she had secretly read at least a dozen books on dance, all of which started out telling you that the most important thing was to have fun and let yourself go. That was always on page one. Then, the next two hundred pages gave you a lot of rules you had to follow or you'd just suck.

She didn't know if Rio was taking a special interest in her or just torturing her, but he seemed to be focusing on her, and everything she did seemed to be wrong.

"Your left foot is slipping."

And . . .

"Your head is tilted too far back."

And . . .

"Your hips are not rotating."

And . . .

"What are you looking at?"

Suzanna was afraid she was about to cry when he stopped them dead in their tracks.

"You do not trust me," he said in defeat.

Suzanna was appalled! Of course she trusted him!

The class was staring at her. What could she say? That she was always thinking about sex—or at least the mysterious deltoids—when she was supposed to be thinking about her footwork? Should she confess to her vision—just a flash—of biting the ponytail holder out of his hair?

Rio gripped her a little more firmly and nodded to the group to continue dancing. Suzanna stared at the floor and Rio commanded:

"Don't look down."

Suzanna looked up at the ceiling.

"No, Suzanna, don't look at the ceiling. Look at your partner. Look at me."

The rest of the session flew by. Suzanna didn't know who she danced with after that or what mistakes she made or if she danced on the inside edge of her foot for even a second. She wasn't sure if she finalized a time for Andy to come over to meet Carla. She didn't even notice that Rio hadn't returned her watch.

When class was over, she walked to her car in a stupor. Unlocking her car, all she could think was:

He knows my name.

CHAPTER 16

Andy showed up for his interview with Carla at ten-thirty the next morning. Suzanna pulled open the front door and led him into the cordoned-off tea shop. She noticed that he'd made an effort: he was wearing new jeans and a pressed checked shirt. Suzanna thought it was sweet that he was taking the interview so seriously. She watched Andy turn his professional eye toward the room. She tried to image how he saw the place: floor draped in plastic, huge gouges in the plaster where Carla had removed the wainscoting, and the dingy mountain laurel walls with their faint framing outlines shimmering like ghosts of bad artwork past.

What a mess!

"This looks great!" he said.

He wandered around the room, running his hands over the walls and woodwork.

"So this is yours?"

"Yeah," Suzanna said, with more than a little pride. "This and the bookstore and the apartment upstairs."

"Wow," he said. "You seem really young to be so established."

"Oh, I'm not that young. I'll be thirty-three in less than a month!"

"That's still pretty young to have all this," he said, gesturing around. "How did you end up here? If you don't mind my asking."

"I don't mind at all. Have a seat," Suzanna said, gesturing to a sawhorse. "It's my place, but I didn't actually do it all by myself."

She perched on a crate opposite him. She told him about moving to L. A. with Fernando and Eric and how they had started in a tiny apartment in Venice.

"The place existed as a tea shop for years before we got here. One of my friends, who you'll meet in the tearoom—Fernando—landed a job as a pastry chef right away," she said. "All the ladies loved him . . . especially the woman who owned this place. When they needed a waitress, he talked Mandy—she was the owner—into hiring me. My other co-worker—Eric—used to come pick us up after work and she got to know him, too."

Suzanna pointed into the bookstore and makeshift tearoom. "Mandy used that alcove as an office and warehouse. It was Eric's idea to put a bookstore in there . . . we call it the book nook."

Andy nodded and Suzanna flushed as she realized how cloying that sounded.

"How did you come to buy it?" he asked.

"Mandy died and her troll of a brother came down from Oregon to run the place. He hated it here and sold it to me for a song . . . seems like only yesterday, but it was years ago."

"And you guys have been running it together all this time? That's pretty amazing."

"Yeah. They're great guys."

"I guess so."

"My friend Carla is doing the renovation," Suzanna said, standing up. "I think she's in the kitchen. I'll go get her. Would you like some tea?"

"No, thanks. I think tea is just brown water."

Andy smacked his forehead with his palm, realizing his faux pas.

"Man! You can't take me anywhere," he said. "Hope that wasn't a deal breaker."

"Not at all—as long as you're better with a screwdriver than you are with your mouth," Carla said, coming out of the kitchen.

From the smell of it, she had a huge mug of Egyptian licorice tea in her hands.

Andy laughed and Carla joined him on the sawhorse after the introductions. Suzanna never ceased to be amazed at the ease Carla felt around men. She felt awkward just standing in the middle of the debris and tried to excuse herself.

"Well, we just got a new shipment of books and they aren't going to sort themselves."

"Sweetie, let Eric handle the bookstore right now. I can't hire Andy without your OK."

Andy looked at Suzanna with a lopsided grin. He was not only office cute, she thought in surprise, he was dismantled-teahouse cute! Maybe Carla and he would hit it off and Suzanna could stop obsessing about Carla reconnecting with Eric. It was a distraction she didn't need.

Worrying about Carla and Eric gives me less time to think about Rio.

"Well, I'm ready to hire him right now," Suzanna said.

"That's why they pay you the big bucks," Andy said.

Carla laughed and squeezed his knee. Suzanna was shocked. Who squeezed a man's knee during an interview? Clearly the words "sexual harassment" hadn't made much of an impression in Napa Valley.

"Well, then, the job is yours," Carla said. "If you want it."

"I'll take it on one condition," he said.

The women waited. Andy stood up and looked at Suzanna.

"I'll help you out if you promise to go to salsa dancing with me," he said. "We need the practice."

Suzanna could feel the heat creeping up her décolleté.

"Well, uh . . ." Suzanna said.

"She would love that!" Carla said.

The three of them turned toward the front of the shop just as Harri was letting herself in with her keys.

"Just make sure you don't mention the salsa classes to the other employees," Carla whispered to Andy before Harri was in earshot. "Suzanna likes to keep things professional around here. Sexual harassment issues . . . you know."

Andy nodded. Suzanna was speechless at how smoothly Carla could handle any situation.

"It's about time you got here," Fernando said, coming out of the kitchen and wiping his hands on a dishtowel.

This was Fernando's standard greeting to Harri, but by the look on his face, he hadn't expected an audience. Suzanna introduced Andy to Fernando and Harri, both of whom gave him the once-over.

Are all my friends sex addicts?

"Well, I'll see you guys tomorrow," Andy said, and headed out the door Harri had left ajar. They all looked after him.

"He is cute," Carla said.

"So cute," Harri said.

"Great butt," Fernando said.

"I have books to unpack," Suzanna said. She didn't have room in her brain for any more cute men.

The bookstore was already open when Suzanna crossed the hall. Eric was at the front counter, studying. He looked up as she stepped into the store.

"Morning, Beet."

Suzanna gave him a nod.

"We got a shipment?"

"Yeah," Eric said, indicating a large box. "Over there. But don't worry about it. I'll unpack as soon as I finish this chapter."

"That's okay," Suzanna said, as she took a box cutter and sliced open a sturdy cardboard box. "I'm pretty worthless next door right now. I'm happy to help."

"Let me at least get it off the floor," Eric said as he effortlessly picked up the box and put it on the counter.

"Thanks," Suzanna said. "Hey, you can go study in the office if you want. I've got this."

Eric gave her a thumbs-up, snapped his book shut, and headed back toward the office. Suzanna watched him go, and as she habitually did, closed her mind to the thoughts that were about to invade it.

She lifted out several used books on the Spanish Armada—obviously a special order for her sister. She registered them quickly and put them in a recycled bag. She looked at her wrist and for the tenth time that day realized that her watch was still with Rio!

She was debating whether she could casually stop by the dance studio to retrieve it or wait until the next class. She shot a look at her sister's bag of books. The dance studio and her sister's house were only a few minutes apart. She could deliver the books and just drop in at DIAGNOSIS:Dance! on the way home. It might seem a little awkward, showing up at her sister's uninvited. She had never actually delivered books to Erinn before.

But still . . .

She shelved the other books quickly and made a speedy inspection of the tables that were now functioning as the tearoom. She wiggled the table with the shim under it. It was nice and sturdy. She wiggled another one. Wobbly! Suzanna dropped to her hands and knees and crawled along the floor, studying the bases of the bookcases for another one of those handy shims Eric had used. She found one and tried to nudge it out from under the wooden bookcase. The bookcase didn't budge. Suzanna stood up and threw her whole weight against the bookcase, which titled back against the wall, surrendering like a fugitive trapped by the police in an alley. She kicked the shim out from under the bookcase base, settled the bookcase back in place, and hoped for the best. She gingerly poked the bookcase. It certainly wasn't what you'd call sturdy, but it wasn't going to topple over, either.

Just like Jenga.

She wedged the shim under the offending table leg, grabbed Erinn's pile of books, and headed upstairs long enough to change into black yoga pants, black shoes, and a yellow T-shirt with a large sunflower on it. She thundered down the stairs and into the backyard to retrieve her bicycle, but decided that riding meant she risked being sweaty when she stopped in—ever so casually—at the dance studio. She rummaged in her purse to make sure she had the keys to the car. It was a shame to miss out on a beautiful bike ride, but a girl had to have her priorities straight!

She crossed the palm-tree-lined streets of Venice into Santa Monica and pulled up in front of her sister's impressive Victorian on Ocean Avenue—one of the last of the old homes on the ocean-front boulevard that was now lined mostly with imposing glass condominiums. The house had been a mess when Erinn first rescued it, but now it was a showcase. The clapboard-clad building featured boxed eaves, bay windows, balconies, elaborate molding, and a steeply pitched roof. There was also a two-story round tower, which reminded Suzanna of her own book nook. Suzanna thought back to the years of helping her parents renovate their barn–house, and often wondered if she and her sister were genetically programmed to save old buildings from disrepair.

She hoisted the bag of books, locked her car, and headed toward the front door, threading her way through her sister's prize rose garden. After she had gotten the house restored to its original glory, Erinn had rototilled the entire front yard and replaced the grass and hedges with a massive rose garden. The new landscaping was not universally loved by the neighbors, but that was something Erinn never seemed to care about . . . or even notice. Suzanna stopped to admire the flowers, with their heady scent, then knocked on the front door.

No response.

Oh, hell!

Deep down, Suzanna realized that she didn't actually have to deliver the books to Erinn in order to stop in at DIAGNOSIS:Dance!, but when she created a scenario, she liked to see it through. She waited another minute, ringing the doorbell and knocking, and finally admitted defeat. She turned—and was startled by Erinn's huge cat, Caro, who had lain down at her feet.

"Caro!" Suzanna said. "You scared me to death."

Caro stood up and leaned heavily against Suzanna's legs. She put the bag of books down and scooped up the cat, which hung limply in her arms, purring in fits and starts like a badly tuned engine. Caro's attention span was pretty short and after a few energetic pats from Suzanna, he jumped down. Suzanna watched him as he padded lightly toward the backyard. He stopped just as he was about to round the corner and meowed at Suzanna.

Surprised, Suzanna followed him. She stood open-mouthed as she realized the cat had led her to her sister, who was photographing flowers in the backyard. Erinn was completely focused, pointing a gigantic black camera with a telephoto lens at a sunflower. Suzanna knew that photography was one of Erinn's hobbies, one that she focused on when she should have been writing. Suzanna cleared her throat and Erinn looked up.

"Hi," Suzanna said.

"Hello," Erinn said, hanging the camera around her neck. "This is a surprise."

"Oh, I know! Sorry!" Suzanna said, holding out the books. "Your books came in and I just thought I'd deliver them."

Erinn took the books. She blinked at them as if Suzanna had handed her dirt samples from outer space.

"How is the play going?" Suzanna asked, unnerved by her sister's silence.

"It's about as big a catastrophe as the Armada was for the Spanish."

"Oh, I'm sure you're exaggerating," Suzanna said. "Don't be depressed."

"I'm not depressed," Erinn said. "Just honest."

"I'm sure you'll figure it out."

"Hope springs eternal, Suzanna," Erinn said. "As Longfellow once said, 'Noble souls, through dust and heat, rise from disaster and defeat the stronger.' Of course, that didn't exactly work for the Spanish, but perhaps it will work for me."

Suzanna remembered why she rarely stopped in to see her sister. She tried another avenue of conversation.

"Caro led me around to the backyard," Suzanna said, bending over and patting the cat. "Who says cats aren't as good as dogs?"

"I don't know," Erinn said. "Who?"

"I better go," Suzanna said. "I know you want to get back to work . . . photographing the flowers."

Erinn had lain flat on her stomach, shooting at a tangle of ivy.

"Go into the guesthouse and grab my 200-millimeter lens, would you?"

"Uh . . ."

"It's the big one. It's sitting on the desk."

Suzanna looked at the guesthouse that was tucked into a corner of the yard. It was a miniature Victorian on which Erinn had lavished a lot of attention and money.

"Okay," Suzanna said, noting the closed door. "Where's the key?"

"The guesthouse is in my backyard. I don't lock it!"

"You keep your photography equipment in there," Suzanna said. "You should lock the door."

"I will not surrender to that kind of thinking."

Suzanna got the lens and held it out to Erinn, who took it without ever looking up, so engrossed in the ivy that speech, apparently, had left her. Suzanna scurried around the side of the house, down the path toward the safety of her car. She turned when her sister called out her name. Erinn was now sitting cross-legged on the grass, tightening the new lens onto the camera. She was not looking at her and Suzanna wondered if it had just been her imagination, and Erinn hadn't called her at all. Suzanna turned back down the path, when Erinn asked, "Where is your watch?"

Suzanna looked down at her wrist as if her carpal bones were going to give her up. Her sister had barely engaged her in conversation for the last ten minutes.

"I can't believe you noticed I wasn't wearing it."

Erinn straightened up and looked at Suzanna.

"I'm a writer. I notice everything," Erinn said.

"I . . . I've got to go . . ."

"I understand," Erinn said, focusing on a hummingbird. "But Suzanna . . ."

Suzanna was looking at Erinn, who was still turned away from her.

"Try to be happy."

Suzanna swallowed and headed back to her life. She thought about her sister as she drove toward the dance studio. She had a mental image of Erinn, years from now, standing in her beautiful, empty house, holding a grotesquely fat cat, an ever-growing stack of books on the Spanish Armanda piling up on the desk.

If I do end up like that, I'm getting a better-looking pet.

CHAPTER 17

Suzanna drove around the block several times, passing the DIAG-
NOSIS:Dance! studio over and over again. She had forgotten how
crowded this part of town got during the day. By the time she found a
parking space, she was so annoyed that she forgot how nervous she
was about stopping in for her watch.

Until she walked in the door—and then anxiety flooded her. She
hadn't taken into account the fact that Rio would be teaching a class
when she got there.

"Oh, hello," the faerie at the desk said in her helium voice. "You're
usually in our evening salsa class, right?"

"Uh . . . yes!" Suzanna said, secretly pleased that the faerie remembered her.

"Well, the afternoon class is just getting started. Better hurry!"

Suzanna looked at her feet. She was wearing leather-soled mary-
janes with a small heel.

They weren't perfect.

But still . . .

Suzanna joined the group of men and women lining up. It was a
much smaller crowd than the evening classes, but there were still a
surprising number of men in the class. That was one of the perks of
living in a city filled with freelance actors, writers, and producers.

Rio started the class—and manned his own iPod. Much to
Suzanna's disappointment, he didn't look surprised that she was

there. Suzanna started to dance with a short, affable Asian man in black workout clothes who introduced himself as Michael. He had a strong, decent lead. Rio called out, "Change partners." Michael smiled, then turned his back to Suzanna and offered his hand to a new partner, one of the invariably tall, slender Amazons whose type seemed to make up the majority in her dance classes.

Suzanna also moved on. Her next partner was a female dance instructor named Paris—a good sport who filled in when there were not enough men. Paris was a really good dancer and a great instructor in her own right, but she was so small that Suzanna felt as if she might crush her at any moment. She avoided looking in the mirror when Paris was leading her around the dance floor. She felt like Goliath being taken for a spin.

When going through the rotations, Suzanna instinctively counted how many "change partners" it would take until she was dancing with Rio. Today, it was only three.

When her turn with Rio finally materialized, he offered her his hand, and the highlight of any dance class began. They practiced a triple spin. Suzanna was thrilled because she had noticed he only did triple spins with women he thought could handle it. He suddenly halted her and turned her toward the class.

"I think it is time to discuss dance etiquette," he said, not looking at Suzanna, who stood there—the dance-etiquette prop. "Ladies, it is important to tie up your hair when you are dancing . . ."

Suzanna felt a heat in the pit of her stomach. Her hair was not tied up—and she was going to have to bear the brunt of this new transgression.

"Wild, flying hair is not attractive," he continued. "It can also be deadly."

Deadly?

One of the women in the class raised her hand. Rio nodded, and she said, in a casual tone, "I think long hair looks great flying around."

"Save it for the bedroom."

The class collectively blinked in surprise. Even though salsa dancing was incredibly sensual, the group always acted as though they were dancing the minuet. Actually mentioning its kinship with sex was pretty startling for a dance class.

"There are rules of dance etiquette and they must be obeyed," Rio continued. "Long hair needs to be tied back because it is unpleasant to get one's hand caught when one is trying to lead. Also, it is dangerous to gets one's hand caught in unruly hair."

Suzanna tried to picture Rio's fingers getting caught in her unruly hair and the hand being pulled off as she changed partners. Normally, anything Rio said about dance was gospel, but she had to admit, she felt as if he were making too big a deal of this. However, if her hair was supposed to be tied up to save the dance world from one-handed instructors, so be it. Rio looked at her. Suzanna sobered.

Rio gave them a few more rules of etiquette, including:

1) In social dancing, couples should share the first and last dance but dance with others the rest of the time.
2) Good dancers should not only dance with those they feel can keep up. They should dance with beginners as well.
3) It is now socially acceptable for women to ask men to dance.
4) The dance world frowns on rejection, so if you are asked to dance, you better have a pretty good reason to say no. (Rio thought the only acceptable reason to reject a dance request was that you had danced so many dances previously that you just couldn't go on.)
5) Men's shirts tend to get damp during a strenuous evening, so it is perfectly acceptable for a gentleman to arrive with a change of shirts.

Suzanna was skeptical. Just as a bathing suit with a ruffled hem signaled, "I have huge thighs and I'm trying to hide them," a man with an armload of shirts was pretty much screaming, "I'm going to sweat all over you."

That's not exactly going to get the girls lining up.

Rio finished his lecture and they danced one last salsa before class ended. The other students filed out and Suzanna saw Rio standing alone by the iPod station. She gathered her courage and walked up to him.

"Hey, Rio, I . . ."

"I know why you are here."

He unplugged the iPod and locked it in a drawer as Suzanna mutely stood by. She decided that since he said he knew why she was here, she need not mention the watch.

"Come with me," he said.

Rio turned on his heels and walked through the mysterious mirrored door. Suzanna stood rooted to the floor. She could not get her legs to move. She was too panicked for even a panic float, apparently. Rio stood in the doorway. She finally got control of her feet and walked clumsily in Rio's direction. She caught a glimpse of herself wearing her sunny yellow T-shirt.

I really have to get more of a grip on my mystique.

Suzanna's heart was thudding in her chest. Rio ushered her into the office and closed the door behind them. The room was dark and her eyes had trouble adjusting after the bright glare of the studio. She had no sense of where Rio was and stood stock still for fear of banging into him. She blinked, frog-like, trying to determine exactly where Rio had gone. Suddenly, she felt his hands on her waist. He spun her around to face him.

Are we practicing a dance move?

His hands started traveling up the inside of her shirt. Suzanna was stunned, but luckily she had enough presence of mind to suck in her stomach. Other than that, she was in a state of near-lyrical hysteria. He spoke to her in Spanish and kissed her neck, but, since she didn't speak Spanish, she had no idea what he was saying.

What's going on?

Suzanna deliberated on this most interesting turn of events. She tried not to think that she was sweaty from class.

But then again, so are you and you didn't change your shirt either, Mr. Dance Etiquette.

Suzanna wracked her brain, trying to remember if she left enough time on the meter for this.

Concentrate, concentrate.

She could not believe that for some heaven-sent, inexplicable reason she was making out with her hot dance instructor. Then the door burst open and they jumped apart. Actually, Suzanna jumped apart and Rio ran a hand smoothly over his ponytail. It was Paris. She flicked on the lights and beamed at them.

"Just need to get some hip-hop CDs for my next class," she said.

She was gone as fast as she'd arrived. Suzanna stared at the floor, mortified, and when she finally willed herself to raise her eyes, she was alone in the room. She peered through the office door out into the studio. Rio was approaching a woman who was seated on the side of the room. He offered his hand and led her out onto the dance floor. Suzanna tried to slink out unnoticed, and somehow managed to propel herself to safety outside. The neon DIAGNOSIS: DANCE! Sign blinked behind her. She casually turned around and looked in the window. Rio was completely absorbed in his next salsa lesson.

She sat in her car, trying to steady her heartbeat. It took her a minute to realize that Rio still hadn't given her back her watch!

That's weird. He said he knew why I was there. Did he think I came to make out with him?

She put her head on the steering wheel and groaned. If she were being perfectly honest with herself, if she had a choice between a make-out session and a timepiece, she had to admit, she could always buy another watch.

It took her forever to drive home. She couldn't concentrate and kept driving the wrong way or overshooting the alley behind the shop. When she finally got home, she made sure Eric was in the nook and Fernando, Carla, and Harri were all occupied when she stumbled into the back office, where she could be alone and think. Had she really been in a fierce lip-lock with Rio? How did such a thing come about?

Too bad I don't speak Spanish . . . there might have been a clue in his murmurings.

She felt as if she'd explode if she kept this to herself any longer. After all, like the ad said: Making out with your dance instructor: $49. 99. Sharing it with a sex-starved best friend: priceless.

"Are you alone?" she whispered to Carla, who was mulling over paint chips in the tearoom.

Carla nodded, gesturing dramatically to the empty room. Suzanna leaped into the shop and grabbed Carla's wrists across the counter.

"You will never believe what just happened."

"Okay."

"No, really."

"Okay, I believe you. I'll never believe what just happened."

Carla could be such a spoilsport. Suzanna looked around conspiratorially, making sure Harri and Fernando were nowhere around.

"I made out with my dance instructor."

Carla's mood changed at once and her eyebrows shot into her hairline.

"It was the most amazing thing. He just grabbed me in the office."

"No explanation?"

"No!" Suzanna replied. "Maybe it's a Latin thing."

Carla snorted derisively, assuring her that, whatever it was, it was *not* a "Latin thing." Eric popped his head in. Suzanna felt herself turning red. Somehow she felt as if she'd cheated on him, which added yet another weird emotional layer to the day.

"So I hear you've found yourself another man," he said.

Carla and Suzanna appeared to be in an eyebrow-raising contest at this statement. How did he know? Did he overhear their conversation just now? Was he psychic? Did he follow her?

Could I get any more paranoid?

"A guy named Andy just called. Said you guys hired him this morning. Wanted to know what time he should come by tomorrow. I told him one of you would call him."

"We will," Carla and Suzanna said in unison.

Two men noisily entered the book nook.

"Well, I guess that's a sign I need to get back to the salt mine," he said, and headed back to the store.

Eric and Harri passed each other in the hallway between the establishments, practically bumping heads. Harri came through the torn-apart teashop on her way to the kitchen. She stopped and looked accusingly at Suzanna.

"This is really impossible," she said. "The tables are set up across the hall, I have to take orders, get them to the kitchen, take more orders, come back to the kitchen, and by the time I deliver the tea, it's cold."

"I know it's hard," Suzanna said as Harri stalked away.

"And I couldn't care less," she said to Carla.

When Harri came back through the construction site again, this time carrying teapots with double tea cozies on them, she shook her head in confusion at Carla and Suzanna, who were hopping around the room like a couple of teenagers.

CHAPTER 18

Ever since she was a kid, before Suzanna went to sleep every night she put an X through the day on the calendar. Carla always said that it creeped her out—crossing out the days made everything seem so final. But Suzanna always saw the X's as a marker for the future. That was especially true now. Every morning, she stared at the calendar and counted.

One day closer to dance class.

This morning, she looked at the calendar in alarm. She had been so focused on her dance class schedule that she had forgotten that her birthday was just around the corner.

Usually she looked forward to her birthday, but this year was different.

She practically sleepwalked into the kitchen, sniffing some heavenly scent coming from the oven. Fernando, still in pajama bottoms, was just pulling a banana-bread loaf out of the oven.

"Perfect timing, as usual," he said.

Suzanna sat at the table, put her head in her hands, and groaned.

"What's up, Moan-a? You've only been awake ten minutes!"

"My birthday is right around the corner."

"I know you're bummed that we promised the tearoom would be done for your birthday and that it's taking forever, but we're going as fast as we can."

"It's not just that," Suzanna said, although she had to admit she was annoyed that the tearoom would not be operating again as promised. "It's a big birthday, and I'm just not ready!"

Fernando put a mug of honeydew oolong tea and a piece of banana bread in front of her.

"What are you talking about?"he asked, sounding confused. "It isn't a big birthday."

"Oh, yes, it is."

"No, it isn't. Correct me if I'm wrong, but aren't you going to be thirty-three?"

"Yes. Exactly!"

"Thirty-three is not a big one," he said. "Thirty is a big one. Thirty-five is a big one. Thirty-three is a big fat nothing."

"Tell that to Jesus."

"Tell what to Jesus?" Eric said, yawning and joining them at the table. His nose had gotten as good as Suzanna's when it came to Fernando's baking.

"That thirty-three isn't an important birthday."

Eric grabbed a cup of coffee—he boycotted tea in the morning— and sat back down.

"I wasn't aware he had opinions about birthdays," he said.

"Jesus was thirty-three when he died," Suzanna said. "And look at everything he accomplished. I haven't done anything worth noticing."

"Don't worry about your birthday," Eric said. "We'll throw you a party Jesus would be proud of."

"I don't want a party," Suzanna said, suddenly exasperated beyond words at her roommates. They never understood anything! "I mean it."

Carla came into the kitchen already dressed with makeup on and ready to go to work.

"Good morning, everybody," she said.

Suzanna got up from the table.

"I can't even get a tearoom reopened," she said as stalked out of the room.

"Well," Fernando called after her, "if you went around curing lepers and raising the dead, you'd get noticed, too."

"Jesus loves you," Eric added for good measure.

She could hear the three of them laughing. She brushed her teeth with all the negative energy she could muster.

The next couple of days went by in a flash. Andy proved to be heaven-sent—Carla couldn't stop raving about him. And he seemed to get along great with Harri, which brightened her mood considerably.

Suzanna tried to steer clear of Fernando and Carla in the tearoom. There were enough strong opinions flying around in there and she thought adding her two cents would just slow things down. Every time she went into the tearoom, they seemed further and further behind.

On her birthday, Suzanna sighed heavily as she realized it had finally happened. She was finally as old as Jesus was when he died. The only thing she had in common with him was that she was also vastly disappointed in some of her friends.

But at least they were honoring her wish to treat her birthday as any other day.

"We're ignoring your birthday," Fernando said. "As ordered."

"Good."

"I'm not even baking a cake."

"Noted."

"You're being a jerk, Suzanna."

Just like any other day.

She decided that she should spend spent the day with Eric in the book nook. He was the least likely to be irritating about her birthday. He was preparing for the book club meeting. It took him days to get ready. This month's selection was *The Count of Monte Cristo*, by Alexandre Dumas—a book he deemed of equal interest to men and women.

Harri showed up early to get the tables set for tea.

"Maybe we should keep these tables here when the tearoom reopens," Harri said to Suzanna. "Then we wouldn't have to set up chairs every month for the book club."

"That might be a good idea," Eric said as he stacked notepads and pens for the club members. "When you're not serving tea, a lot of people grab a book and just sit for awhile. Since you brought the tables in, customers stay in the store an average of thirty percent longer."

"How do you figure that?" Suzanna asked.

"I made it up," Eric said. "It sounded so business school. I thought it would impress Harri."

Harri laughed.

"Well, you won't be able to impress me much longer," she said. "We're graduating in two months."

Suzanna jerked her head up.

"Two months? Are you kidding?"

"Did you think we'd be in school forever?" Eric said.

Actually, Suzanna did think they'd be in school forever, but she couldn't admit it. She sat down at one of the tables.

"Do either of you have any plans. . . I mean, for after you graduate?"

She saw them exchange a look.

This can't be good.

"Well, I guess I might as well tell you," Harri said. "I've gotten an offer at Bash Gesas and Company."

"Who? What?"

"They're a really prestigious accounting firm in Beverly Hills."

"Did you know about this?" Suzanna asked Eric.

"Sure," he said. "I wrote her a letter of recommendation."

"Do they care what one student thinks of another at . . . prestigious accounting firms?"

"I think I hear Fernando calling me," Harri said, and dashed out of the bookstore.

Eric sat down with Suzanna.

"I didn't write the letter as a fellow student," he said. "I wrote it as the manager of a bookstore."

"Oh, and who wrote letters for you? Fernando?"

"I wasn't actually planning on going anywhere just yet."

"What do you mean by 'just yet'?"

"I really hadn't thought about leaving," he said. "But I've always assumed when I do leave, I could count on you to recommend me."

He stood up before Suzanna could think of anything to say. She watched him leave. Her head was pounding. She grabbed her bike from the backyard and pedaled to the bike path as fast as she could. As the scenery flashed by—outdoor cafés, swing sets, lifeguard stations—Suzanna tired to make sense of her life.

She had been so wrapped up in herself—her annoyance at her friends, her need for a change, her . . . whatever it was she was having with Rio—that she never stopped to think that other people in her life might be feeling the same way. Yet, the evidence was all around her. Fernando needed a new tearoom. Carla wanted a break from Napa. Harri would be gone after graduation. And the unthinkable: Eric might one day leave, too. Was it her fault that everyone was so discontented? Had she taken her eye off the ball for too long? Suzanna turned her bike back toward the Bun. Perhaps it was not too late to make everyone happy again.

I should not have been a jerk about my birthday party.

I should have been more understanding about how long the tearoom was taking.

I should forget about Rio.

Suzanna rode morosely down the bike path, so lost in her thoughts that she pedaled farther than usual and was panting when she finally got home. She locked her bike in the backyard and let herself in the back office, where she sat in cool darkness. She closed her eyes and put a bottle of cold water to her forehead. She got up and walked down the hall, realizing that she had abandoned Eric, which was hardly professional. She peeked in the bookstore and saw him standing behind the counter, head inclined toward a woman whose face she couldn't see... although she seemed familiar. She watched as Eric came around the counter and took the woman in his arms. She gasped as the woman laid her head against his chest.

It was Carla.

Suzanna swiftly retreated to the hallway. She tried not to listen, but couldn't help hearing Carla saying:

"I feel bad lying to her."

"I know. I know. But this isn't like the last time we lied to her."

"Lying is lying," Carla said. "Maybe we should just tell her. Not ambush her."

Okay, maybe they aren't talking about me.

"It's not going to be an ambush. Suzanna will find out soon enough, right?"

So much for that.

"Right."

"So just keep it quiet for now. Promise me."

"Okay. Okay."

Suzanna leaned against the wall, trying to make sense of what she had just heard.

It's like high school all over again.

Suzanna heard a steady pounding coming from the construction area and realized Andy must be at work.

Suzanna walked determinedly toward the sound of the hammering.

Time to get back in the game.

Andy stopped hammering when Suzanna came in the room. "Hey," he said.

"Hey, yourself," Suzanna said, looking around the room. "You know, to the untrained eye, it really doesn't look like you're making a lot of progress."

"Yeah, well, to the trained eye, it doesn't look much better."

"I won't keep you," she said. "I was thinking. We really should go salsa dancing soon. Tonight."

"Tonight?" he asked. "Wow—that is soon."

"Well, why put it off? Let's say seven-thirty?"

"Uh . . . well . . . isn't this your birthday? Don't you have other plans?"

"No . . . I don't want any other plans. I want to go dancing."

"I don't know, Suzanna. I'd have to go home, shower . . ."

Suzanna looked at her wrist—still no watch.

"What time is it now?" she asked.

"It's four o'clock . . . but I haven't finished for the day."

"Sure you have," she said with a huge, slightly addled smile. "I'm the boss, and I'm saying you're done for the day."

"Are you sure that will be cool with Carla?"

"I guess you didn't hear me . . . I'm the boss and I said you could go home."

"Oh . . . OK. Monsoon on 3rd Street sound good? I've heard they have an awesome dance floor."

"Perfect," she said. "I'll meet you there."

Andy scratched his head with a hammer as she turned on her heels and stalked up the stairs to the Huge Apartment.

Four can play at this game.

Suzanna took a quick shower, then wrapped her hair in a towel and her body in an oversized bathrobe. When she opened the bathroom door, Fernando was standing in the hallway, waiting for her.

"Carla is being impossible," he said.

"Oh?"

"Yes! I'm ready to tear out my hair. She's taken over the whole renovation—she doesn't give a crap about my vision."

"I thought the design was her vision."

"No," he snorted. "It was my vision . . . and her execution. She's added a whole new dimension to the word 'executioner.' "

Suzanna took the towel off her head and handed it to Fernando, who started vigorously rubbing her hair. Nobody could subdue her curls like Fernando.

Suzanna bent at the waist and braced her arms on either side of the hall, so Fernando wouldn't pull her off her feet while he worked furiously.

"Well, you guys have to work it out."

"She's a tyrant," he said. "Even Andy said so."

"Andy said Carla was a tyrant?"

"Not in so many words. But he's definitely on my side."

Fernando flapped the towel—the signal that her hair was done—and Suzanna straightened up.

"Do you like the tearoom?"

"Yes, but . . ."

"We all have to make sacrifices," she said. "Besides, we're in the home stretch."

"So you're saying 'suck it up'?"

"Well, my sister would think that was a lazy way of putting it . . . but yeah."

Fernando turned and went into his room. Suzanna jerked open her bedroom door. She was surprised to find Harri lying on the bed, face buried deep in the pillow. She looked up and squinted at Suzanna. Suzanna could tell she had been crying.

"I . . . I didn't know you were in here," Suzanna said.

"I'm sorry to bogart your room. I just needed a quiet place to go," she said. "I know I should be downstairs working with Fernando or Eric."

"Oh, no problem! Are you okay?"

Harri buried her face and started crying again. Suzanna, on guard, sat on the corner of the mattress and stiffly patted Harri's back.

"I've had so much fun here," Harri said. "I didn't realize until today how much I was going to miss you guys. I'm going to graduate and be all by myself."

"You won't be by yourself, you'll have . . . a prestigious accounting firm in Beverly Hills."

"I know." Harri sniffled. "But you and the guys have such a great life together. I know you get tired of them, but . . . I was just working away, laughing with Eric about something, and I just got so damn sad about leaving."

"I guess the grass always looks greener on the other side," Suzanna said, as she started to try on various little black dresses.

"Are you getting ready to go somewhere?"

"Andy and I are going salsa dancing tonight."

"Oh? He has another hour and a half of work—"

"I told him to knock off early."

"Well," Harri said. "You're the boss."

"That's exactly what I said," Suzanna said.

She went to the dresser and started her makeup. Harri sat lotus style and watched Suzanna.

"Do you really think you should be dating an employee?"

Suzanna poked herself in the eye with the mascara wand. She turned and gave Harri a Popeye squint.

"A, I'm not dating Andy, and B, he's not an employee."

"That's not the way it looks to me."

"Well, things are not always what they seem."

"Thank you, Confucius," Harri said. "You're paying him to work here. . . that makes him an employee."

"No, he's a freelancer. You're an employee."

"Same thing . . . and I don't see you dating me."

"We're going dancing, that's all," Suzanna said, trying to sound cosmopolitan.

"It's what we do."

"It might be what you hope to do," Harri snorted. "But it's not what you do. Besides, do you even know how to dance?"

Suzanna tried to rub off the mascara that had splattered on her cheeks. She took a few shallow breaths as she realized how close she had gotten to giving away her secret.

"I . . . I'm not horrible."

"What underwear are you wearing?"Harri asked.

"What?" Suzanna asked, relieved that Harri's attention was diverted from dancing. "Afraid I might get hit by a bus and have to go to the hospital?"

"No," she replied, "but I've always thought that if you put on your best lingerie, you were secretly looking to get laid."

"Well, I can't say I've ever thought about it."

"I'll bet you're not wearing pantyhose tonight."

"Pantyhose aren't even in fashion," Suzanna replied, adding mascara furiously.

"Did you shave your legs?"

"Of course I shaved my legs . . . that's just good manners!"

Suzanna hoped Harri would drop the subject, because she had, indeed, not only shaved her legs but had put in a new blade to do so *and* had wriggled into her really small red bikini panties with a bow on each hip that actually untied. Not the best circumstantial evidence, for sure.

But none of this is really for Andy. I need to get away from Carla and Eric . . . and there's always a chance Rio might show up at the club.

"I just want you to be careful," Harri said, "I mean . . ."

Suzanna stopped with the makeup and looked at her. She looked decidedly uncomfortable.

"What?"

"Well, I was thinking . . ." Harri said. "You and Andy don't really know each other. Do you really want to spend your birthday with somebody you hardly know?"

"What is with you, Harri?" Suzanna asked. "First you think I'm out to seduce him and then you tell me I shouldn't be going out with a stranger."

"Well, they aren't mutually exclusive."

"Look, it's my birthday and I just want to do something a little different, that's all."

The bedroom door opened and Carla stuck her head in. She looked surprised.

"There you are," she said to Harri. "We've been looking all over for you."

"I better get back to work," Harri said. She turned to Carla. "Suzanna is going dancing tonight. With Andy."

Carla was silent as Harri left the room. She waited for Harri to be out of earshot, then looked at Suzanna, who was trying on various heels.

"You told Harri about dancing?"

"No . . . not exactly," Suzanna said. "Can't a woman decide to go to a club on her birthday?"

"I guess," Carla said. "But some people might want to spend their birthday with their best friends."

"I wouldn't know."

"Why are you being so short-tempered about everything?" Carla said. "We just want to celebrate with you, that's all."

"Who does?"

"Fernando, Eric, and me—who do you think?"

Suzanna tried to focus on the evening's potential. She was not about to get into a decades-old argument with Carla. Not on her birthday. Suzanna tried to control her thoughts so she could put together a coherent sentence, instead of just letting loose.

"I think you and Eric can celebrate without me."

"Are we going to go over all this again? That's ancient history!"

"Is it?"

"I'm not even going to dignify that with an answer."

How convenient.

"Eric and I have always been friends," Suzanna said. "And we always will. But I have to admit, having him around all the time has made me lazy. I always had a date for the movies if I needed one."

Now he's getting a degree and might be moving on.

Suzanna was as mad at herself as she was at Carla. But it was so much easier to be mad at her friend. She knew that if there had ever been a time when she could have been in a relationship with Eric, that time was long past. Suzanna tried to take comfort in the fact that she was too smart to mess with something as good as her friendship with him.

She thought back to an evening in Napa when she and Eric were watching *Dick Tracy* on HBO. They were seniors and the Carla-Eric thing was long past. Suzanna was thinking about hitting on him in a casual, friendly kind of way, when Madonna and Mandy Patinkin starting singing a torch song called "What Can You Lose?" As Suzanna inched closer to Eric's shoulder, she heard Madonna's warbling as she asked that age-old question: Should you spill your guts or hang on to the relationship you've got? Suzanna listened intently to every word . . . but Madonna just repeated the refrain, she didn't come up with the answer.

If that wasn't fate slapping some sense into her, then there was no such thing as fate. And she was a big believer in fate. Look at the whole thing with Rio! No, Eric was yesterday's news, to be sure. Carla could have him.

"Tonight is not about Eric, I'll tell you that much."

"OK . . . but seriously, Suzanna. Andy is such a sweet guy."

"This isn't about Andy, either."

"I know that. It's about the dance teacher," Carla said. "So it really isn't fair to be using Andy."

Hell!

"I just don't want to see anybody get hurt," Carla said.

Suzanna was flabbergasted. First and foremost, she loved the fact that Carla seemed to be viewing her as this siren who was tearing through Los Angeles with all these men at her heels. But was she using Andy?

"I'll keep that in mind," Suzanna said, summoning as much world-weary vixen-ness as she could muster.

"Come on, Suzanna," Carla said. "Just stay home with us."

"Not a chance," she said. "I'm making some big changes and I'm starting now."

She finished dressing, adding a necklace and earrings. She rooted around in her jewelry box for another watch, but decided against it. The sight of her naked wrist always came as an erotic shock and she rather enjoyed it.

She promised Carla she would behave (*HA!*) and dashed out of the bedroom. She practically smashed into Eric on the stairs.

"Hey, rocket, slow down," he said, holding her at arms' length to look at her. "Wow, you look amazing!"

"Thanks," she said, feeling a flush creeping up her well-moisturized cleavage. "I gotta go, Eric, I'm going to be late."

She wriggled free of his grasp and headed down the stairs to the car. He followed her.

"I was hoping we could have dinner," he said.

Even as distracted as she was, she was surprised and intrigued by this statement.

"Well, sure, Eric, I'd love to," she said. "But not tonight."

"Hey, that's cool," he said. "But let's do it soon. I . . . I really miss you, Suzanna."

"I don't know how you could miss me," she said. "I'm right here."

"Are you?"

Stalling for time, she dug through her purse, got out her keys, released the lock with the remote, and then looked at him. He was such a wonderful, caring man; she could see that. And she realized that this was the first birthday in twenty years she hadn't spent with him.

"Where are you going?" he asked, holding the car door open.

"I'm going dancing," she said, inching toward the truth.

"Looking like that?"

Suzanna couldn't help but be pleased by his reaction to her tight black dress and heels. She got into the car carefully, arching her feet seductively. Eric smiled and kissed her softly on the cheek. "Happy birthday."

He closed the door and stood in the driveway until she pulled out into the street.

Suzanna's mind was whirling, but she decided to focus on the evening ahead. After all, dancing was supposed to be her stress reliever, not her stress inducer!

CHAPTER 19

Suzanna had heard that Monsoon on the 3rd Street Promenade was a bit tamer than some of the salsa clubs she'd learned about at the studio, primarily in that the patrons at Monsoon weren't hostile toward either full-fledged adults or beginning dancers. Monsoon was primarily an Asian-leaning restaurant that, for reasons known only to the whimsical restaurant gods, turned into a salsa club on Wednesday evenings. One of the reasons Suzanna wanted to hit the club early was because she knew that, as the evening progressed, they would be outnumbered by better dancers and would look like a couple of losers. This way, she'd be warmed up by the time Rio showed . . . if he showed.

She parked in one of the behemoth municipal parking garages that dotted Santa Monica's downtown and said a silent prayer that she would remember where her poor car was languishing when the evening was through. She had, on more than one occasion, come to the wrong garage, insisting to the beleaguered parking attendant, as he drove her around each floor in his golf cart, that her car must have been stolen. He would reply, through gritted teeth, that he was pretty sure she just left her car in another garage. It happened all the time, he would say. The parking garages all looked alike.

Suzanna opened the lighted mirror on her visor to do minor repair to her lipstick. She tried not to think about all the drama at the Bun.

Was Carla right? Was there a possibility Suzanna and Eric might get together after all these years? Or, was Carla lying and secretly having fabulous make-out sessions with Eric behind her back? Were Andy and Fernando going to stage a coup? And what about Eric? He definitely noticed Suzanna's brain had been otherwise occupied these last few weeks. Should she confess?

She put everything out of her mind. She was determined to have a good time tonight.

As she walked up the promenade toward the club, she passed several street performers, all of whom seemed to be confident in their abilities as entertainers. Some of them were really good: a youngish guitar player channeling Nat King Cole's singing style and a little girl about eight years old who did an unnerving Michael Jackson impression. There was a woman who banged on an old plastic Sparkletts bottle and created really interesting percussion effects. There were also some odd acts to skirt: a very large man in an Elvis suit and white mime makeup who pretended he was a mannequin never failed to spook Suzanna.

Who does he think he's kidding? Mannequins don't sweat.

Suzanna took a deep breath and entered the restaurant. Walking into Monsoon, she tried to adjust to the confusing mood lighting . . . were they going for a combo English fog/Malaysian nights thing? The interior resembled an upscale Tiki Room with a dash of India thrown in. She couldn't decide if the architect was being serious or playful. Monsoon was split into many mysterious rooms, with the bar being the first space you saw as you came in from the street.

Once she adjusted to the low light and could make out the features of the room, she noted that the bar, thankfully, was hospitable looking.

She sat, starting her nonchalant wait for her non-date. The bartender, tall and slim with rosy cheeks, barely looked old enough to be in a bar, let alone behind one serving drinks. He had jet-black hair that stood up in an alarming imitation of a tidal wave. He gave Suzanna a welcoming smile. She ordered a glass of shiraz, which seemed to pass for wine sophistication in Los Angeles, and he gave her a sly smile.

"No *mojito* for you?" he asked.

"I'm sorry?"

"You have the look of a lady who would drink a mojito."

"Oh, well, I don't know what that is . . . but I guess I'll have one," she said in her most friendly, flirtiest tone, which she hoped signaled, "Oh, yeah, I'm just a breezy kind of barfly."

"It's a Cuban drink . . . rum, sugar, club soda, and lots of fresh mint, we make a good one."

She watched him pull components for her drink from every corner of the bar . . . glass from here, ice from there, rum from a top shelf, green stuff—which turned out to be mint—from a little mystery compartment near the cash register. She couldn't help but notice how gracefully he moved. The energy of bartending must be so different from running a teashop, she thought. The bartender must have realized that he was being scrutinized, because he turned around and gave Suzanna a big smile as he finished preparing her drink.

She peeked around the bar, trying not to look toward the door. She wasn't really sure if she wanted Andy to show up at this very moment or not. After all, she was in the midst of a mild flirtation with the bartender, was she not? This is one of those occasions when she knew Fernando would be egging her on and giving her great lines to toss around, but, she had to admit, it was exhilarating to be navigating these hormone-laced waters on her own.

The bartender put the Cuban concoction in front of her.

"It was Hemingway's favorite drink when he lived in Cuba," he said, still smiling.

Those choppers can't be real. Porcelain or BriteSmile?

You had to love a bartender—especially in greater Los Angeles—who knew anything about Hemingway, including his drink and country of choice.

I sound like my sister! Again!

Suzanna concentrated. Erinn was the last person she wanted in her head right now.

"Besides," he continued, history lesson closed, "most of the ladies who come in for salsa order a mojito."

"Is it that obvious I'm here for salsa?" she asked, her voice registering somewhere in the vast expanse between flirtation and panic.

"Well, you're dressed up, which is usually a sign," he said as he cast a quick glance over the bar at her legs. "And you look like a dancer."

Wow! This guy is good!

Suzanna casually shot a look at her legs and noticed that she did indeed have a good deal more muscle tone in her calves that she'd had a few months ago. Her confidence took a huge leap forward.

"It's my birthday."

"Well, then, it's on the house," he said, wiping his hands on a towel and offering his hand. "My name's Big Daddy."

She burst out laughing. His smile died. Suzanna tried to recover, but feared the damage was done.

"I'm sorry," she said. "You just seem awfully . . . uh . . . young to be calling yourself Big Daddy."

"All the girls call me Big Daddy," he said. The brilliant smile returned and Big Daddy leaned toward her. "I'm bigger than I look."

He beamed and headed off to the other end of the bar to serve another customer.

Suzanna tried to remain casual and sipped her drink while she pondered this rather unashamed penis reference.

Maybe that's the new bar talk.

Her analysis of the situation came to an abrupt end as Andy entered the bar. He blinked in the semidarkness, and Suzanna waited patiently for his eyes to adjust—no sense hailing a blind man—and then gave him a tiny wave.

Andy gave her a sheepish smile and settled into the chair next to her. He looked decidedly out of place in this trendy watering hole— he was dressed more for country line dancing than for a restaurant that was soon to unfold into a smoldering salsa club. Suzanna reminded herself that this was not a date and that she shouldn't care how he looked.

But she did.

Big Daddy returned before she and Andy had even said a word.

"Hey there, buddy," Big Daddy said, "What can I get ya?"

"This is really good," Suzanna said, offering her drink to him. "It's a mojito. Try it."

Andy took a small sip, but shook his head.

"Uhmmm . . . I'll have a beer. What have you got on tap?"

The ubiquitous beer-on-tap conversation ensued, with Andy settling on a Portuguese import recommended by Big Daddy. Again,

Suzanna was struck by the uncommon grace of the bartender... maybe it was because she had dancing on the brain, but every move he made seemed choreographed.

All was revealed when the restaurant turned into the dance club. Before the dance floor opened, there was an introductory salsa lesson—and Big Daddy was the instructor. There were maybe fifteen people in the class—young, not so young, gorgeous, and not so gorgeous. Suzanna felt that she and Andy fit in just fine. They started with the basic footwork and Andy smiled at her in obvious relief— they actually knew what they were doing!

Big Daddy grabbed Suzanna's hand and pulled her to the front of the class.

"Come here, birthday girl," he said, twirling her around. "I see we have an expert here."

Suzanna could tell she was blushing. She didn't know if he was making fun of her or not. But it appeared he was serious, as he demonstrated some couples' steps to the class. Miraculously, she didn't screw up and she was pretty sure it really did look as if she had been on a dance floor more than once.

Everyone was watching them as Big Daddy said, "When you put the steps together . . . it looks like this."

He spun Suzanna around and she executed a perfect double turn. She snuck a peek at Andy and he was grinning from ear to ear. Big Daddy released her and the class gave her a round of applause. Big Daddy announced that class was over and that the band would be starting in a few minutes. He thanked her for dancing with him and said he hoped he'd get a chance to dance with her during the evening. The fact that he did this in an incredibly theatrical manner for all the class to enjoy and not in an intimate whisper did not dilute the absolute thrill she was feeling.

This was the stuff of salsa dreams!

I wish Fernando and Eric could have seen that!

Suzanna was surprised by her thoughts. Wasn't the whole point of salsa to get away from Eric and Fernando?

Uh, no . . . Rio was the whole point of salsa.

Andy noticed a small table that was open. He took Suzanna's hand and they grabbed it while the band set up. They ordered another round of drinks and the uncomfortable silence of first non-dates set in.

"The renovation is sure going well," he said.

Suzanna was about to say she didn't want to talk about business tonight, but then she realized that she really didn't have much else to say.

"Yeah . . . I love what you're doing with the place," she said.

Suzanna looked around the room, as much to avoid stilted conversation as to see what action was taking place. She knew it was too early to start hoping Rio would show—the great dancers didn't arrive until late in the evening. She was relieved to see that the eclectic mix of people who took the dance class had not miraculously been replaced by amazing-looking dancers, although there were some of those, too. Basically, Andy and she could still fit right in—if they decided to actually dance.

Big Daddy was tearing up the dance floor, spinning and twirling a woman in a filmy 1940s style dress. She had updated her look with a really tiny pair of thong underwear, which was on full display every time she spun. One would have to assume this was for effect—and God knows, it was effective! Every man in the room had his eyes glued to her skirt.

"Aren't those girls in our class?" Andy yelled over the music. He indicated Sandy and Alexia, the *La Femme Nikita* sisters.

Suzanna nodded affirmatively, and she was suddenly aware at how out of place she was. She stared at Sandy and Alexia as they effortlessly fit into the scene. While she was worrying about every move she might make, Sandy and Alexia were drinking mojitos with casual abandon. They were in conversation with two guys and the sisters laughed coyly, their impossibly Los-Angeles-white teeth glowing as they tossed their perfect manes of hair over their shoulders to indicate their pleasure.

"What are their names again?" Andy asked.

"Oh, I don't remember."

Suzanna wasn't exactly sure why she lied to him. But if he didn't remember the names of those two gorgeous girls, it would seem a little odd that she did.

"You should ask one of them to dance," she said, before she could stop herself.

Why, why, why? Why have I said this? I don't mean it, I don't want him to, but there it is—I said it.

Suzanna hoped maybe he hadn't heard her, but he took an uncharacteristically large pull on his beer and stood up. She tried to arrange her features so that she looked happy that he was going to leave her to her own devices, but he suddenly put his hand out—just like in dance class.

"May I have this dance?"

Suzanna looked into his eyes and could see he was just as nervous as she was—which, in some weird way, made her feel a little better. She put her hand in his, and he led her to the floor.

While they were not the best on the floor, they weren't the worst, either, and frankly, that was about the best Suzanna had ever hoped for. "Not being the worst" was her yardstick. She willed herself to get over the competition factor—nobody cared how she was doing but her. Nobody was looking at her, nobody was judging her. And besides that, thong-salsa-girl pretty much had everyone's attention anyway. Suzanna finally relaxed and started to really have fun. She and Andy went from "practicing" what they'd learned in class to actually dancing! Suzanna was breathless with victory and dance moves. She even waved happily to Sandy and Alexia.

"Let's sit this next one out," Andy said, breathless.

Suzanna nodded vigorously. They went back to their table and ordered another round of drinks. Suzanna was so happy she could barely contain herself. She was so thirsty that she downed her mojito in a few quick gulps and ordered another one.

"Careful there," Andy laughed, while he sipped his beer.

The evening progressed magnificently. Dancing, drinking, more dancing.

While on the dance floor, Suzanna suddenly lost her timing as she spotted Rio and Lauren entering the club. Andy saw them, too, and he gave her one of his thumbs-up. Suzanna was galvanized by the sight of them: Rio was dressed to kill in all black and Lauren looked nine feet tall (in a good way) in a low-cut taupe wrap-around top and a skirt that looked like it had been made from running water.

Suzanna had no time to freak herself out, because Big Daddy was suddenly tapping Andy on the shoulder, asking to cut in. Big Daddy offered his hand to Suzanna, who looked at it as if she didn't know what a hand was.

"I think he wants to dance with you," Andy said, as he left the dance floor.

Suzanna snapped out of her bunny-in-the-headlights mode. She noticed that Rio had looked at her. She started to dance as if her soul depended on it.

CHAPTER 20

"We've got a birthday girl in the house," Big Daddy announced.

And the crowd went wild.

Suzanna was a little tipsy, but she knew better than to drink too much. She was not a fun drunk, and if she let alcohol get the better of her, she'd have absolutely no control over her panic swells. The last thing she wanted to do was float above the dance floor in front of all these people. Even if they couldn't tell she was floating, she could— and that was all that mattered.

A hand reached out for her as the music started to pulse. It was Rio, guiding her to the floor. She couldn't believe it. She was in a club, dancing with Rio—and she wasn't even paying him. She took a deep breath and focused. She wanted to remember every second of the dance.

The song was called "La Ruñidera"—it was one he played in class all the time, so Suzanna was familiar with it and knew she could keep up. Her feet seemed to have a life of their own. She felt so light, this could have been the beginning of a swell, but she knew she was not going anywhere. She was here—in the moment—living out a dream. She caught a glimpse of Andy, who was dancing with one of the twins. He pointed to his watch. Suzanna almost stumbled, but Rio caught her.

Andy knows about the watch?

Rio and Suzanna continued their seductive back and forth, with a rope spin and a butterfly turn thrown in, but Suzanna was distracted. As she swirled, she tried to find Andy in the crowd. The song ended, and Rio led her back to her table without a word. Andy was already at the table. He exchanged a nod with Rio as Suzanna sat, breathless. Rio disappeared into the crowd.

"You looked great out there," he said.

"I . . . I saw you tap your watch."

"Yeah," he said, tapping it again. "It's getting late. Maybe we should call it a night."

Suzanna relaxed. Her secret was safe. She looked around the club. It appeared Rio was leaving with Lauren. There wasn't any reason to stay. There would not be another dance with Rio. She felt her lip tremble, but nodded. As Andy guided her toward the door, Big Daddy called out, "Good night, birthday girl!" Suzanna turned and waved. It really had been a fun birthday.

Then why do I feel so empty?

When they got outside, Suzanna struggled to find the armhole of her jacket. Andy straightened it out and held the jacket for her.

"Where are you parked?" he asked. "I'll walk you to your car."

Suzanna smiled. Whenever she went out with a guy, she had several "potential boyfriend" tests, and Andy passed all of them. The first was "no smoking." The second one was "the sharing of food or drink": Andy had gamely sampled her mojito. The next was "hold the coat." This was Suzanna's own adaptation of "hold the car door," which she thought was goofy and time-consuming. Again, Andy passed. But the big one was "walk me to my car after dark." Again, bingo!

It was hard to find a guy who passed all the tests. So far, only Eric and Andy had gone four for four. And neither of them was going to end up her boyfriend.

Maybe I need to look at Andy a little differently.

The streetlight was illuminating them. She looked at him and envisioned a long, romantic birthday kiss.

Nah.

"I'm in the garage," she said. "Where are you?"

"I'm in the opposite direction, but I'm happy to walk you."

"That's OK," Suzanna said. Her rule was that he ask; he didn't have to follow through. "There are plenty of people around. Thanks for a great evening."

She kissed him on the cheek.

"I'll see you tomorrow," she said.

Suzanna was aware that he was watching her as she made her way up the street. She stopped at the corner and turned.

"You're going home, right?" he called to her.

She smiled and gave him a small thumbs-up, then disappeared around the corner.

She could see Rio leaning against her car in the parking structure. He was smoking a thin cigarette. He looked at her and lazily blew a smoke ring. Suzanna tried to steady herself on her heels as she walked toward him. A panic swell overtook her and she swam toward him, six inches above the ground. He put out his cigarette and looked at her as if nothing unusual was going on.

"I believe this is yours," he said.

He reached into his jacket pocket and held out her watch.

Pop! She was back on the ground. She reached out with quivering fingers and took it from his outstretched palm. He caught her hand.

"Let me help you," he said.

Suzanna held her breath as Rio fastened the clasp. She concentrated on her breathing when she felt his lips brush her wrist. She felt lightheaded. She remembered from class that Rio always advised focusing on a specific spot on the wall when you felt dizzy, so she concentrated on the red and green EXIT sign. Rio put his hands on her waist and pulled her close.

Are we going to dance?

He pulled her tighter, reached slowly under her skirt, and squeezed her butt.

That would be a no.

Suzanna closed her eyes and abandoned herself to Rio's advances. He continued his featherweight kisses until he reached her neck. Suzanna couldn't decide if she should concentrate on the hands massaging her backside or his breath on her neck.

Happy birthday to me.

Suzanna heard a car nearby and opened her eyes. Rio appeared to be deaf to anything but her body as a truck of teenagers drove by them, honking and hooting. Suzanna gave them a tiny, self-conscious wave. When she returned her attention to Rio, he had already unzipped her dress to the small of her back. Another car was approaching and Suzanna was now completely out of the moment. She caught his hand as it started its second advance up her leg.

"Let's go somewhere."

Rio looked at her, his maddeningly bored expression still in place. "Where?"

"To your place?" Suzanna asked.

"No."

"Uh . . . well . . ."

Suzanna tried to take stock quickly. She certainly couldn't bring Rio back to the Huge Apartment. She stole a glance at her Smart Car.

Even with dance lessons, I'm not that flexible.

"Perhaps another time," Rio said, rezipping her in one practiced move.

"No!" Suzanna said loudly. She tried to conceal her panic.

There has to be a place.

Then it hit her.

"My sister lives just up the street. She has a guesthouse in the back and it's never locked. We can go there."

Rio shrugged. Suzanna wasn't sure if that meant "OK" or "Your birthday is going to end in disappointment, just like all the rest." She waited, hoping he would clarify.

"I will follow in my car," he said. "It's a BMW."

Suzanna decided not to mention that she knew his car . . . she'd been hit by it. There might even be a dent where it had collided with her bike. If they ever got married, she would have the cutest "how we met" story to tell the kids.

She drove out of the car park and waited for the BMW to show itself. For a moment, she feared that he might change his mind. She gripped the steering wheel tighter and glanced in the rearview mirror. Still no Rio. She caught her reflection in the mirror and rubbed some mascara flakes off her cheeks. A horn startled her. It was Rio, engine roaring, behind her.

She looked at the clock. It was almost midnight. She shot a look at her cell phone on the passenger seat.

Should I call Erinn?

She decided against it. Erinn would be asleep and they could sneak into the backyard without a sound.

Thank God that ugly cat isn't a guard dog.

Suzanna pulled up to the curb in front of Erinn's house and Rio joined her. She got out of her car and clicked the car alarm. She jumped when her horn sounded—just the quick little beep that let her know that the alarm was on. She looked over at Rio, who was leaning against his car and watching her. She decided to be bold and walked toward him, never taking her eyes from his.

God, I'm hot!

Without a word, Rio stood up, embraced her, and started kissing her. They toppled onto the hood of the BMW. Suzanna tried to get the ponytail holder out of his hair. If this fantasy was going to continue at this pace, she was ready to go Fabio. The ponytail holder got stuck and Suzanna yanked.

"Ouch," he said. "Oh, you like it rough?"

He spun her around and threw her back on the hood, face down. Suzanna worried about Erinn's neighbors.

Well, maybe if anybody comes by, they'll think he's a cop and he's just arresting me.

Suzanna shut her eyes tight. This kind of foreplay was way out of her realm, but she figured she was thirty-three now and maybe some nasty adult sex was just what she needed. Thirty-three ... the magic number of adulthood.

What would Jesus do?

Suzanna clamped down on her thoughts ... she didn't really want to be thinking about Jesus just then. She tensed as Rio lifted her skirt. She waited. She could feel a slight breeze on her exposed bottom. A few seconds passed. Was Rio staring in appreciation of her newly firm ass? Could he see the bows on the sides of her undies in the darkness and was thinking about untying them? She waited.

Smack! Smackity-smack-smack!

Suzanna's eyes flew open as she realized Rio was spanking her.

I'll probably have to leave this part out when I tell our kids that story.

She tried to get into it, but it just wasn't happening. She flipped herself over and started kissing him, trying to get the train back onto a more romantic track. Suzanna was relieved to find that Rio seemed happy enough to forgo the S and M. He pushed against her and drove them both onto the car hood. His ponytail holder finally snapped, and his curls covered his face.

This was more like it! Her head nearly exploded from excitement, but deep inside, Suzanna felt another panic swell coming on.

No . . . no!

She tried to relax, knowing that as long as he was on top of her she could never float away. She started to run her fingers through his hair, but her stroke stopped abruptly. His hair was so curly, her fingers only got through about an inch. She could feel her legs starting to float on either side of her. She clamped them firmly around Rio's knees and he moaned. He thrust his pelvis against her.

"Who is my dirty girl?"

Is that supposed to be sexy? Am I supposed to answer that?

Pop! She was back.

"Do you like this?" he asked, rotating figure eights with his hips.

Suzanna tried to curb her annoyance. She couldn't believe it. He was what Carla called "a talker." Suzanna and Carla were both much more into the nonverbal type of lover.

Don't think about Carla. This is your dream. Stay focused.

Rio had said more to her on the hood of this car than he had in all the time she'd known him. She now understood why he kept his mouth shut. Exasperation was creeping in, but she was determined to see this through. She braced a hand against his chest and pushed him off her.

"Let's go," she said, taking him by the hand and leading him through the side gate.

When they got to the front door of the guesthouse, Suzanna gripped the doorknob and Rio started kissing the back of her neck. Now that they were off the street, Suzanna let herself relax into the sensations of his hands and mouth. Her breathing quickened as she felt his fingers inching up her skirt. She felt one of his fingers hook the side of her panties and slide them down her legs. She stepped out of them. She put her arms around his neck and his kisses got rougher. She could feel her chin being rubbed raw and knew she would have the telltale whisker burn in the morning—which thrilled her.

Blind with desire, she reached behind her and felt for the doorknob. She hoped it wouldn't squeak and destroy the moment. She gave it a turn.

The door was locked.

CHAPTER 21

She knew she couldn't sit in the car in front of her sister's house all night, and she sure as hell wasn't ready to go home, so Suzanna drove blindly around, trying to gather her—what? Wits? Dignity?

Her bare bottom stuck to the leatherette seat. She tried not to relive her last moments with Rio, but she went over it again and again anyway.

The disdainful look in his eyes when she told him she couldn't get the door open made her miss his bored expression. He had spun around without a word. She ran up the path after him, grabbing at his sleeve. He turned back to her.

"I think I can find the key. Just hang on."

"It is too late," he said.

The moon was insanely bright and they could see each other clearly. He wasn't leaving—just looking at her. Suzanna smiled her most seductive smile. He inched closer to her and Suzanna's hopes soared.

"You have spinach in your teeth," he said, and continued his retreat.

Horrified, Suzanna clipped the offensive greenery with her nail as she hurried after him.

"It's mint!"

She realized in horror that she was pathetically waving the offending herb at his back as he stalked away. She threw it to ground as if it were a lit match.

I wish it were a lit match. I could set myself on fire and be done with it.

She watched as he walked down the street. She never knew what he was thinking when he had that hooded-eyed uninterested look on his face. But there was no mistaking what his back was telling her tonight.

She was history. Yesterday's news. Toast.

How do you say "toast" in Spanish?

She drove up the coast for over an hour, made a U-turn in Oxnard, and headed south again. She turned up the California Incline and pointed the car aimlessly up and down the Santa Monica streets. As the car dealerships on Santa Monica Boulevard gave way to the coffee houses on Broadway, then to closed Main Street shops in Venice, Suzanna finally turned toward the boardwalk, exhausted. She looked at the clock on the dashboard—it was nearly one o'clock. Her birthday was over and Rio was gone. She sighed. She'd been through varying degrees of heartache before, and was surprised that this one really didn't rate very high. It was nothing compared to finding out about Eric and Carla. But of course, nothing had ever come close to that one.

It surprised her, as she got closer and closer to home, to realize that Rio was actually kind of an asshole. A really hot asshole, but an asshole nonetheless. It occurred to her that Erinn would be disappointed in her right about now. Erinn thought swearing was lazy. But right now, Suzanna felt that "asshole" was the absolutely most perfect description. Her real friends wouldn't treat her like that! She felt guilty about the way she had been treating her friends of late—and she swore she would make it up to them.

And as much as it hurt, if Carla and Eric had hooked up again, she would be supportive. Well, she would pretend to be supportive. All her friends deserved to be happy, and Suzanna would not stand in their way. She had a lot of thoughtless behavior to make up for.

The Smart Car pulled into the alley behind the shop and Suzanna got out as quietly as possible. She wondered if salsa class was going to be any more awkward than usual? Or maybe she should quit and start dancing someplace else. There were times when Suzanna tried to flatter herself, to come up with some excuse why this wasn't all her own fault. Well, Rio had to shoulder some of the blame, she admitted that. But tonight, she was thinking pretty straight. She knew she didn't mean anything to Rio. And he didn't really mean anything to her. Just another fantasy gone wrong. She bet the local dance studios were full of women just like her—pantyless, terrified women in their thirties afraid no one would ever love them, throwing money and themselves at their instructors.

Suzanna noticed the light was on in the tearoom. She looked closer and saw Andy. Had he come back to work? It was the middle of the night—that was crazy!

She walked into the front yard. Andy was in the tearoom all right, and so was Harri. Harri and Andy?

Oh my God! Even Harri is getting lucky!

Suzanna crept up to the window and looked inside the Bun. She closed her eyes, afraid she must be losing her mind. When she opened them again, she beheld the same unnerving sight:

The tearoom was finished!

She flattened herself against the wall between two of the windows. It wasn't possible. The room had still been covered in plastic and paint buckets just a few short hours ago. She peeked in again. Now the room was softly lit with candles. The candlelight flickered over the mismatched bone china and played up soft shadows on the new tea-colored walls. She saw Harri and Andy again, but realized there were more people in the shop as well. She counted Erinn, Eric, Fernando, and Carla, too. Harri came close to the window and Suzanna ducked again.

What was going on?

She listened for Harri's footsteps to disappear and then looked in again. The room was so beautiful that she wanted to cry. The fact that it was impossible for the room to be done and all her friends to be there in the middle of the night made her want to cry, too, but for other reasons. Was she going crazy?

She couldn't hear what anybody was saying, but by the collective body language, she could tell that everyone was upset and on edge. She wondered if she had died and was witnessing her own funeral reception. She dismissed that idea immediately—surely there would be more people at her funeral. The patrons of the Bun knew that, even if it were a funeral, Suzanna would make sure it was a party.

She bit down on a knuckle as she realized what was going on. She steeled herself and looked in again. Against the far wall, above the double doors leading into the kitchen, was a beautiful banner that read HAPPY BIRTHDAY, SUZANNA. It was hand lettered in tea colors. She steeled herself, crept around the back of the building, let herself in without turning on the lights, and felt her way up the stairs. She would face them—and soon.

But not without underwear.

As she wriggled into the first pair she could get her hands on, pieces of the last few hours fell into place. The conversation between Eric and Carla about keeping a secret from her. Harri trying to convince her that she shouldn't be dating employees. Carla being shocked that Suzanna was going dancing. Andy stalling.

They had the party planned and she had ruined it.

She'd only been thirty-three for less than twenty-four hours and she was ruining everything. She was the Anti-Jesus.

As horrified as Suzanna was at the prospect of facing them, she was determined to make this up to her friends. She started back down the stairs, avoiding by instinct every creaking step on the staircase. The sad little book nook was dark and silent, but she could hear voices buzzing in the teashop.

"There's a LoJack on her car," she heard Fernando say. "Maybe we should call it in and see where the car is."

How dare Fernando even suggest such a thing? That would totally infringe on her rights as an adult—not to mention making them all look like idiots because the LoJack people would find the car in the driveway. Suzanna sighed in relief when she heard Eric say:

"We can't do that. The car is registered to her. She's the only one who could call."

"Well, we have to do something," Erinn said. "She's been gone for hours."

Suzanna could hear the terror in her sister's voice. She braced herself to go inside . . . hoping some plausible lie would come to her. But even if it didn't, it wasn't fair to keep her friends and family in suspense any longer.

They'll probably be so relieved I'm okay, they'll forgive me for ruining the party.

That thought cheered her up and gave her enough confidence to step into the room. She stared at everyone and everyone stared at her.

"Surprise," she said.

"I think that's our line," Erinn said.

Suzanna stared at the floor. She couldn't think of anything more to say. She certainly couldn't explain why she was so late—the humiliation would float her. She heard a rustling and lifted her eyes from the floor. Erinn was putting on her coat. Harri took her cue from Erinn and gathered up her belongings as well.

"I think I'll get going, too," Harri said, kissing Suzanna on the cheek. "The important thing is, you're safe. Happy birthday."

"Thanks," Suzanna said.

"All's well that ends well," Harri said.

"All's well that ends," Erinn said, and the two women left.

Suzanna looked around the room.

"It's beautiful," she said. "I don't understand . . . it was a wreck this afternoon."

"It was a ruse," Fernando said.

"A ruse?"

"We were faking you out!" Fernando said. "The place was finished two days ago, but we left it looking like we still had weeks to go, so we could surprise you for your birthday."

"Well . . . you did! I'm totally surprised."

"Go to hell," Fernando said, and stalked out of the room.

"Look, I better go, too," Andy said. He looked sorrowfully at Suzanna. "I came back for the party. I didn't mean to rat you out. It's just that . . . when you didn't come home . . ."

"That's okay," Suzanna said. She hadn't really thought of accusing Andy of anything, so it was easy to be magnanimous. She kissed him on the cheek. "Thank you for coming to my party."

Suzanna hugged him. She realized that it was silly to start acting like the hostess of her disastrous birthday party at this stage of the game. It was as if she were standing on the deck of the *Titanic*, kissing people and waving them off cheerfully as they struggled into lifeboats. But at least it gave her something to do.

"That's okay," he said in a low voice. "Listen, Suzanna, when you didn't show up, I went back to Monsoon. Rio was there and . . ."

Rio went back to the club?

"I'm just going to walk Andy to his car," Suzanna said to Carla and Eric. "Be right back."

Suzanna took Andy's arm and hurried outside. The air had a slight chill to it, but Suzanna was sweating anyway. She knew that whatever Andy had to say was not going to be good.

"I went back to the club to see if anyone had seen you. Rio was there with Lauren . . ."

"I didn't see Rio," Suzanna lied.

"I know. He said he hadn't seen you after we left."

He said he hadn't seen me? What a loser.

Suzanna recovered from the shock of Rio's lie. She couldn't very well bust him, since she was lying, too.

"Oh. Well, then. What did you want to tell me?"

"Rio and Lauren are moving to New Zealand."

Suzanna waited for her heart to stop. But it kept on beating. In fact, it didn't skip a beat.

I guess I'm really over him!

The thought surprised her. She had told herself in the past that she was over guys, but she was usually just trying to convince herself. Now her only regret was that "You have spinach in your teeth" were the last words he'd said to her.

As far as endings went, *Casablanca* it wasn't.

"Yeah. They're leaving tomorrow," Andy continued, breaking into her thoughts.

"I guess we'll have to find another instructor."

"That's just it, Suzanna, that's what I wanted to talk to you about," Andy said, shifting from foot to foot. "I'm not going to take any more classes."

"Oh, no," Suzanna said. "It's not because of me, is it?"

Andy tilted his head in confusion.

"Why would it be because of you?"

She hoped he couldn't see her blushing. Sometimes Suzanna's ego surprised even her.

"No reason."

"I'm moving," he said. "I really loved working here and it made me want to open a place of my own . . . a B and B up north."

Suzanna caught sight of a shadow. She turned to see Fernando walking toward them.

"Hey, Fernando, I'm sorry . . . I'll only be a minute . . ."

"I need to be in on this conversation." Fernando said. Suzanna had never heard him sound so serious.

What is going on?

"I'm going with Andy," Fernando said.

"Right now?"

"I'm going to open the B and B with him."

Suzanna blinked. It was too much information, too fast. She thought about all the hours Andy and Fernando spent alone. She had always prided herself on her gaydar. How could she not have seen this coming?

"You're gay?" she asked Andy.

"No, I'm not gay. Why would you even ask that?"

"Do business partners need to have the same sexual orientation?" Fernando asked.

"But . . . but . . ."

"Look, Suzanna, all of us have been hanging on to this arrangement for far too long, and you know it. The tearoom is finished and you can have a fresh start. I need one, too."

He grabbed her wrist so she wouldn't float away. How was she ever going to find another friend like that? Who would keep her grounded? She swallowed and tried not to cry.

"You can have my gingerbread recipe," Fernando said.

Suzanna sputtered. She willed herself to not wreck the moment—after all, she had created it.

"Where are you going to go?"

"Vashon Island," they said in unison.

"But you hate Vashon Island," Suzanna said to Fernando through tears that refused to stop.

Fernando grabbed her and hugged her so hard it hurt. It hurt on so many levels.

"People change, Suzanna," he said into her hair. He released her. "Look, I'm going to go get some coffee with my new business partner. You have some other people to talk to . . ."

Suzanna sniffled. The guys wished her happy birthday one last time and headed down the street. She looked back at the tearoom. She had no choice but to go back in.

Maybe Carla and Eric had gone upstairs, now that they know I'm safe.

She was half right. Carla was nowhere to be found when Suzanna came back inside. Eric was seated at one of the tables, head in his hands. She spotted her birthday cake on a side table. It stared at her accusingly. She swallowed a lump in her throat—she knew it was a red velvet cake, her favorite—and that Fernando had made it for her.

"Anyone want some cake?" she asked Eric, trying desperately to remain in hostess mode.

Without waiting for an answer, she picked up a knife and started slicing into it.

She hurriedly cut two large pieces, hoping to make the cake look well-loved. She put the plates down in front of Eric, who stared at the offering as if he'd never encountered cake before. Suzanna took a hefty bite.

"Hmmm . . . yum," Suzanna closed her eyes.

"Suzanna, we need to talk," Eric said.

Suzanna got up and studied the remodeled tearoom.

"This is gorgeous, isn't it? Carla really outdid herself."

"Yes, she did . . . Suzanna—"

"It's so funny. I overheard you and Carla talking about the party . . . you said you didn't want to lie to me. I thought you guys were back together. How crazy was that?"

Eric looked at her. She knew him too well not to know she had surprised him . . . and it wasn't that she'd overheard him. Her heart sank.

"You . . . you weren't talking about the party, were you?"

Eric shook his head. Suzanna walked over to the table and lowered herself into a chair.

Whatever he has to say, I deserve it.

"I've been offered a job back in Napa when I get my degree. I didn't want to tell you until after your birthday. I didn't want to ruin the day for you. I've decided to take it."

"Is it because you want to be with Carla?"

Eric slammed the table and stood up. Suzanna could see his muscles tensing under his shirt as he paced the room.

"No, damn it. Not because I want to be with Carla. That's ancient history—to everybody but you."

"So it's not because of Carla?"

"No, Suzanna, it's because of you."

"Me?"

"Yes, you. When I found out you were taking those . . . stupid dance lessons . . ."

"Oh. Yeah. Andy told me he told you guys about that."

"Andy didn't have to tell me! I've known for months."

Months?

"You used the wrong credit card at the dance studio. So, I got the bill."

Suzanna looked down at the table, ashamed. Now that it was all behind her, she realized how silly she had been. And she could tell by the sound of things that it was too late to fix it.

"I waited and waited for you to tell me. Dancing isn't a crime," he continued. "I mean, what's so important about dance lessons that you had to hide them?"

"I . . . I just wanted some space."

"Well, congratulations, now you've got it."

"But I don't want it any more. I want things to go back the way they were."

"They can't," he said, grabbing both sides of the table and glaring into her eyes. His voice softened. "They can't."

She watched Eric as he turned his back on her and left the shop. Suzanna wandered around the room. She shook a few of the tables. Not one of them wiggled.

I better put that shim back under the bookcase. I'm already in enough trouble.

She took down the "Happy Birthday, Suzanna" banner, gently folding it and putting it next to the cake. She walked into the hallway that separated the tea shop from the bookstore. She could see a light coming from the back office. Eric must be in there. She hesitated, wanting to see him, but decided he had said all he had to say. She climbed the stairs to the Huge Apartment. Fernando's bedroom door was open—he must still be out with his new partner. She looked down the other hall, to her room, where Carla was presumably already asleep; the door was old, and when the light was on, you could see it outlined in the doorframe. The door was dark.

Suzanna sat down at the kitchen table, took a deep breath, and listened. The entire building was silent. She couldn't have had more space if she lived on the moon.

CHAPTER 22

Suzanna put a kettle of water on the stove. She opened the cupboard and looked at their vast selection of teas: besides the usual favorites, there were some new offerings, thanks to Fernando's ever-reaching research. She chose *gueifeicha*—"concubine tea," a current favorite of the household, thanks to the "green" nature of the tea . . . it was a pesticide-free, biologically grown oolong tea. Every step of the tea preparation stabbed at her like a knife. Signs of Fernando's and Eric's devotion were everywhere—from the tea she was drinking to Eric working away in the office at three in the morning.

She kept looking at the stairs, hoping Eric would come up, but there was no sign of him. All her rummaging around in the kitchen did wake Carla, however, who stepped sleepily into the kitchen. She sat at the table and put out her hand . . . their secret signal that she'd like some tea, too.

"I guess Eric was right; we shouldn't have kept the tearoom a secret," Carla said. "That was probably one of my worst ideas ever."

"No, it was a great idea. I just was so self-absorbed, I ruined everything."

"Yeah."

"You don't have to agree with me."

"But I do. I agree wholeheartedly."

"Do you know Fernando is leaving?"

Carla nodded. "And before you say anything," she said, "I didn't try to lure Eric back to Napa."

"I didn't think you did."

Carla gave Suzanna a look that she'd been using since they were six. It said, *Who do you think you're kidding?*

"Okay, I'm too tired to debate this, anyhow."

"Suzanna, you just really blew it, you know."

"Hey, lighten up. It's my birthday!"

"Truly yesterday's news, girlfriend."

Suzanna put her head on the table and rolled it from side to side.

"I can't believe they're leaving me," Suzanna said, her head still on the table.

"Well, I hope last night was worth it."

"It totally wasn't! I've blown my life apart for one night of creepy foreplay."

"Eeewww."

"You have no idea. And to top it all off, he was a talker."

"Too much detail, Suzanna. Seriously."

They both groaned.

"Listen, Suzanna, this is none of my business, but . . ." Carla reached out and squeezed Suzanna's arm. ". . . that's never stopped me before, so here goes."

Suzanna stopped rolling her head and waited. When Carla didn't say anything, she put her head up and looked at her friend, who was wiping away a tear.

"I've waited all these years for you to figure it out, but you never did. I was selfish and should have told you sooner. I don't know why I didn't. I'm sorry. I'm so sorry."

"Wait! Wait! What? I don't understand."

"When Eric and I broke up in high school, it was because. . . ."

"I am SO listening . . . go on."

"It was because he said he was in love with you."

"What?"

"I know . . . I know . . . I should have told you, but I thought if I told you, I would never get another chance. But I respected his wish and nothing. . . . I swear . . . nothing has happened between us in all those years."

Suzanna couldn't stop it. She started to swell and floated up to the ceiling. Carla continued to talk to her empty chair as if nothing were happening.

"I know you think Eric is coming back to Napa to be with me . . . and it isn't true. He's still in love with you."

Pop! She was back in her chair.

"What?"

"He's still in love with you."

"He told you that?"

"He didn't need to tell me. . . . it's been clear that you two have been in love with each other all this time. You're just both two stubborn or too afraid of being rejected or ruining your friendship or whatever it is . . . to admit it to each other."

"I don't know what to say."

"Please just say you'll forgive me—and that we'll still be friends."

Suzanna got up and poured more hot water into the teapot. It amazed her how clear her feelings were—first about Rio, now about Carla.

"Of course I forgive you. I mean, it's not your fault that Eric and I never made a move toward each other."

"But I was just being selfish."

"Yeah, okay. You can beat yourself up about being selfish," Suzanna said. "But I know you love me and Fernando as well as Eric. I can see it in every detail of the tearoom—and I haven't even thanked you!"

The two women embraced. Suzanna, usually the emotional one, held her friend, who cried fifteen years' worth of guilty, lonely tears. Suzanna knew what that felt like. Who was she to judge Carla?

"You need to go talk to him," Carla said. "Make this right. Don't wait another fifteen years."

Suzanna nodded and started down the stairs, but turned back.

"Are you sure?" she asked Carla.

"Sure I'm sure."

She tried again to head down the stairs.

"But," she said, turning back to Carla. "He didn't actually say he loved me. What if you're wrong?"

"Suzanna, you said you wanted some change in your life. Isn't this worth risking everything for? Think of the change. Just think."

Suzanna took a breath and headed downstairs one final time. She caught a glimpse of herself in the mirror. She had to admit, she looked like hell. But if she had a chance at a future with Eric, she wasn't going to miss another instant. She wasn't sure exactly what she was going to say when she got to the office, but she was startled to find him standing in the middle of the bookstore when she opened the door, and she had no time to formulate a speech.

"You're working late," Suzanna said.

Eric flipped on the lights, tossing a harsh glare across the tiny bookstore.

"Well, I want to make sure everything is in order . . . now that you know I'm moving back home."

Suzanna took his hand in both of hers.

"You are home, Eric."

Suzanna could tell he was looking at her, but she couldn't meet his eyes. She stayed focused on their hands. He slowly released his and walked away from her. She closed her eyes and bit a knuckle, trying not to cry. Praying that he wasn't leaving the room. She could hear him walking around.

"Suzanna, I know you wanted to have some space to yourself. And I guess Fernando and I crowded you—but we didn't realize you were unhappy."

"I was just confused. You guys didn't crowd me at all. Or, if you did, I liked it. I still like it."

"No, you were right to try to carve out a place for yourself. We all get it. We all agree with you. A fresh start will be best for all of us."

"Well, I think . . . I think we should all sit down and discuss it."

Suzanna got up the nerve to face him. He was shaking his head.

"Fernando is dead set on going, Suzanna. You know how he is, once he makes his mind up."

Suzanna squeezed the bridge of her nose with her thumb and index finger, willing herself not to cry. She couldn't bear the thought of the tearoom without Fernando in it. He had been instrumental in every day of its existence. And now, with the remodel, she'd lost every bit of his influence. All she had now was a clean slate. She suddenly hated that they had redecorated. She wanted the old tearoom back.

"I guess we've all just been too scared to make any changes," Eric said. "We always joked about you being the scared one who had to be talked into things, but you turned out to be the brave one."

"I don't understand what you mean."

"Well, dancing lessons aren't exactly on a level with saving the world, but you took a step, Suzanna. It shook us all up. We've got to move on. It's time."

"No, it isn't," Suzanna said. "I've tried it. Change is overrated. Really."

"We can't go back to the way it was," Eric said. "I know I haven't . . . stepped up to the plate. But that's in the past now. I don't blame you for hating me."

"I don't hate you," Suzanna said. Eric was standing in the doorway leading to the hallway. He had one foot out the door. "I . . . I love you."

"Could you repeat that?"

"Forget it—saying 'I love you' is like a magician doing a trick. It loses something if you do it again. Your audience starts to see the cracks."

"I don't understand. Why are you telling me this now?"

Eric looked at her, and she saw so much pain and regret that she had to look away.

"I guess I can tell you because it doesn't matter any longer. It's all over."

Suzanna suddenly felt she was falling. It was the opposite sensation to floating. The ground was shifting out from under her. She tried to steady herself. She reached out toward a bookcase. What was happening?

Earthquake!

The bookcase, the one she had forgotten to balance, started to fall. Eric tackled her, pushing her out of the way of the falling mass of splintering lumber.

She woke up in a pile of shelves and books. Eric lay still on top of her. She waited, afraid to touch him. She tried to reconstruct what had happened. The earth had been tilting. The bookcase had started to topple, and she knew it was going to crush her, but she was immobilized. Eric had been safe in the door frame, but had come back into the room to help her.

A sob caught in her throat as she felt him breathing against her rib cage. She shook a couple books off her right shoulder and reached up and stroked his hair. He groaned. She knew he was going to be fine. He was also going to be annoyed as hell that she'd taken the shim out from under the bookcase, but they could work past that.

Suzanna didn't remember exactly what had happened, but she would never forget the look in his eyes as he crashed into her and pushed her to safety.

Carla had been right.

If she knew anything, she knew Eric loved her.

PART FOUR

UPTOWN

CHAPTER 23

Suzanna stood in front of the antique full-length mirror in Erinn's second-story bedroom. She examined the intricate lacework of her wedding dress. Until you really studied it, the pattern looked so simple, but when you looked closely, you could see all the exquisite detail—all the work and imagination—that had gone into it.

Sort of like life.

The bookcase had broken Eric's leg in two places. Except for a lump on his head, that was the extent of the damages, for which everyone was grateful. Luckily, she and Carla were able to free him, and he dragged himself to a sitting position. They had all been through California earthquakes before and knew getting an ambulance would take some time, so they settled in the best they could. Suzanna stayed with Eric while Carla went into the tearoom kitchen and made some chamomile tea—on a butane stove they kept on hand for emergencies. Native Californians, they all knew not to turn on the stove after a natural disaster.

The epicenter had been just north of Santa Monica, in Malibu, the quake measuring 6. 0 on the Richter scale.

"Man, that was one major quake," Fernando had said. He and Andy had come back to the Bun as quickly as they could maneuver through the chaos.

"A 'major earthquake' registers a seven on the Richter scale,"

Erinn, who had also made her way to the shop with her cat, said. "A six is a 'strong' earthquake."

"I stand corrected," Fernando said gallantly.

Andy had pulled the wooden "The Rollicking Bun: Home of the Epic Scone" sign off the porch and used it for a stretcher. They managed to get Eric into the front of the store, and once Carla had come downstairs with tea and food, they decided to stay outside. The building had been through worse—although you couldn't tell by looking at it—but just to play it safe, Carla and Andy wanted to thoroughly inspect the place.

Not a bad call, having an architect and carpenter on hand after something like this.

It was well into the morning hours when they were finally able to get Eric into an ambulance. As the two paramedics were setting up the gurney, Suzanna asked if she could go with him, but the ambulance driver said no; she would have to follow in her car.

Suzanna took Eric's hand.

"I'll be right behind you."

He was sitting on the gurney, but asked the paramedics to give him a minute before they strapped him down. He kissed Suzanna's hand and looked at her.

"Listen, Suzanna. I'm not that bad off, and it might be hours before they get to me. You should stay here."

Suzanna was horrified. Had she read this wrong?

It wouldn't be the first time.

"But I want to be with you," she said.

Was that so hard?

"I know," he said, looking around at all the broken glass, shattered doors, and splintered wood that was strewn all over the street. "But it looks like nobody on the boardwalk has gas or electricity. We've got backup equipment and lots of food. We've got to help out."

"You're right," Suzanna said. "I'll do what I can."

Eric pulled her closer.

"Suzanna, I know it's taken me almost two decades, so I guess there isn't any rush . . ."

One of the paramedics came over, but Eric asked him for just two more minutes.

"I wish I could do this right, but it doesn't look like I'll be getting down on one knee anytime soon . . . but, as signs from God go, this was pretty spectacular, wouldn't you say?"

Suzanna nodded, afraid to speak. Afraid to break the spell. Afraid she might ruin everything.

"Will you marry me?" he asked.

Suzanna tired to hold back her tears. When she knew that wasn't going to work, she tried at least to let out a ladylike sniffle, but it was no use. She blubbered. There was no other word for it. And sobbed. And gagged. She did manage a nod. It was probably the most pathetic acceptance of all time, but she didn't care.

The paramedics looked as if they were afraid they were going to have to cart the two of them away instead of just Eric, so they hurriedly laid him down, strapped him in, and drove off, Suzanna sniveling in their wake.

Erinn came up beside her and held out a tissue.

"You have mucus running from your nose."

Suzanna took the tissue and honked. The blubbering continued.

"That was not pretty," Erinn said, putting her arm around her sister. "But it was certainly beautiful."

The Bun became the neighborhood headquarters in the next few weeks, as the boardwalk got itself back on its asphalt feet. Andy, Fernando, and Carla, who all had places to go, stayed instead and helped get the stores in working order. Suzanna wanted to insist they return the tearoom to its mountain laurel glory as a tribute to Fernando, but he would have none of it.

"I always hated mountain laurel," he said. "The new design is my masterpiece. Go with it."

"It's actually my masterpiece, but whatever," Carla groused.

Eric received his diploma (although he had them mail it—that leg wasn't going to last through a graduation ceremony) and Suzanna held a small graduation party for him and Harri at the grand reopening of the Rollicking Bun. With state-of-the-art earthquake-proof bookcases for the nook.

Eric also very politely blew off the job offer in Napa. He and Suzanna were going to make a go of it as the newlywed owners of the Bun. Just like the building, they would be the same—but different.

Suzanna turned from the mirror and looked down into Erinn's backyard, where the wedding was going to take place in less than an hour. Their mother Virginia was arranging flowers for centerpieces and ordering Fernando and Harri around. It certainly didn't matter to her that she was in the midst of catering professionals. She was the mother of the bride, damn it, and attention must be paid. Suzanna tapped on the glass and her mother looked up. Suzanna motioned her to come upstairs. Virginia nodded, gave a few more marching orders to Harri and Fernando, and headed into the house. Fernando and Harri looked up at Suzanna and mouthed the words *Thank you.*

Virginia slipped into the room. Years of university life had steered Virginia away from the free-flowing, gauzy, shepherdess-style dresses she had favored when she was younger. But she still had a slim figure and she was showing it to advantage in a flowing slate gray pantsuit with a long duster jacket. She glowed at Suzanna.

"Honey, you look perfect."

Suzanna looked at herself again in the mirror. She had to admit, she'd scrubbed up pretty well. The bedroom door squeaked open, and Erinn, face scrunched up behind her new video camera, came padding into the room.

"Just pretend I'm not here," Erinn said, circling them. "Don't look at me! Just be natural."

"Erinn, shut off the camera. Seriously!" Suzanna said.

"No! You'll thank me later."

"No, I won't. Please shut off the camera."

"Mother, don't look at the camera, please. Look at Suzanna," Erinn said, ignoring Suzanna.

"I'm not sure what to say," Virginia said, her head at an unnatural angle, as if she were sitting for a tintype.

"Tell her she looks ethereal," Erinn said, climbing up on the bed without removing the eyepiece from her face.

"I already told her she looks perfect."

"Erinn, I mean it, put the camera down," Suzanna said to obviously deaf ears. She raised her voice. "I'm the bride, damn it. You have to do what I say!"

Erinn, still standing on the bed, looked up, surprised. She shut off the camera.

"In case you're interested," Erinn said. "It's 'you have to do as I say.'"

"Was I that annoying when you were growing up?" Virginia asked Suzanna.

"No, Mom. It's way more annoying having your grammar corrected by your sister than by your mother."

"Thank God. One less thing to feel guilty about."

Why is Mom feeling guilty?

Erinn sat down on the bed next to her mother and they both looked at Suzanna as if they had never seen her before.

"Well, come on, you guys, say something!" Suzanna said.

"I am so happy," Virginia said, pulling a handkerchief out of her sleeve. "I wish your father could be here."

"I wish he could, too," Suzanna said, tilting her head back so her mascara wouldn't run.

"He'd be so happy," Virginia said. "He loved Eric."

"I know."

"We all love Eric."

"Oh, trust me, I know." Suzanna could hear the resentment and pettiness creeping into her voice and decided to squash it.

"And you seem so happy." Virginia got up and took Suzanna's face in her hands. "And you are so very, very beautiful."

Virginia kissed Suzanna's forehead and put her arms around her. Suzanna rested her head on her mother's shoulder.

"Well, weddings will do that to you, I guess," Erinn said. She was uncomfortable with displays of emotion.

"Beauty is not caused, it *is*," Virginia said.

Virginia and Suzanna dissolved into tears. It was one of Martin Wolf's favorite quotes, from a poem by Emily Dickinson.

"Oh, crap, that was great," Erinn said, picking up her camera. "Let's try that again . . ."

Suzanna and Virginia looked at Erinn, who was squinting at them from behind the giant lens like a Cyclops with a film degree.

"From 'Beauty Be Not Caused . . . .' . . . . and . . . . action!"

Suzanna and her mother looked at each other and burst out laughing. Erinn came out from behind the lens, confused for a moment, but then joined them in rollicking guffaws. The three women collapsed on the bed. When they were all laughed out, Virginia sat up, wiped her eyes, and said:

"I'm glad we have a minute to ourselves before things heat up. I want to tell you two something."

Suzanna and Erinn exchanged an ageless sisterly this-doesn't-sound-good glance and sat up, one on each side of their mother.

"I'm retiring," Virginia said.

It took a moment to sink in. Suzanna really couldn't picture their mother without the mantle of professorhood. But perhaps this was good news. In a few years there would be grandkids, and long trips up the coast to the see the barn would be wonderful.

"And I'm moving," Virginia said. "To New York."

Suzanna and Erinn gasped in shock.

"To New York?" Suzanna asked, hoping perhaps she had heard it wrong.

"Why?" Erinn asked.

"Well, girls," Virginia said, "I'm lonely up there in Napa by myself."

"Well, move here," Suzanna said. "You can have Fernando's room."

"Thank you, sweetheart . . . . I'm lonely, but I'm not that lonely."

Suzanna looked hurt and her mother kissed her on the top of the head the way she did when the girls were small.

"I mean . . . I'm not ready for that step just yet. I've watched so much change lately . . . with you girls . . . and your friends. You two are getting married, little Harri got her degree, Fernando is moving to Vashon Island. . . ." Virginia looked at Erinn, who was nakedly waiting to be included. "Erinn . . . got a new camera. It's all been exhilarating to witness, but I have to admit, I don't want to be left behind. I want to shake things up, too."

I started this. My mother is moving three thousand miles away because of me. Does no good deed go unpunished?

"But I don't want you to go," Suzanna said in a small voice. "New York is too far."

"It's only a plane ride away," Virginia said. "Don't you remember, we always said that to Erinn when she'd call from New York?"

"Yes, I do remember," Suzanna said. "You'd say it to her and then you'd hang up and cry for half an hour."

They all laughed. Then they all cried. Then they laughed again. How could Suzanna begrudge her mother a new beginning?

And, besides, New York is only a plane ride away.

Carla knocked on the door. She walked into the middle of a crying jag.

"Wow, you guys, lighten up. You're all swollen!" Carla said.

Carla and Virginia headed down to the backyard. Suzanna took pity on Erinn, who was awkward in the best of situations, and agreed to let her videotape her final preparations: lipstick, flowers in her hair, and perfume.

"Skip the perfume," Erinn said. "It's bad for the camera."

Suzanna tried to act natural. Erinn hit the "stop" button.

"I need a new tape," she said. She opened the window and yelled down to Andy, who was serving as the wedding's jack-of-all-trades. "Hey, Andy, there's a mini DV tape in a box on the desk in the guesthouse. Would you grab it for me? The door isn't locked."

Suzanna froze. She tried to pin a tea rose in her hair and sound natural as Erinn closed the window.

"Oh, that's right. You never lock the guesthouse."

Erinn released the shot tape from the camera and stuck it in a small plastic case without looking at Suzanna.

"Oh, I wouldn't say I never lock it," she said, and then looked Suzanna in the eye in a way that only a sister—even a sister ten years younger—would understand. "I did lock it once."

How did she know? Sisterly sixth sense? A writer's sixth sense?

Suzanna knew she could never bring herself to ask. And did it really matter? All that mattered was that Erinn had saved her from making a huge mistake that night.

I owe you one, Erinn.

The next half hour passed quickly, even with Erinn videotaping everything. The next thing Suzanna knew, she was being escorted down the aisle by Fernando. She saw Eric, leaning on a cane next to a flower-strewn lectern. She tried to stay focused on him, tried to blank everything else out—especially that god-awful camera.

This was about Eric. And her. And their new beginning.

As Fernando guided her rhythmically toward the lectern, Suzanna caught sight of Caro out of the corner of her eye. The cat was batting at something red. He hurled it into the air, caught it in his paws, and then pounced on it. Suzanna could feel herself panicking.

My panties! From that night with Rio!

She felt herself flushing. Should she grab them? She couldn't! Everyone was looking at her. She eyed the cat again. The panties winked at her in equal parts glee and condemnation. She remembered trying to explain about Rio to Eric, but he didn't want to hear about it. Rio could be part of the past, he said. He had nothing to do with their new life.

The damn cat can have the panties.

As they reached Eric, Suzanna paused to give Fernando a kiss. There were so many tears on his cheek, that her kiss slid right past it and she kissed his ear. She looked at Carla, who was sitting with her parents. She blew her a kiss and Carla caught it in the air. She walked over and handed Virginia a rose. They hugged.

"Go Yankees," Suzanna whispered.

Suzanna sought out her sister, who came out from behind the camera long enough to tell Suzanna to stop looking into the lens. Suzanna turned back to Eric. She took a breath.

The future was now.

As she took Eric's hand, she realized that, since the earthquake, she hadn't had the slightest sensation of floating.

They turned toward the minister.

"Dearly beloved, we are gathered here . . ."

Suzanna's spirit soared, but her feet stayed firmly on the ground.

Recipe for Medieval Gingerbread

1 lb jasmine honey
Bread crumbs—about 1 lb finely ground unseasoned bread crumbs in a combination of white and wheat (which gives us another way to use up old bread, hurray!)
Ginger—1 tbsp
Cinnamon—up to 1 tbsp
Ground white pepper—up to ½ tsp
Pinch of culinary lavender

Bring the honey to a boil, reduce heat, skim off any scum, and make sure honey does not boil over. Add spices, slowly beat in the bread crumbs. Add just enough bread to achieve a stiff, well-blended mass. Remove from the heat and turn the mixture into a bowl. Let cool. When cool, take a rolling pin and spread the gingerbread out evenly into a square shape, ½ to 1 inch thick. Trim the edges with a knife, then cut into small slices to serve. Decorate with small leaves (real or candy) attached to each piece with a clove. If you use real leaves, make sure they are not poisonous.

Photo by William Christoff

Celia Bonaduce is a producer on HGTV's *House Hunters*. This is her first novel. She lives in Santa Monica, California, with her husband in a beautiful "no-pets" building. She wishes she could say she has a dog.

You can contact Celia at: www.Celiab.name

The lives and loves of the Wolf sisters continue in Celia Bonaduce's

A COMEDY OF ERINN

An eKensington e-book on sale September 2013!

CHAPTER 1

Erinn Elizabeth Wolf leaned on the fence that kept visitors from sliding down the bluff into the ocean. She glowered at the young couple snuggling on *her* bench —in *her* park. The young man and woman occasionally looked at the water, but spent most of their time sinking into each other's eyes.

The sun was just dipping into the water. The world was suddenly filled with coral, russet, violet, periwinkle, and cornflower. Erinn was getting impatient, very impatient. She decided to take matters into her own hands.

She joined the couple on the bench. Nudging the young woman aside with her hip, she heaved her oversized bag onto the bench and hunkered down.

"Look at that sunset," Erinn heard the young woman sigh softly." God's masterpiece."

Erinn snorted.

"God wouldn't have a prayer creating a sunset like that," she said." This is a masterpiece only city smog could produce."

The couple ignored her. It was obvious Erinn was going to have to crank up the annoyance factor. She studied the couple. Gauging that they were liberal arts students from one of the local universities, Erinn formulated a plan. With a quick prayer, asking forgiveness from her beloved Democratic Party, Erinn said, "Since he's now out of office, I think Dick Cheney is really coming into his own, don't you?"

The couple left their spot on the bench—he frowning, she beaming with politically correct good will.

That's one way to get your bench back.

Erinn glanced at the rapidly advancing sunset and realized she had not a moment to spare. She reached into her bag and pulled out a battered, hand-held video camera. She quickly and expertly adjusted her settings and started panning steadily over the horizon. She was getting pretty good at her camera work—if she did say so herself.

The view at Palisades Park in Santa Monica, California, was the billion-dollar vista featured in movies since cinema's golden era. Although Erinn had lived in Santa Monica for nine years, she never got used to the incredible beauty the park offered.

Whenever Erinn was shooting, she was nimble—and confident in her movements. But as soon as she shut the camera off, a transformation took place. She suddenly appeared heavier and slower, as if gravity had taken hold of her—as if she were rooted to the earth. When the sun had gone, Erinn stowed her camera and made her way home. She didn't walk far, as she was the owner of another masterpiece—one of the few remaining Victorian houses on Santa Monica's main drag.

While Erinn would never be mistaken for the stuff of fairy tales, the courtyard of her house looked like something out of *Beauty and the Beast*. The old climbing roses that crawled up the lacy wooden pillars also disguised layers of peeling paint on the porch. An uneven walkway curled quaintly toward the side yard.

She retrieved a large silver key from a keychain that looked like a medieval jailer's and fitted it into the front door lock. The door squeaked open, and Erinn was home.

She shrugged off her coat, hung it on an old-fashioned hall tree, and carefully put her camera aside. She caught a glimpse of herself in the mirror and rearranged a few bobby pins, hoping to control her wild, coarse hair. Even with her hair pulled back in a severe ponytail, corkscrew tendrils tended to escape. Her hair was still mostly pepper, but now with a sprinkling of salt. Erinn had made no attempt to halt the aging process, which she knew was practically a sacrilege in Southern California—but she stood firm against useless vanity. Even so, without the weight of the camera bag on her shoulders, hints of the graceful young woman she used to be were still evident in her posture and the way she moved. Almost miraculously she had remained an extremely attractive woman.

Not that she cared.

Not that anybody cared.

The doorbell rang. She peered out. A man in ripped jeans, a tight T-shirt, and carrying a skateboard was trying to open the gate. Erinn instinctively stepped out of sight, but kept her eye on the man. He managed to get the latch open and headed up Erinn's path. He marched up to the porch and knocked.

It suddenly occurred to Erinn that this must be someone who wanted to rent the guesthouse.

"Damn it, Suzanna," she cursed under her breath.

Her younger sister, Suzanna, was worried that Erinn would lose the house if she didn't generate some income. She had placed a rental ad on craigslist without Erinn's knowledge or consent. Erinn balked when she heard about it, but promised her sister she'd keep an open mind and at least meet with a few people.

The man, in wraparound sunglasses, knocked on the door again.

She yanked open the heavy wood-beamed door.

"Hey there, how you doing?" asked the young man, as he removed his glasses. He put out his hand by way of introduction." Craigslist."

He had the casual gait of a man—Erinn would put him at about twenty-eight—at ease with himself. He was also extremely well built, with biceps peeking out from under the sleeve of his snug T-shirt.

"That's an interesting mode of transportation," Erinn said, indicating the skateboard.

"Yeah," he said." It's a pain in the ass sometimes, but it's a real chick magnet."

"Pardon?"

"The babes really go for a guy on a skateboard."

"*I* don't."

"Well, you're not a . . ."

He propped his skateboard against the house and stepped inside, without invitation. Erinn followed him. He walked around, whistling appreciatively.

"Wow, this place is awesome," he said.

He walked into the living room and started to pull open the curtains.

"Dude! You have an ocean view . . . why do you have the curtains shut?"

"If you must know, I like to keep to myself. I like the privacy," Erinn said." Besides, I find Southern Californians vastly overestimate sunshine."

"Well, it's a cool place anyway," he said as Erinn closed the curtains. He squinted in the darkness." You could do a spread in *Better Caves and Gardens*."

The cat rubbed against the young man's legs.

"Sweet! I love animals," he said, scooping up the cat." Whoa! This is one fat cat!"

Erinn reached out and patted the cat, a large, flat-faced, silver point Himalayan.

"His name is Caro," she said.

"Hello, Car-ro," he said, pronouncing two r's.

"It's pronounced with one r," Erinn said." Car-o. It's Italian for 'dear one. ' "

"Isn't that what I said?"

"No . . . you said '*Car*-ro' . . . that's Spanish for 'truck. ' "

"Well, no offense, dude, but Truck's a much better name for this guy," said the young man, as he put the cat down and headed toward the kitchen.

Erinn kept her face impassive. This boy was not winning her over.

"Wow, nice kitchen, Er . . . do you mind if I call you 'Er'?"

"Massively," said Erinn.

"What about Rinn? Or Rin Tin Tin?"

Does he want the guesthouse or did he just come here to insult me?

"Why would you call me Rin Tin Tin?"

"Just shortening the process, dude. That's how nicknames are made. You start out with something that makes sense, like Rinn, and pretty soon you're Rin Tin Tin. It's totally random."

"I didn't catch *your* name," Erinn said.

"Jude . . . Raphael."

Common ground at last.

"Ah!" she said." As in the artist!"

"As in the turtle," Jude said." Hey, let's go check out my guest-house!"

He stood and followed a stormy Erinn into the backyard.

If love could have kept this place up, Erinn would have had no worries. But like everything else about the Wolf residence, the yard was looking a little down-at-the-heels. The one-room guesthouse was nestled in a patch of large fig trees. It was a miniature Victorian, complete with a tiny porch and hanging swing. Its bright red door stood out from the greenish tone of the rest of the exterior, and its window boxes overflowed with geraniums.

"This is it," she said, trying to hide the pride she felt in the place.

Jude stood back and looked the building over.

"Huh."

Erinn turned on him.

"Is there a problem?" she asked.

"Nah," he said." I'm just not really big on these gingerbready kind of places, ya know? They're kinda gay."

"Gay?"

"I mean . . . not in a bad way. Like . . . not even in a gay way, you know?"

"Shall we go inside?" asked Erinn, since she hadn't the faintest idea.

She clicked on the light but didn't step inside. Her eyes scanned the room lovingly. Jude stood on the porch looking in over Erinn's head. The room had an open floor plan, and every inch of space counted. A small kitchen was fitted into one corner and a bathroom was tucked discreetly into another. There was a wrought-iron daybed that functioned as a seating area as well as a bed and a tiny, mosaic-tiled café table and chair set. Even in this small space, there was an entire wall of bookcases. Erinn turned to Jude.

"Is this gay, as well?" she asked, as she walked into the room, Jude at her heels.

"Hey! If you're gay, I don't care. Really," Jude said." I'm, personally, not gay. I'm, you know, metro/hetro. But whatever floats your boat, I say."

"Thank you. I was so worried it might be offensive to you somehow, if I were gay."

"Whatever, Erinn. I mean . . . gay is as gay does, right?"

"Well, obviously, that's true," Erinn said." But I don't do as gay does, because I'm not gay."

"Whoa . . .you know that old saying . . . something about . . . you're protesting a shitload."

"Are you perhaps thinking of 'The lady doth protest too much?' from *Hamlet*?"

"Moving on, Erinn," Jude said." Your sexuality isn't the only thing in the world, right? There's food, the beach, the theater . . ."

Erinn winced and walked around the room, trying to ignore the cretin who was taking up much too much space—and oxygen—in her little sanctuary. She started opening blinds, to make the room seem somehow bigger.

"I don't go to the theater," Erinn said.

"What do you mean?" asked Jude, trying out the daybed." Erinn Elizabeth Wolf, the famous New York playwright, doesn't go to the theater? That's crazy!"

Erinn almost choked, she was so surprised by this comment. Any use of her full name by someone other than her mother usually meant she was being recognized. Jude had his back to her and was studying a line of books in the bookcase. He turned to look at her.

"Did you realize your initials are E. E. W. ? EEEEEEwww wwwww."

Erinn tried to ignore Jude's inept attempt at winning her over with a nickname. But she definitely wasn't finished with the conversation.

"You . . . you've heard of me?" she asked.

"Sure. I was a theater major. You're in the history books."

Erinn tried—and failed—to hide her dismay. She was surprised to hear that, at forty-three, she was already considered a relic and consigned to history. She tried not to let on that Jude had delivered a verbal slap.

"Not the *history* books, exactly . . . but . . ." he said.

"But . . . like . . . you know," offered Erinn, who could see he did not mean to hurt her feelings.

"Well, yeah."

Erinn sat down at the mosaic table. Jude continued to look around the room and stopped to admire a photograph. It was a close-up of a wrinkled old man playing checkers.

"This is cool," Jude said.

Erinn studied the picture, lost in thought, remembering the first time she saw Oscar, sitting in the little park across from her loft in Manhattan. He was always so focused on his game. That was nearly twenty years ago . . . by now, he was probably dead, or just another lost New York memory.

"I took that years ago," she said.

"You took that? Awesome."

Erinn warmed to the praise.

"Well, I've always been interested in the visual arts. I'm actually learning how to shoot an HD camera and I'm thinking of trying my hand at editing, too. I like to keep up on those sort of things."

"Hmmm," Jude said." That's pretty cool for somebody . . . uh . . . not totally young . . . to be into that stuff."

"Let's talk about you, shall we?" Erinn asked, as her good will ebbed away.

"Sure," said Jude, grabbing the chair opposite her." Well, let's see . . . I'm in the business . . . television mostly. I mean, in this town, isn't everybody?"

Erinn looked at Jude thoughtfully. What could Suzanna have possibly been thinking? She said she would look for a fellow artist, but she'd sent someone in *television.* Erinn realized that her mind had wandered, and she tried to tune back in to whatever it was Jude might be saying.

" . . . but, you know, until I can produce my own work, I pick up assignments wherever I can."

Erinn watched Jude as he picked up the rental agreement on the table.

"Well, I don't think you really need to read that just yet . . . ." she said, trying to grab the document that would have damned her to her own personal hell should he sign it.

Jude picked up a pen from the table. Erinn watched in silence as he lost interest in the document and started doing curls with the pen, watching his bicep rise and fall with the motion. He was mesmerized. Erinn coughed, hoping to get his attention. Jude looked up and smiled sheepishly.

"I read that you should work out whenever—and wherever—you can," he said.

"Oh? You read that?"

Jude laughed." Well, I downloaded a workout video to my iPod so I could listen to it while I was skateboarding. Same thing."

Erinn arched an eyebrow. Jude suddenly looked up at her.

"What about Tin Lizzy? That would be an awesome nickname for you!"

"You know, Jude, I'm not sure this is going to work out."

He looked up." Oh? Why not?"

"Well," Erinn faltered." I just think that, if two people live in such close proximity to each other, there should be some symbiosis . . . if you get my drift."

Jude looked at Erinn for a minute, then smiled.

"Oh, you mean 'cause I'm in such good shape," he said." Don't worry about that. I can help you get rid of that spare tire in no time."

"No, no, no," Erinn said." I appreciate your offer. Although I wasn't aware I *had* a spare tire."

"Oh, big-time."

"It was more along the lines of, well, I don't feel we're . . . intellectually compatible."

Jude frowned.

"I'm not smart enough to rent your *guesthouse*?"

He held up the rental agreement and waved it in her face.

"Is there an I. Q. test attached to this?" he asked.

Erinn stood up so fast she knocked the chair over, and stormed out of the guesthouse. Jude sprinted after her, and Erinn wheeled on him.

"I'm sorry, Jude, but clearly this isn't going to work."

"Tell me about it. You think you're some sort of god because you wrote one important play a hundred years ago? Nobody can even make a joke around you? I'm out of here."

"I assume you can see yourself out?"

"If I can find my way around your huge ego, yeah," Jude replied, as he walked toward the main house. He stepped over the cat, which was sunbathing on the walkway.

"See ya around, Truck."

Apparently, Jude had not succeeded in giving *her* a nickname, but poor Caro did not escape unscathed.

Erinn went back into the kitchen, stung by Jude's comments. To distract herself, she put up a pot of soup. She pulled out her large stockpot, added some homemade chicken stock, and started scrubbing tubers in a fury.

Who does he think he is, talking to me that way? she thought. *I dodged a bullet with that one.*

The phone rang. Erinn wiped off her hands and reached for the cordless, hesitating just long enough to grab her half-moon glasses and checked the caller I. D.

It was Suzanna.

Erinn put the phone down without answering it. She took off her glasses and returned to her soup.

CHAPTER 2

Erinn made sure the front door was securely bolted for the night and walked into her living room. She flipped on the light and admired the heavy, dark furnishings.

Sunshine, for God's sake. She bristled as she thought back to that half-wit Jude's reaction to this thoughtful, peaceful room.

She sat down at her computer—a twenty-four-inch behemoth that looked out of place on a highly polished claw-foot desk. She settled in to pay a few bills online. Caro pounced upon her, eager for attention. Erinn opened her eyes and scratched him thoughtfully.

"The bills won't pay themselves, Caro," she said, as she held the cat up and looked into his green, unblinking eyes.

With a sigh she went upstairs and changed into her men's striped pajamas, brushed her teeth dutifully for two minutes, and headed back downstairs to the kitchen. One of Erinn's little rebellions was that she brushed her teeth before she had her late- night hot chocolate.

Caro padded softly down the steps behind her.

Erinn's kitchen, like every room in the house, was a monument to a more gracious era. The room was square, and the cabinetry was white with glass window inserts, so all the contents were proudly on display. A KitchenAid mixer, a Cuisinart, a Deni electric pressure cooker, a Vibiemme Domobar espresso machine, all had a place in the Wolf kitchen. If times were tough, they weren't always.

As Erinn stirred her cocoa, she heard a key jangling at the back door. She grabbed another mug and smiled slightly as she started another serving of hot chocolate. The key continued its clanking, grinding medley for several seconds. Finally, the back door swung open.

"Hi, Erinn. I was in the neighborhood . . . ," offered a voice from the door." Can I come in?"

"Don't let the cat—" called Erinn, as Suzanna wrestled with the key still jammed in the lock.

Caro scooted out the door.

"—out," Erinn finished.

Suzanna flung herself into the room, laden with bags from Mommy and Me, Two Peas in a Pod, and the Wildfiber Yarn Store. Suzanna was seven months' pregnant and was taking to the experience like Mother Nature to spring.

"I can give you a new key," Erinn said.

"That's OK. This way you hear me coming," Suzanna said." I don't want to scare you."

She set her new purchases on the table and dumped out several maternity outfits and skeins of orange, brown, and lime-green yarn. Erinn picked up the yarn and examined it—could this be for the *baby*?

"It's not your lack of skill with a lock that scares me," Erinn said.

Suzanna was in her mid-thirties. She had recently married Eric, the object of her desire since high school. Suzanna owned the Rollicking Bun Tea Shoppe and Book Nook on the other side of town.

"I thought orange and green were safe for either sex," Suzanna said.

She and Eric had decided that they didn't want to know the gender of their baby beforehand.

Erinn watched as Suzanna continued to unload her bags.

"God! I love shopping," said Suzanna.

"You were shopping? At this hour?"

"Erinn, it's eight-thirty. People shop at eight-thirty."

Suzanna tossed a small box to her sister, who caught it clumsily.

"I bought you a lipstick!" she said." Try it! It will look great with your . . . pajamas."

Ever since Suzanna had gotten married, she'd been obsessed with Erinn's single status. She was on a one-woman campaign to get Erinn out in the world.

Suzanna and Erinn had not been close as children. Erinn was nearly ten years older, and had moved to New York City when Suzanna was still young. Since moving to Santa Monica, the siblings had gotten closer, and as she examined the lipstick, Erinn doubted the wisdom of this. She eyed the waxy red tube with suspicion.

Suzanna snatched it back. She grabbed her sister's mouth and forced it into pucker." Don't move. . . ."

Suzanna finished the application, whipped out a mirror from her purse, and handed it to her sister. Erinn inspected her new lips.

"If one is a sheepdog, why try to look like a Pekingese?" she asked, as she returned the mirror.

"Well, Scooby-Doo, you could do with a little lift, that's all. Don't you remember when people used to say you looked like Valerie Bertinelli?"

Erinn nodded, trying not to gag on the waxy taste of the lipstick.

"Well, since she's been on Jenny Craig . . . not so much."

"And one lipstick will do for me what a year on Jenny Craig did for Valerie? I think not."

"Baby steps, big sister. Baby steps."

Erinn was grateful for her sister's concern, but missed the days when Suzanna was in awe of her and treated her with respect instead of with incessant camaraderie. While her sister reloaded her bags, Erinn covertly wiped off her new lipstick and took a hefty sip of cocoa.

"Well?" Suzanna asked.

"Well what?"

"Did you find a tenant for the guesthouse?"

"No, I did not," Erinn said." And I have to say, I don't think Craig nor his list are the way to go."

"You aren't trying."

"It's my guesthouse, Suzanna. I don't have to try. They do."

"Well, keep looking."

"Let's change the subject, shall we?"

Erinn had pulled out her big sister voice, which wasn't really fair. She knew Suzanna would cave in.

"OK," Suzanna said." How's the new play?"

Erinn got up and went into the living room. Suzanna had started casting yarn onto a set of large circular needles and had to scoot after her sister to catch up.

"How long have you been practicing that casual delivery?" Erinn asked.

"Uh . . . all week, if you must know," Suzanna said, following closely at her sister's heels.

Erinn thumped down on the sofa and put a pillow over her head.

"Erinn, come on! I'm worried about you. You stay holed up in here day after day, not talking to anybody. . . ."

"That is not true," Erinn said, from under the pillow." I had a very interesting conversation with a nice couple I met in the park just this afternoon."

Suzanna sat next to Erinn. She pulled the pillow off her sister's head and tossed it aside. Erinn noticed the corners of the pillow were a little frayed, but, hey, get in line.

"Listen, I'm not just talking to you as a sister," Suzanna said." Mimi was in the shop yesterday, and she said you've been avoiding her."

Mimi was Erinn's agent.

"She shouldn't be discussing my business with you!"

"She's worried about you. She says she needs something to sell."

"And what if I don't have anything right now? She'll drop me?"

"How should I know? Hey, we forgot our cocoa," Suzanna said.

"I'll get it," Erinn said.

Erinn headed back to the kitchen. She tested the temperature by dipping her little finger into the cocoa. She put the cups in the microwave to reheat. While she watched the cups go around and around, she suddenly noticed how quiet it was. Leaving the cocoa to its carousel ride, she dashed frantically back into the living room, but she was too late. Suzanna was staring intently at the computer screen.

Erinn tried to block the screen and said, "It's not ready!"

"Just a peek!"

"No! It's still rough."

"I'll make allowances."

Erinn couldn't budge her sister. Suzanna countered every move like a prizefighter —years of sisterly combat had her trained—and the two women stared at the screen.

MRS. FURST

John, you may be the president, and this might be the
White House, but it's still our home . . . where the buffalo
roam and the deer and the antelope play."

Erinn turned off the monitor and started to pace.

"It's hopeless," she said." I'm hopeless."

"It's not that bad," Suzanna said." It's very patriotic."

"Do you think Mimi will like it?"

"Oh, who cares if she likes it? She's an agent . . . she only cares
ten percent," Suzanna said, as Erinn chewed on a thumbnail." I, on
the other hand, am your sister. So I care one hundred and ten percent."

Erinn turned, mid-pace, and stared at her sister.

"That's a good line," she said, going back to the computer." That's
a very good line. I bet I can use that."

Suzanna smiled wanly. She started to twist her hair nervously as
Erinn's fingers blazed over the keyboard.

"Sorry, Suzanna, you need to go. I need to write!" Erinn said
without looking up." Could you let yourself out? And let the cat in?"

"Sure," Suzanna said, kissing Erinn's hair." Good night."

Erinn glanced up as her sister waddled away in the muted light of
the living room. She saw the little girl who used to look up to her.
How did it come to this? Erinn wondered, as she stared back at the
computer screen.

How did it ever come to this?

CPSIA information can be obtained at www.ICGtesting.com
Printed in the USA
LVOW12s0840120813

347434LV00001B/1/P